NEW CASTLE LIBRARY

The Scent of the Gods

The Scent of the Gods

a novel by

Fiona Cheong

W. W. Norton & Company

New York · London

TO LEICESTER

Some of the historical data presented in this novel draw upon the *Hikayat Abdullah*, or, *Autobiography of Abdullah Munshi*, as translated by A. H. Hill.

The text of this book is composed in Aldus with the display set in Tiger Rag. Composition by PennSet, Inc. Manufacturing by Courier Companies, Inc.
Book design by Charlotte Staub.

First Edition.

Library of Congress Cataloging-in-Publication Data
Cheong, Fiona.
    The scent of the gods : a novel / by Fiona Cheong.
    p.   cm.
    I. Title.
    PR9570.S53C467   1991
    823—dc20   91-22594

ISBN 0-393-03024-5
W.W. Norton & Company, Inc., 500 Fifth Avenue, New York, N.Y. 10110
W.W. Norton & Company, Ltd., 10 Coptic Street, London WC1A 1PU
1 2 3 4 5 6 7 8 9 0

55744

Acknowledgments

Thanks first of all to my teachers at Saint Anthony's Convent, and to my mother, Doris Cheong, for their gift of beginnings; to my father, Daniel Cheong, who inspired this book unwittingly; to James McConkey, for his wisdom and kindness; to faithful friends, whose spirits accompanied me throughout the writing—Katheryn Rios, Juliana Whitmore, Deidre Jackson, Marjorie Maddox, JoElaine Wasson, Edward Hardy, William Evans, John Lauricella, Mabel Lee, and Angela Yeo McKenzie. My gratitude also goes to Rebecca Dietz, whose listening woke important voices; to Zofia Burr and James X. Lucey, whose poems lit pathways through countless writing blocks; to Danny Brink-Washington, for his patience near the end; to my editor, Jill Bialosky, for her act of faith. I remain indebted to Edward Washington, for his irrepressible sense of play; in the lonely hours, you sustained me.

The Scent of the Gods

One

We used to play hide-and-seek underneath Great-Grandfather's house, where the sand was soft and the dark wove threads like cool smoke, and stone pillars glimmered smooth white at the edges of the dark. Between the pillars ran the water pipes, a network of hanging paths. They smelled old, long-used, and full of balance. Underneath them we would crawl, pillar to pillar, hiding from my cousin Li Shin, who knelt at his pillar with his eyes closed and counted one two three four five six seven eight nine ten. When evening came we would hear the grown-ups arriving home and walking above our heads. Then we would know it was time to go inside. Then we would stop playing. "If you play hide-and-seek at night, the devil will come and play with you," Grandma said, and told us about the boy who had gone off to hide, and when the other children called his name, he did not answer. They called and called, until the grown-ups stepped outside to find out what had happened. The grown-ups found the children standing in a circle on the grass. The older ones were still calling for the boy, telling him the game was over. But when the grown-ups walked towards them, the younger children began to cry.

"Did the devils take the boy?"

"Yes."

"How did they take him?"

"Someone called the boy's name. He thought it was one of the other children, so he answered."

Inside Great-Grandfather's house there were many rooms. They were big silent rooms, with tall red doors, and windows that looked out to the trees, and some windows that looked out to the road. All the windows were oblong. They had red wooden shutters that latched onto two nails in the windowsill, because the grown-ups did not want to hear them bang about in sudden winds. The house was filled with grown-ups. They slept in the big silent rooms that we were not supposed to enter unless we were called there, where the same wood floor ran in and out of doorways emptying smoothly into corridors. There were many corridors. They had pale green walls. On the walls hung old brown-edged photographs of our dead relatives, who had lived in the house before us. Their photographs hung there on iron nails, and when our amahs wiped off the dust, the lines of the faces would reappear, still clear.

In May, when the dry season arrived, the heat would sink into all our rooms, so heavy, and still as stagnant water left in old clay flowerpots sitting on the grass, forgotten. Then doors were left open and we were told to leave them open or the heat would choke us. Only grown-ups were allowed to close the doors. These grown-ups were our aunties and uncles, who went to work in the morning and came home at night. Grandfather used to come home with them, but one day when I was five years old he started to cough out blood, and an ambulance came and took him to the hospital. Three months later, he died. "Your grandfather drank river water," said Grandma. "Now he must go back to China, just like the chrysanthemum." She did not tell us that it was tuberculosis that had killed him. All she said was that we were like chrysanthemums. Chrysanthemums were Chinese flowers, because they were growing in China ten thousand years before someone took them and planted them in a foreign place. We were like that, she said. And wherever we happened to end up, our souls knew before we were born where to return us to the land. That was a law, like the law that called for all the generations of one family to live together under one roof, just in case. "Just in case of what?" my cousins asked. "Just in case means just in case," Grandma said, to teach us that in the face of so many terrible things possible, meaningful answers were not spoken.

On hot afternoons my cousins would pull off their shirts as soon as they came home from school.

They would walk around wearing only their shorts. They were boys, so they could do that. Since I was not a boy, I had to wear a T-shirt with my shorts. Once I took off my T-shirt, but Auntie Lily found us outside where we were playing soldiers near the cemetery trees, and she said to my cousins, "Are you mad? Esha's a girl."

The cemetery trees stood behind the house. They were old, old trees. They grew close together, shading the graves of our dead relatives, whose belongings remained in those rooms where, because we lived in Singapore, equatorial light tumbled like bright water through the oblong windows.

We lived here, Grandma would say, because of war and poverty going on in China. In olden days, she told us, we Chinese were a great civilization. We invented porcelain, paper, and fireworks. Then in 1644, China was invaded by the Manchus, and we became a nation of peasants, who had to make a living off small plots of bad farmland rented from cut-throat landlords. "Not even such suffering could weaken Chinese people's loyalty to homeland," said Grandma. "But people have to fill their stomachs." So in 1830, our great-grandfather packed his few clothes and schoolbooks into a gunny sack, swung the sack over his shoulder, and trudged down to the wharf to find work on board a merchant's junk. This was how poor people paid for their passage out of China. This was why the Chinese who showed up in Singapore at the time were mostly men. They came to Singapore because trade was booming here, and jobs were abundant, and the men who came intended to return to China after they had made their fortune—the ones who were leaving China forever traveled much farther, to America, where they went in search

of the Gold Mountain. But many of those who came to
Singapore did not return, either. In 1830 a throbbing
downtown had already sprung up around Keppel Harbor,
and after putting in a hard day's work, the men would go
to the gambling houses and opium dens. "These men were
peasants, you remember. They were not used to handling
money in a city." At first, the men would bundle up most
of their earnings into small brown packets, which they
sent home to their wives and families in China. But soon
they were sending home less and less. They lost their
money to gambling, or they became opium addicts. Every
day it became harder for them to return to China.

"Was our great-grandfather like that? Did he have a
wife?"

"No. Your great-grandfather was fifteen years old when
he came. A schoolboy."

"Did he lose his money in an opium den?"

"No. He knew how to keep his money."

"How come he never went back to China?"

"It was easier for him to fit into life here. He grew used
to it."

"He didn't miss his family?"

"Young folks do not take long to get over such things."

"Did he have brothers and sisters?"

"Probably."

"Do we have relatives in China?"

"Of course you have relatives in China."

"Do you know where they are?"

"No. But they are there."

Our great-grandfather's name was Wei Hsu. When he
first arrived, the grown-ups teased him, calling him Siuchai, because everywhere he went, he would bring a book.

A *siuchai* was a successful candidate at the County Examination held once a year in China. It was the first in a series of public examinations used to qualify you for a position in the Imperial Service. Sons of blue-collar workers such as barbers, coolies, and coffin-makers were automatically disqualified even from taking the examinations. Since our great-grandfather came from a long line of coffin-makers, everyone knew that the people who called him Siuchai were making a joke, and it was a double joke because they were in Singapore. They were no more in China. In Singapore the people served a different Emperor, called the King of England, who spoke English and ruled from the other side of the earth. This was why our great-grandfather stopped speaking Mandarin, which in China he used to study because it was the language of scholars. He put away his schoolbooks, feeling foolish for having carried them all this way, and with the money he earned as an errand boy in a British bank, he bought an English dictionary.

As an errand boy, our great-grandfather would make coffee, deliver letters to other banks, and empty wastepaper baskets. While he was working, he would practice his English in his head. When he picked up a coffee cup, he would think to himself, "Coffee cup. For Mr. Williams, black with two cubes of sugar." This was how he taught himself to think with English phrases. He would repeat any order that was given to him, so that he could hear the words twice. Then he would break up the order, move the words around, and try to put them back together by himself. If he had time, he would write the words down in a small notebook, which he carried in his back pocket. He would learn to spell a new word with the help of an

Irish office girl named Ena, who taught him how to use his dictionary. Ena was not a real office girl. She was the bank manager's daughter. The bank manager and his wife had adopted Ena when she was eleven years old, and had taken her back to England to live with them and go to school. When our great-grandfather met her, she was sixteen, only a year older than he. She would come to the bank because in the house that was provided for her family, she would get lonely and miss her friends. She would talk to our great-grandfather about Ireland, which she said she remembered very clearly. Sometimes she would talk about England, which she said was her home now, but it was not the same as Ireland. In this way, our great-grandfather learned a great many words, and phrases, and sentences, and as his English grew better, he began to tell Ena a little about China.

After Ena's family returned to England, she would write to our great-grandfather, who would write back on the same day that he received a letter from her. This went on for many months. In the meantime, our great-grandfather graduated from errand boy to interpreter. As an interpreter, he helped to settle disputes between the British authorities and Chinese-speaking merchants. For this, he received a higher salary, enough for him to save and to lend out. When he wrote to Ena, he would tell her about his new work, and what he wanted to do with his money. He was a young man now, fluent in the English language, and he had strong dreams. One of his dreams was to open a finance company officially in his name, which could be passed down to his descendants as a family business. This turned out to be a successful dream. But suddenly Ena's letters stopped arriving. Our great-grandfather continued to write to her, but she did not write back. He never found out why. Soon he got married. He married a Straits-born Chinese from Malacca, a businesswoman several years older than himself, who had come to Singapore for a holiday. This was in 1836. Our great-grandfather was then twenty-one years old.

❀

"Were they in love?" my cousins asked, on the seventh evening of Grandfather's death, in late September 1963.

We had just spent all afternoon watching Grandma burning piles of spirit money out by the roadside. Spirit money came in the form of thick yellow squares of paper carrying red Chinese characters brushed on with firm, bold strokes, to show the gods we were not wishy-washy. We knew that Grandma burned spirit money so that Grandfather would have it to buy food on the Other Side.

We had watched the paper squares melt to ashes, and then we had followed Grandma back to the house and out onto the back porch, where we now sat listening to her voice dip and stretch like a breeze loose in the grass. She was in her storytelling mood.

"Your great-grandfather had a good business head," we heard her say.

It was almost dinnertime. The trees surrounding us had turned soft to the night and somewhere a bird was calling, lonely in its sound.

"No, Grandma," said Li Shin, who was eleven years old back then. "Ena and our great-grandfather, did they love each other?"

"Love," said Grandma, "does not guarantee anything,

except in the pictures. In real life you have destiny, and you have hard work."

She was sitting near a window that opened out from the kitchen, and in the light that fell onto the porch, I could see how she kept her hands folded in her lap, neatly, the way she had taught me, many times, to fold my hands so that people would know that I was a proper young lady. These things were important, she told me. Men were going to treat me according to how I behaved. One day when I was older, she said, I would understand what she meant, and I would be grateful that she had taught me the proper graces.

I could hear our amahs in the kitchen, lifting lids off the pots on the stove. I could hear them putting the lids back, and dishing food into serving bowls with wooden ladles.

"Why did she stop writing, Grandma?" asked Li Yuen. He was nine that evening. He sat perched on the porch rail like a shadowy bird.

"Over a year had passed since they last saw each other," Grandma answered. "Too much can happen in a year."

Li Shin pushed his hands into his shorts pockets. He was standing near the steps that led down to the grass. I could see him looking stubborn with his head tilted to the side. "Why did it matter?" he said. "True love conquers all, like Edward and Mrs. Simpson."

Leaves were quivering behind his head, a breeze moving in the mango tree that grew out of a patch of bare earth between the house and the grass. My father had helped to plant that mango tree a long time ago when he and our uncles were boys. My father, who had died in an automobile accident, which had also killed my mother and my cousins' parents, had been Grandma's second son. My cousins' father had been her first, her eldest. I knew very little about either of them, aside from that they had planted that tree. I was six months old when they died.

"Edward and Mrs. Simpson," said Grandma. "You and your Edward and Mrs. Simpson. He was a big-shot king. It makes all the difference—your history teacher did not explain that to you?" She moved to make herself more comfortable in her seat. She was sitting in a big rattan chair padded with fat red cushions, red for good luck. "Ena lived in England," she said quietly. "Simple things matter."

"Why didn't our great-grandfather go there?" Li Shin said.

"He did not have the right passport."

Li Yuen threw his arm around one of the wooden posts that ran up to the roof. "Why didn't he go to get the right one, Grandma?" he asked, resting his head on the wood.

"Whatever passport you had, that was what you had," she said. "You could not change your passport."

"Why not?" Li Shin asked, still stubborn. "We were already part of the Empire."

"Yes," said Grandma. "We were part of the Empire. We were the Empire's coolies."

Li Yuen let go of the wooden post. "But Grandma," he said, swinging his legs back and forth as he gripped the rail with both hands, "our great-grandfather was an interpreter."

"To them, he still looked like a coolie. A dressed-up coolie."

"Why did he look like a coolie?"

"Because of his eyes."

"What kind of eyes did he have?"

"Same kind of eyes as you."

Li Yuen stared at her, and then he burst out laughing. "I'm not a coolie!" he cried. Throwing his head back, he laughed and laughed.

Grandma shook her head. She was smiling, but her smile seemed a little sad. Li Shin did not smile. He looked at Li Yuen as if Li Yuen had just turned into a donkey or a baboon.

No one expected me to say anything. Chinese children were not expected to say much, girls even less so than boys. My duty was to watch and listen. So I watched. The sky was darkening fast above the treetops, melting purplish blue like a bruise. Li Yuen's voice was cooing into the coming night, "I'm not a coolie, I'm not a coolie." He made his words float like a song that I could hear pass over the grass and into the cemetery where our dead relatives lay, scattered throughout the trees. Some of their graves were hidden in the lalang, the tall sharp-edged jungle grass that Li Shin told us had once sprung up all over the island, wild and healthy as fire.

In that year other parts of the island were already changing. Over dinner the grown-ups talked about new roads appearing in such-and-such a district, and about the factories in Jurong, on the west coast. We did not pay them much attention, then. The lalang was still growing where we lived, and around Great-Grandfather's house there were no factories. There were no new roads. We lived without the sounds of traffic, or school bells, or church bells. On some nights we would hear army trucks rumbling past on the narrow road outside our gate. They would be taking recruits to the barracks two miles away. But that was only on some nights, and very late.

In the daytime we would hear only the trees. Great-Grandfather's house was surrounded by trees. In the front there were coconut trees growing just inside the fence, their gray trunks leaning into the air like the necks of dinosaurs. Across the road was a rubber plantation left over from the days of the British. British ships had brought over seeds from South America and now rubber trees ran on for miles, making tall green rows. Between the rows the ground was covered with leaves, and crackled softly when my cousins and I walked on it. Every day, more leaves were breaking off to float down and settle on top of the older leaves, and there were layers gathered from all the days that had already passed. We would take off our shoes when we stepped onto the plantation, and we would tie our shoelaces together so that we would not lose the shoes. Then we would wade through the leaves, hearing them shift around our ankles like magic green water. Once, Li Shin pretended to be blind. He closed his eyes and threw his arms out, and said, "Make sure I don't bump into trees." Li Yuen and I took his hands and led him between the rows, even though this was a game we were not supposed to play. Grandma had told us, "Never stick your tongue out at other children, and never pretend to be blind or deaf. One day the wind will change and your face will get stuck forever." Although we seldom disobeyed her, when we walked in the green light of the rubber trees it seemed that not even the changing of the wind could harm us.

None of the other trees were so safe. The trees that grew up to the sides of Great-Grandfather's house, and in the back where the cemetery was, grew so thickly tangled, only the kampong Malays knew how to walk among them, since the Malays were descended from Singapore's original fishing tribes, not from immigrants—an immigrant's method of surviving the equatorial jungle had always been to cut it down.

In those days I did not know much about the Malays, only that most of them lived in secluded villages in the jungle, and the Malay word for such a village was *kampong*. This was why they were called kampong Malays. Their villages consisted of sandy compounds with wooden houses built on stilts. The houses had atap roofs, made with leaves from the nipa palm. Coconut trees grew everywhere for shade, there was not a single road, and everyone in the kampong shared a common bathing area. This usually meant one or two showers surrounded by a zinc wall fitted with a swinging wooden door. It was an old-fashioned way to live, but then the Malays were old-fashioned people. They did not mix well with other citizens, because most of us were Chinese, and the Chinese believed in progress. This was what we were told.

When I was older, I would know the Chinese had always looked down on the Malays as a backward people who had proved their ignorance by choosing not to follow in the footsteps of our British forefathers. When the British ruled Singapore, they had allowed us to set up our own schools. The Chinese had seized this opportunity at once, recognizing it as an opportunity to better ourselves. Our first schools held classes in the provincial dialects, mainly Hokkien and Cantonese, which were spoken by most Chinese immigrants. But soon our schoolchildren were also learning Mandarin and English. As we progressed,

more and more of our classes were held in English, and
soon we had English-speaking schools as well as Chinese-
speaking schools. Even in the Chinese-speaking schools,
the pupils studied English as their second language.

The Malays, however, chose to stick to their ancestors'
way of life. They were Muslims, disciples of the prophet
Muhammad. Religious education was very important to
them, so their children attended religious classes which
taught them to pray five times a day facing the sun, but
which did not teach them mathematics or science or English. This was how they fell behind, Grandma told us.
The parents miscalculated. "If you want to preserve the
customs of your ancestors, you must teach them to your
children in the home," she said. "But your children must
go to school. They must learn to recognize changes. Then
they can know how to adapt old traditions to new situa-
tions. This is how we Chinese have survived all this time.
It is not easy." She did not call the Malays ignorant, but
shortsighted.

The Malays knew how to carve a passage through the
jungle. They carried parangs, long sickle-shaped knives,
which they would wave in front of them as they walked,
swinging the blade from side to side to cut away the
underbrush. This was the work they used to do for the
British, and now they did the same work for the local
government. They did not seem to see that such work
foretold its own end. They were not preparing themselves
for the day when there would be no jungle left in Singapore, and also no kampong. "If you do not prepare, you
get no choice. You must take whatever is handed out to
you. That is your karma." What Grandma did not say
was that in Singapore, karma was flowing more and more

from whether your family was Chinese or Malay or Indian, rather than from the Angels of the Universe and
their Maker. What she did not say was that Muslims did
not have to accept their karma.

But we would learn this lesson soon enough.

Two

When the businesswoman became pregnant, she wrote home to her aunts in Malacca, telling them she wanted to hire amahs. Her aunts wrote back that they would screen the neighborhood's girls for her, and send her those whom they could tell had been brought up properly. In those days, being brought up properly meant that a girl did not (what the old folks would say) run around with boys—although boys, because they were boys, could do all sorts of things, even things forbidden to girls. If a boy and a girl made love and she became pregnant, people said it was her fault for running around. The boy was thought of as "the one who got caught," and some people would even go so far as to say who could know for sure if he was the father. It was assumed that if an unmarried girl became pregnant, she must have al-

lowed many boys to make love to her. There was no room
for accidents, no room for passionately committed mis-
takes.

And so in Great-Grandfather's time, the house became
filled with virgins. All of them came from Malacca, and
when they arrived they were all fifteen or sixteen years
old. They had taken a bus from Malacca south to the town
of Johore Bahru, and from there the ferryman had rowed
them across the Straits into Singapore. The entire passage
had been paid for by the businesswoman. So when the
girls arrived, she owned them, more or less.

My cousins asked Grandma why those girls would come
all this way just to become somebody's servants.

"They came to find husbands," she said. "Rumor was
that opportunity was much better here than in Malacca.
Singapore was a newer port than Malacca, but it was
already busier, and the men were richer."

The Malays called those girls Peranakans. They were
Straits-born, like the businesswoman, and like us.
"But remember," Grandma would say, "your great-
grandfather himself was born in China." This made us
different from his wife and her amahs, who would have
had to trace their way back through hundreds of generations of intermarriages before they could lay claim to
their original Chinese ancestors. Those ancestors were the
merchants who had run the old Spice Route. They had
arrived in Malacca long ago, in the time before the
Europeans.

"Some people say, those merchants came to this region
as long ago as 500 B.C. They used the northeast monsoon
winds. In those days, there were little kingdoms here,
ruled by kings and princes. The merchants brought silks,

and porcelain, and medicines, and they would use these things to trade for tin and gold. Then when the winds changed direction—which meant that the southwest monsoon was in season—the merchants would start their journey home."

"Did they have wives in China?" my cousins asked.

"Some of them. Others were unmarried. But in those days, people still followed tradition. If a man wanted to marry, he would go among Chinese women to pick his choice. He did not even look at a woman who was not Chinese—if it was a wife he wanted."

And then, sometime in the twelfth century, the merchants began to go among the Malay women of Malacca.

"Some books say, since by that time the merchants owned shops in Malacca, they needed wives to look after their shops because when supplies ran out, the merchants would have to return to China to get more. But probably this was not why they got married."

My cousins asked why not.

"A Malay woman was not going to marry a Chinese man just to become his shopkeeper. No one is so stupid."

"They fell in love, right, Grandma?" my cousins said.

We did not know yet how the merchants had listened too long to the sound of the rain at night, and it had made them lonely, made them tired of stroking themselves to the shaking leaves outside their huts, to the from-time-to-time thump thump of hard ripe coconuts wind-knocked to the sand, made them remember the woman-smells they had discovered as boys, tugging underneath their classmates' skirts behind frenzied countryside bushes after school. When they walked among the villagers in the morning, the smell of their loneliness set the women's hearts beating. The women had noticed these men before, these foreigners, whose clothes held the spices they carried on board their boats, and held the ocean, salty winds. When the men stopped in front of the first sweet-smelling fruit stand, the women were ready. They watched the men pick up the yellow bananas. They watched the men cradle the yellow bananas fondly in their hands.

"How come the Europeans weren't here yet, Grandma?"

We still did not know what it meant, that in the time before the Europeans, Malays and Chinese tossed about on each other's sheets and made love up there in Malacca.

"The Europeans still did not know the earth was round."

"They thought it was flat, right, Grandma? They thought if they sailed too far, their ships would fall off. How come the Chinese knew the earth was round?"

"We could read the stars. In olden days, many people read the stars. Indians, Africans, Arabs, all of them came to Malacca to trade."

"Did they fall in love with Malay women too?"

"Some of them stayed and married Malay women."

The most celebrated of all of Malacca's mixed weddings took place in 1459, when Sultan Mansur Shah took Princess Hang Li Po as his bride. Princess Hang Li Po was the daughter of Emperor Yung Lo, of China's Ming Dynasty. She arrived in Malacca with five hundred beautiful handmaids, and all of them lived on a hill that soon became known as Bukit China.

Even when we heard that story, Li Shin asked only about the Emperor. "Even the Emperor did not follow tradition anymore, Grandma?" he said.

"Oh, for the Emperor, there were different traditions," she replied. "When that royal wedding took place, it was as if Malacca and China were getting married. Now trade between the two countries was like a family business. This was very good for China." She smiled. "So you see? The Emperor acted wisely."

❀

After dinner that night Li Shin stepped out onto the porch to practice his walk. Li Yuen and I were in our bedroom, which was in the back of the house, facing the cemetery. We listened to Li Shin outside the windows, pacing up and down the porch floor. He was going to be a soldier when he grew up. He was practicing to walk so that an enemy listening would not know where to point his gun in the dark. If you were a soldier and you couldn't do that, he would say to us, his voice lowered to a hush, filled with warning, if you were a soldier and you didn't know how to walk across a wooden floor with the enemy near and always waiting, if you couldn't move in your own house without making a sound, you could die from one careless creak. The enemy was a soldier too, and soldiers had to shoot to kill. If not, they would get killed themselves. That was just the way things were.

He did not speak like this in front of Grandma. In her presence he was careful not to say how he was going to be the best soldier in his platoon. Grandma did not want to hear it. She wanted Li Shin to study an apprenticeship under our aunties and uncles, so that someday he could run the finance company that had been passed down to us, that had been started in our great-grandfather's day by our great-grandfather himself. She wanted Li Shin to marry a Chinese girl from a good family, and the Chinese girl to have a son, and the son to be the firstborn son of the next generation in our house, who would be here to take over the family business when his time arrived. Neither I nor Li Yuen would be allowed to marry until this son of my elder cousin's was born. Such was the tradition in our family. And it was my cousin's duty as the firstborn son in our generation to make sure this tradition was not broken.

Enough traditions had been broken already, said Grandma. People did not even remember the things that had kept our ancestors alive, that had kept families in harmony with the universe. Every tradition had its beginning, she said, in the time that the universe itself began. Those were the days before heaven and earth separated, and the gods themselves had lived among human beings. "Imagine what people are throwing away," said Grandma, "when they decide to throw away traditions." And we would know that she was not talking just about the spice merchants with their Malay wives. She was also reminding us of Grandfather's daughters from his first wife, the woman he had married when he was twenty-five years old. "Too young to have common sense," said Grandma. "Just like his father at that age."

Just as our great-grandfather had married the businesswoman from Malacca, our grandfather had married a Straits-born Chinese from Penang. According to Grandma, that was the root of all the trouble. First, the Penang wife did not give birth to any sons. "Weak blood," said Grandma. "Too much mixing in the family." Unlike the businesswoman, whose grandfather had been an immigrant from China, the Penang wife was a true Peranakan, with a string of Malay grandmothers in her family background. She ended up having five daughters, but not one son. Second, the daughters disappeared as soon as they got married. It was true that daughters should live with their husbands' families, said Grandma, but that was not what happened. Our grandfather's daughters had moved out of the country completely. Some of them were living in Indonesia, because their husbands had jobs in Djakarta. One daughter was even living in Brunei. "Brunei, imagine," Grandma would say. "A Muslim country. Nothing but desert and oil refineries." That was the daughter who had married an Australian geologist. None of them kept any of the traditions. Their husbands were rich, but no one ever came to visit, not even for Chinese New Year. And they never sent any *angpow* to their father. No small red packet of money had ever arrived in the mail, and no letters, no photographs of grandchildren. Surely there were grandchildren, said Grandma. They would be our cousins. But they would be older, as old as our aunties and uncles. If they had children, those children would be our nieces and nephews, and they would be our age. But probably they were growing up without hearing any stories. Probably they did not know about the spice merchants, or about our great-grandfather Wei Hsu, or even about our grandfather. It would be for them as if they had no past, and for us as if we had never been.

I listened to my cousin Li Shin walking outside on the porch. Sometimes his footstep fell so soft I almost did not hear it on the wooden boards. How he was going to keep peace with Grandma and still become a soldier, I did not know. I heard the wood dip ever so slightly underneath his feet, its sound shy, almost invisible.

✿

We never wondered why Li Shin wanted
to be a soldier. It seemed perfectly natural, and honest,
an instinct with which he had been born. Wherever we
walked, he would scan the territory, searching for warning
signs in trees growing along the road, in bushes bordering
sidewalks, in cars and buses that passed us more slowly
than usual. He gravitated towards war stories, their details
circling him like a fish net. He made those stories games
for us to play.

Often we would play at founding Singapore. In the back
of the house, where the grass grew spiky red-green and
sparked off white light blades at noon, it would be the end
of January 1819. British Colonel Farquhar (my cousin Li
Shin) would be sailing up the Singapore River with his
Malacca men (Li Yuen being one of them), and I would
be sitting in Grandma's chair on the back porch, pretending I did not know that they were about to arrive. I was
the Temenggong, ruler of the island Singapore, which in
those days was known by its Indo-Malay name, Pulau
Singapura, "Lion City Island," a legendary name given
by an Indian prince said to have spotted a lion while he
was out hunting in the jungle. This legend came from a
time when the Malays called the island Temasek, "Fishing
Village."

When Colonel Farquhar arrived, the island was still
covered with jungle, with the Orang Laut living in huts
along the coast. The Orang Laut were sea gypsies of the
Gelam tribe. Our history books described them as prim-
itive people who collected bark from the gelam tree and
used it to make awnings and sails for their boats. The

23

Temenggong did not live among them. He had a house set back some distance from the river mouth. The house stood at the edge of the jungle, facing an open space.

Li Shin would walk up to the porch, and ask if the British Empire could set up a trading station on the island. I would say, "Yes," and he would produce a piece of paper from his pocket, and both of us would sign our treaty. Next, Li Shin would ask where the best place would be for him to pitch his tents. "Wherever you please," I would say. He would look around the "open space," in the middle of which had stood a shady eugenia tree, and he would say, "I think the best place is here, on this open space." Then he would order his men to cut down bushes and to put up the tents, and also to dig a well underneath the eugenia tree, which was the mango tree that grew near the railing of our porch.

In 1819 the Temenggong had not said anything about cutting down the bushes around his house, nor had he said anything about digging a well underneath his eugenia tree. But Li Shin explained that the British did not have to ask anyone's permission in such matters. Everywhere they went, it was expected that they would cut down bushes, so that they could build not only drinking wells but also roads, market centers, schools, hospitals, and whitewashed brick houses with square verandas and wide staircases. All the new British buildings would have tall silver flagpoles, he said. On top of every flagpole would fly the Union Jack, red, white, and blue.

While I sat on our porch and watched, Li Shin would walk about the grass, checking the work of his men. Then he would order them to erect a flagpole. The flagpole would be thirty feet high, and it would stand by "the seashore," and as soon as it was erected, the men were to hoist the British flag. The British flag was a piece of rectangular cloth cut from an old bedsheet, which our youngest uncle, Uncle Tien, had painted into the Union Jack for us. At this point in the game, Li Yuen would go over to the wooden shed that sat in the far right corner of the yard, and he would look inside for the bamboo pole that Uncle Tien had broken in half for us. When he found the half that was our flagpole, he would take it over to where the frangipani tree stood, close to the tall grass that grew alongside the cemetery trees, and he would plant our flagpole in the frangipani soil. The tall grass became the South China Sea. The frangipani tree marked our shoreline. The soil around it was strewn with petals, smooth white petals that upon falling soon curled brown and lay as if burnt in the red sand. Li Shin called them seaweed. He would stand beneath the tree, facing the South China Sea and carrying the British flag with both hands. When the flagpole was ready, he would shake the flag loose and hang it on two nails that stuck out at the top of the pole. He would announce solemnly, "I hereby declare Singapore a Crown Colony of the British Empire. All bow to His Majesty, the King." Then he and Li Yuen would take a step back, click their heels, and salute the flag.

We never made games out of the stories that Grandma told us. But there was one story I was especially fond of, which she first told my cousins after our parents died. This was a story about some people who had lived long ago, in China. The people lived near a river, and every day the women would go to the river to wash their clothes. One day while they were washing their clothes, one of the women noticed that she had no reflection. Frightened, she called to the other women to come and look. When the other women came to see what was the matter, they saw that they, too, had no reflections. The river water stretched out before them sunny and blue, like the sky above their heads, except where a willow tree grew bending over the water's edge. There, the river was leafy green.

Slowly, the women realized that they were dead. Then they knew that soon the gods would send a messenger, who would take them to the Other Side. They fell to the ground and prayed on their knees for the gods to let them go home one last time, so that they could see their families. While they were praying, the messenger arrived and took them to the Other Side. But on the seventh day the women's prayers were answered, and when midnight fell upon the countryside, their spirits entered their homes to say goodbye.

On that seventh night of Grandfather's death, Li Shin was out on the back porch practicing his walk until nine o'clock. By then I was falling asleep. I was tired because all afternoon the amahs had been busy cleaning the house and they had forgotten to make sure that I took my two-o'clock nap. But Li Yuen was still wide awake. He was sitting in his bed, drawing, when at nine o'clock we both heard Grandma in the kitchen doorway. She wanted to know why my elder cousin was still outside. We heard her voice, restless and wandering, coasting on the night air like a water lily blown across a pond. I saw

Li Yuen look out the window a second. We both knew that in a few hours it would be midnight. Our aunties and uncles had already gone to their rooms, and the house was almost ready to greet Grandfather's spirit. We could hear our amahs closing the windows and lighting the candles.

In all the rooms that night, the floor had been washed and waxed, the furniture had been dusted, and even the windowsills had been wiped clean. There were fresh oranges in the bowl that sat on the kitchen altar. More oranges had been left on the kitchen table. And in the dining room, a white lace tablecloth had been laid out. It was hand-sewn, and very old. Grandma had brought it with her from China, in 1929, the year she arrived in Singapore to marry our grandfather. She was eighteen years old then. Our grandfather was forty-eight. His Penang wife had died of a heart illness five years before, and his two elder daughters were already married and gone. His other three daughters, who were old enough to understand why he was importing a young bride from China, welcomed Grandma into the house and then they left, one by one. It could not be helped, Grandma explained to us. It was not uncommon in those days for a man to marry a much younger woman, one who could bear him several sons for posterity. But our grandfather's having grown-up daughters complicated matters. When Grandma arrived, she realized that she was only a year older than her bridegroom's youngest daughter. No one had prepared her for this. Her marriage had been arranged for her by her father and the village matchmaker, both of whom had told her that our grandfather had five daughters, but not how old they were. It had not occurred to Grandma to ask. She was a young country girl with no experience, she said. It had not occurred to her that life could so fill itself with complications that she herself did nothing to invite.

When she found my cousin Li Shin on the porch that night, he did not follow her into the house immediately. We could hear him asking her questions. "Why did our great-grandfather come to Singapore?" he wanted to know. "Why didn't he go to Malacca?"

"Oh, by then, the Europeans were here," she answered. "Dutch in Malacca, British in Singapore. And the British had a better reputation than the Dutch. Also, it was known that the British liked Chinese people. We were hard-working, and we obeyed their laws. They did not like the Malays, you know. They thought the Malays were lazy."

"Why?"

"Because the Malays were not as obedient."

"Was it wrong for us to be obedient?"

"It was not a matter of right or wrong. We survived, and we prospered. Remember this—if you have money and education, you have a chance to become boss. Why do you think the Chinese are in charge of Singapore now?"

"It doesn't seem fair, Grandma."

"Why not fair, Li Shin?"

"The British took the island from the Malays. Now that we have it, we should have Malays in our government too."

"There is a Malay minister."

"Only one."

"Most Malays are not educated enough, Li Shin."

An amah passed by the room, and through the doorway we saw her white blouse wave briefly in the dark corridor.

She was carrying two lighted candles in glass bowls on saucers. We listened to the bowls rattling against the saucers as the amah went off down the corridor. Each bowl was filled a quarter of the way with water, to extinguish the flames before they reached the bottom of the bowl.

On the porch outside, Li Shin had stopped asking questions. A silence was beginning between him and Grandma, and we heard the silence plant itself like a sharp slivered moon stuck high in the sky. "Come inside now," we heard Grandma say. "Do not make your grandfather's spirit angry."

"Yes, Grandma," we heard Li Shin answer.

They entered the house, and the door closed after them. The key turned in the lock. Then the porch was silent. Li Yuen sat still in his bed and I watched him as he listened to the frogs and crickets, their cry rising outside behind the trees.

I was lying in bed with my eyes closed when I heard Li Shin enter the room. Li Yuen was putting away his drawing pad. I could hear him sliding it underneath his bed, and his pencil rolling on the floor when he dropped it. I heard Li Shin ask him, "Were you drawing?"

"Yes, why?"

I opened my eyes.

Li Shin was walking over to the dresser that stood between their beds. They slept across the room from me, with Li Shin's bed closer to the windows, because he was not afraid of ghosts.

"You should be practicing arithmetic," he said, pulling open the top drawer of the dresser. "You don't have to practice drawing. You always get A's in that." He looked into the drawer and took out a pair of light blue pajamas with dark blue trim and dark blue buttons.

Li Yuen stared at the pajamas. "Those are mine," he said. "Grandma gave them to me. They're too small for you now."

"They're not too small," Li Shin said, because he wanted to keep the pajamas. They had been a gift from his parents. They had been several sizes too large that year his parents brought them back from Japan, but he had grown into them eventually. He had been wearing those pajamas for the past three years now, sparingly, so as to make them last. But he had grown too tall lately. The sleeves strained to reach his wrists, and the trousers dangled above his ankles. Grandma had told him the pajamas made him look like a poor farmer's son.

I watched him put them back into the drawer. He pulled out another pair, then glanced over his shoulder to make sure that I was asleep. I closed my eyes. I could hear him peeling off his shorts and underpants. Then he whipped on his pajamas. He had recently begun to dress this way, no longer comfortable at being naked with me in the room. I could not understand it yet, nor could I understand why lately he was so shy around schoolgirls. I had heard about this shyness from Li Yuen. Although the school my cousins attended, St. Augustine's, was an all-boys Catholic school, next door to St. Augustine's was Our Lady Queen of Peace. Li Yuen said that during recess they could hear girls laughing on the other side of the high stone wall that surrounded St. Augustine's football field. Then, after school, there would be girls waiting at the bus stop, and girls walking along the sidewalks. Li Yuen said that whenever he and Li Shin walked past those girls that traveled in groups, and many girls did, the girls would pretend not to see them when actually the girls were talking about them. He knew this because the girls made sure of it. They would speak loudly, saying things like "St. Augustine's or St. Patrick's?" Or "How old do you think?" Or "Probably going to be a priest. Too bad." Sometimes Li Yuen would look straight at the girls, and then they would start giggling. But, he said, Li Shin never looked at the girls. And Li Shin would blush if a girl even looked at him, or asked him a question.

It was easy to catch Li Shin blushing, because he was so fair-skinned. In this way he took after his mother, Grandma said. Both Li Yuen and I were darker. We took after our fathers.

"Why don't you practice your arithmetic?"

"I hate arithmetic."

"You can't keep getting C's and D's."

I opened my eyes again. Li Shin was walking over to the door, rolling his underpants into his shorts. He dropped them into the clothes basket. Then he walked back to the dresser and picked up the alarm clock that sat near the lamp. He started winding it. "What kind of future are you going to have?" he said. He put the alarm clock back on the dresser, turning it to face his bed.

"Who cares about arithmetic?"

"The government cares. They won't admit you into the university."

"Maybe I don't want to go to the university."

I knew that Li Yuen did not know yet whether he wanted to go or not. He only wanted to argue.

Li Shin switched off the lamp and got into bed. "You

have to go to the university," he said. I could hear him talking softly in the dark. "Don't be stupid. Otherwise, you will end up as a coolie."

Li Yuen said nothing. Probably he wanted to stop talking about arithmetic, because he was not like Li Shin. Li Shin loved to study. He could sit with any book for hours without even going to the bathroom. But Li Yuen had been told by one teacher after another that he had a problem with concentration. It was written over and over again in his report book. He could not pay attention, his teachers said. He daydreamed too much. Perhaps he could learn some discipline from his brother. But Uncle Kuan had told Grandma not to worry. Uncle Kuan said the teachers were not being fair. The teachers always knew Li Shin first. Li Yuen was only in his third year at school, but already a rumor was circulating that he was not as smart, although one teacher had said that Li Yuen was simply more playful. This was too much pressure on a boy, Uncle Kuan said.

I suspected that Uncle Kuan was right. Li Yuen had told me once he could beat Li Shin in only one subject, art, which was not a real subject. And he could run almost as fast as Li Shin could, but track was not a subject at all.

"Do you want to be a coolie?"

"No."

"You'd better practice your arithmetic."

Li Yuen was looking outside the windows. I looked out, too, and as I remembered Li Shin practicing his walk outside, I thought about the Portuguese who had conquered Malacca in 1511, driving the last Sultan, Mahmud Shah, into exile. The Portuguese had been among the last people to find out about the spice trade. They could not

read the stars, and they had used Chinese-invented gun-
powder to fight. It had not seemed fair to us that they
had been allowed to win the war. But when we told
Grandma this, she explained that the gods did what they
did, and it was not our place to ask questions.

Outside the windows a wind was picking up in the trees.
I closed my eyes. The Dutch had arrived one hundred
and thirty years later to conquer the Portuguese. After
the Dutch had come the British. I imagined the ancient
air tight with the sounds of men fighting, and cannonball
explosions, and bleeding heads torn off shoulders dressed
in olive-green uniforms. What had happened to the souls
of all those dead soldiers? There must have been millions,
all the different armies of foreign souls accumulating over
centuries, let loose. I saw them sailing home in invisible
spirit-boats that packed the oceans.

The wind outside wove gently in between the leaves.
It knocked on branches as it went, bending the cries of
the frogs and crickets into a low lullaby song that rose
and fell, rose and fell. I could hear Li Shin breathing in
his bed. He was almost asleep. It worried me a little that
he wanted to be a soldier, but then I could not imagine
him with his head blown off. So I thought of him as a
peacetime soldier, since the only wars I had heard of had
happened so long ago. After all, wars were outdated
things. They were like traditions. Modern people did not
engage in them.

"Li Shin," I heard Li Yuen say.

"What?" Li Shin mumbled.

"Do you think Grandfather will come into our room
tonight? To look at us?"

"Maybe."

"Will he try to wake us?"

"No."

"Are you scared?"

"It's only Grandfather. Now stop asking me questions and go to sleep."

Li Yuen settled down in his bed, and after a while I could hear him snoring, soft little hums like cotton wool.

Nothing disturbed our house that night, except for a dream that woke Li Shin sometime between midnight and one o'clock. In it, Li Shin saw our grandfather standing near the trellis that ran around the outside of our house. It was a white wooden trellis surrounding the pillars that held up the floor, and since as far back as we could remember it had been broken in one corner near the back. Our grandfather was standing beside that corner in the dream. He was dressed in long white trousers and a white shirt, and he wore a red bow tie. He smiled at Li Shin. Then he bent down and began to crawl into the hole in the broken trellis. Li Shin called out to him to wait. But our grandfather turned around and shook his head. Li Shin asked him didn't he want to change his clothes first. Our grandfather smiled. He put out his hand and signaled to Li Shin to stay where he was. Li Shin reminded him that Grandma would scold him if he walked back into the house with sand on his white trousers. Our grandfather smiled again. Then he turned away and continued crawling, moving slowly through the wide dark space underneath our house. Li Shin watched his white suit recede into the darkness until our grandfather was just a tiny spot of cloth.

As soon as the spot of cloth vanished, Li Shin found himself sitting up in bed. For a moment he was going to wake us. Then something changed his mind. "What?" we asked him later. But Li Shin did not know. He sat there listening to the silence in our house, the sound of our aunties and uncles sleeping. Outside our windows the trees were silent too, a clean stillness that night covering the branches like lace. Li Shin told us that he heard the old grandfather clock chime one o'clock. Slowly, he got out of bed and tiptoed into the corridor.

"Weren't you scared?"

"I don't know."

All the lamps had been turned off everywhere in our house, since ghosts were afraid of electricity. Grandma explained it as negative energy. We had to burn candles instead, the light-heat from candles giving off positive energy.

When Li Shin stepped into the corridor, he saw short white candles burning in round glass bowls on the floor. They sat in a row along one wall. He walked towards the dining room, and saw candles burning in there, too. But the candles in the dining room were altar candles, the tall red kind that burned in pairs on the kitchen altar. He counted fifteen of them on the dining-room table. They stood in a circle, their flames shining softly off Grandma's wedding tablecloth.

Across from the dining room, the door to Grandma's room stood shut, as it always did at night. But on that night Li Shin saw a bright red banner draped across the top. There was Chinese handwriting on the banner, flowing gold characters hand-painted on the red silk. But he could not read the handwriting. He had chosen Malay as his second language in school, since Malay had been declared our country's national language.

He stood looking up at the handwriting on the banner. Then he came back to our room and got into bed.

"And then what happened?" we asked.

"That's all," he said. "I fell asleep."

"What?"

"It was the middle of the night. I fell asleep."

We could not ask anyone about the banner. That morning we went to look for it. The time was only half-past six and Grandma's door still stood shut, but the banner was already gone. Li Shin guessed that the amahs had taken it down. He told us not to ask Grandma, because he did not want to have to tell her about his dream. It would worry her. We asked him why it would worry her. "Grandma's superstitious," he said. "You know that." Li Yuen asked him if the dream was supposed to mean something. Li Shin said no, that it was only a dream and we were not to think about it anymore. Otherwise we would grow up superstitious too. It was all right for Grandma to be superstitious, because she came from the older generation. But it would not be all right for us. We would be considered backward, he said, if we grew up superstitious.

So we never told anyone.

Three

There was a monsoon drain that ran near the coconut trees outside Great-Grandfather's house, where the grass slipped away and then continued on the other side of the drain onto the road. In June you could run to the monsoon drain and stand looking down the steep cement from up there on the edge, and smell leaves rotting on the far dark bottom, and see moss growing in crooked cracks up the sides. And while you were still running, before you reached the drain, you knew already that when you stopped you would be standing at neither the beginning of the drain nor at the end of it, but in the middle somewhere, and that which direction you decided to turn did not matter because the drain would still be running, as if it were the longest drain in the world and ran straight into the horizon, then past the horizon and onwards forever. And you could believe this, believe that a monsoon drain ran on forever, if you did not know already that it went only to the sea. But there were things you knew. There were things you did not know, too, but some things you knew.

In December the floods would arrive, and the road held beating rain. My cousins took mahjong paper from the storeroom and went into the red room, where they knelt on the floor and made paper boats while the rain swept through the trees around us. Mahjong paper was thick and smooth. It helped the boats to have nice firm shapes. The grown-ups kept the mahjong paper in rolls, and my cousins would take out one roll at a time. A roll contained twenty-five sheets. When my cousins unrolled them, they would place books at the corners to flatten the sheets. They would fold each sheet into four parts, tear off each part, and fold it into a paper boat. As soon as the monsoon drain outside began swaying in the muddy brown flood-water, they would throw open the front door and race banging down the veranda steps. They would run across the grass, clutching their white plastic bags filled with boats. I would stay behind and watch. Grandma said that Chinese girls did not play in the rain. Once I heard her. She was on the veranda shouting into the bright slanting rain, Li Shin. Li Shin, she shouted. Look after your brother. You know what will happen if he falls into the drain, the floodwater will carry him to the sea and send him back to China. But my cousin Li Shin ran on. He ran and did not stop until he was at the gate. Then he stepped through the gate, onto the road, and there he walked about, wiping rain off his face so that he could look closely at what was on the ground, although out there, there were only patches of weak grass, yellowish green and trying to grow in the stony earth beside the road. Now and then I saw him cross the road. He stood on the other side, staring into the trees with his hands in his pockets. Then he swung around and crossed back.

On our side of the road Li Yuen was running along the drain. He laughed and chased his boat down the water. His voice drifting across the grass came through the red-room windows and melted past me into the room. I heard him fade over the big empty floor.

The floor in the red room was an open space, because that was where we played. The red room was the only room in Great-Grandfather's house that had so many windows, tall thin windows that ran in a single row down one long wall. The windows had red silk curtains. Grandma said that silk was discovered in 2640 B.C. by the Emperor's wife Si Ling, who used to sit in the Imperial Gardens watching silkworms. Three thousand years after her death, the merchants invented a land route that allowed them to carry silk into Europe. This was called the Silk Route. Only the bravest merchants could travel on it, because the Silk Route crossed mountains and deserts where the nomad robbers lived.

In the red room there were also books. They sat on bookshelves made out of trees that grew in China, called rosewood, and lined two walls from floor to ceiling. Many of the books had once belonged to our dead relatives. They gave off faint dusty colors when the afternoon sun shone on them. Some of them were our great-grandfather's account books. Those sat on the highest shelves, divided up by colors. The ones on the far left were red, in the middle they were blue, and to the far right they were green. They were books that we were not allowed to play with, or talk about. They involved the old days, when people were leaving China to escape the warlords. The books hid names of many people so far thought dead, who had actually escaped, and also names of the people who had helped them.

On one side of the room, in front of the lower book-shelves, there were chairs and tables all made of rosewood and arranged in a row, facing the middle of the floor. The tables had small round marble tops. On them were lamps fitted with stiff white lampshades like pleated skirts. Underneath the lampshades sat human shapes. Each shape sat clinging to a wooden pole and held up the pleated skirt like an umbrella. All the shapes looked like mountain hermits and sages. They had round faces with fat cheeks, they were bald, and they wore robes.

The chairs were old-fashioned, too. They had dragons carved into their backs, and curved legs like scepters. One night in August 1966, when I was eight, Uncle Wilfred told Grandma that he knew a foreign businessman who would pay good money for them. But Grandma said the chairs belonged to us, to Li Shin and Li Yuen and me. When we grew up, each of us would own two chairs. She said that if we were in trouble, we could use them, and that by then we would know what she meant. Uncle Wilfred shook his head, saying, who could tell what the chairs would be worth by then? Strike while the iron's hot, he said. But Grandma told him we deserved some kind of legacy. She said those chairs had been made by the ancient craftsmen. In them was a history that when we were older we would no longer be able to remember by ourselves, if the Prime Minister had his way. Uncle Wilfred did not argue with that. But later we heard him tell another uncle that he thought Grandma was over-reacting.

In August 1966, Singapore was celebrating its first year as a republic, so the Prime Minister was going around making public speeches. Li Shin said that Grandma was worried because the Prime Minister wanted us to call ourselves Singaporeans, not Chinese. Why did that make Grandma worry? I asked. He told me Grandma did not want us to forget her stories. Why did the Prime Minister want us to call ourselves Singaporeans? I asked. "Because that's what we are, Chief," Li Shin said. "Chinese people come from China. We come from Singapore." He reminded me that it was something to be proud of. "We did not become a republic by choice, you know. We have no natural resources. One small island. Other countries have good soil, they can plant food. But only jungle trees can grow here, did you know that? We don't even have our own water. We have to buy water from Malaya. So people were frightened when the federation kicked us out, even the Prime Minister. You don't remember?

I remembered learning in school that Singapore used to be part of the Federation of Malaysia. Why did the federation kick us out? I asked. "Their leaders thought we were developing too fast. They called the Prime Minister headstrong, like the proverb, bull in china shop." I asked, what did that mean? Li Shin explained that the Prime Minister had wanted not only Singapore to industrialize, but the other federation countries, too. And the Malaysians did not want this. They thought the Prime

Minister was moving too fast. They said he was trying to make too many changes too soon. He was not cautious enough. But also, he was Chinese. And Singapore's population was mainly Chinese. The Malaysians were afraid that the Prime Minister's ambition was to gain control over the whole federation. They did not want this, either. Most of them were Malay and they did not want to be controlled by a Chinese country.

So who was right? I wanted to know. The Malaysians or us? Why did the Prime Minister want to industrialize everyone?

"The Prime Minister says it's important to industrialize," Li Shin answered. "That's how Singapore has managed to survive. Besides, we have to keep up with the modern world. You don't want to live in a backward country, do you, Chief?"

A backward country. In school I had been told that in backward countries, children had to have their teeth pulled out without anesthesia, and also, you could die from a simple cut on your foot. So I said, "No." I did not want to live in a backward country.

Late afternoons that year the yellow dust sank low in the trees, so low it shivered over the road and was everywhere above the grass, and we stood in it as if between sheets of slow calm water. In school I learned that evenings on our island came that way, coated in yellow dust, because Singapore was in the tropics, and we were situated one degree and eight minutes from the equator. The equator was an imaginary line that divided the earth. When Pin Nyun, my classmate who sat two desks in front of me, asked Sister Katherine, the geography teacher, how could anything imaginary divide the earth, Sister Katherine said that just because something was imaginary did not mean it could not have consequences in the real. She told us to write that down, and that when we were older we would understand. When we were older, she said, we would know how something as imaginary as the equator could explain humidity, which was real, and our island had plenty of it. Humidity was moisture catching light and sending it down through the trees, the yellow dust.

I had started attending the Convent of St. Catherine of Sienna, a large school with cream-yellow walls and a green tiled roof, where I had to wear a uniform. My uniform was a blue pinafore, which I would slip on over a white blouse. I also had to wear white socks and white shoes. On weekday mornings I would put on my uniform and then my cousins and I would leave Great-Grandfather's house and we would walk out to the main road, where we would catch the half-past-six bus. My cousins wore uniforms, too. They wore white shirts and navy-blue ties, and Li Yuen wore navy-blue shorts, since he was twelve years old and still in primary school. But Li Shin, who was fourteen and already attending secondary school, wore long white pants. They would get off the bus with me at the bus stop near St. Catherine. We would walk to the main gates together, which were green wooden gates connected to a high brick wall that surrounded the whole school compound. Outside the gates stood a shady old mango tree. My cousins would stop there, and say, "Okay, 'bye, Chief." Then they would leave me and walk on quickly, so that they would not be late for General Assembly at their own school, which sat on another road but not far away.

General Assembly in all schools began at exactly fifteen minutes past seven o'clock. First was the Raising of the Flag. We would line up on the field and form neat straight rows, and then all the pupils, and even the teachers and the school principal, had to stand at attention to sing the "Majullah Singapura." After that, we would say the Pledge. During all this, if you moved even a little bit, the prefect in your row would take down your name and give you a detention mark. As soon as your detention marks added up to six, you had to stay after school to be punished.

None of my classmates had ever been to detention class, but we had heard from some of the older girls that it was not so bad, that it depended on who happened to be the supervisor for that day. Sister Josephine was all right. She only made you sit on a bench for an hour. The bench would be placed in the middle of the room and you had to sit up straight and face a blank wall, and you could not slouch, otherwise you would have to stay an extra hour. Sister Judith was the best. She taught art, and if she was in charge, she would make you practice calligraphy, or make you help her with some kind of charity project. Sister Calista was the worst. She made you wash toilets with a hand sponge.

I was careful not to collect any detention marks. Li Shin said that all I had to do was not talk during class, not talk in the school corridor except to greet teachers, not run in the school corridor, not fight with my schoolmates during recess, not unbutton my blouse collar no matter how hot

I felt, and always carry a piece of white chalk in my pinafore pocket so that I could whiten my shoes if they got a little dirty. These rules were taught to us so that we could practice discipline, he said. He said that the Prime Minister said discipline would turn us into a rugged society. A rugged society would mean that we were tough. It would tell the world that even though Singapore was small, we were not a nation of softies, not like when the British were here. When the British were here, we were softies. Li Shin said that was how come the Japanese were able to take over. He said that on December 8, 1941, Japanese planes began attacking us from Johore. It was half-past four in the morning when British antiaircraft guns opened fire all around Changi Prison. That was the first day of World War Two in the Pacific, but the battle with the Japanese lasted for us only till February 15, 1942. By then, the Japanese had cut off our water supply from Malaya, and the British were forced to surrender Singapore. Sometimes when I listened to Li Shin talk about the Japanese, it frightened me.

As soon as the Japanese took over, they renamed our country Syonan, "City of Lights." Li Shin said this was what Singapore looked like to soldiers on board the warships coming in from the sea. He said that up close, once the fighting between the British and the Japanese had ended, Singapore was a mess, worse than a kindergarten playground during recess. Many buildings had burned down, leaving broken walls standing by themselves, ash-black and still smoky. Some buildings were still burning. The streets were filled with dead bodies and smelled of urine. And in the harbor, oil fires kept exploding from the tankers, red flames on the water.

The part of the story that frightened me the most was about Operation Clean-up. The Japanese sent out an order for all Chinese males between the ages of eighteen and fifty to report to the Kempei Tai at noon on February 21, 1942. The Kempei Tai were Japanese secret police. They were famous for chopping off the heads of people who disobeyed or offended them. Most of the Chinese men in Singapore obeyed the order. They reported to the designated assembly points, which were wide-open spaces without trees, where they were made to stand in the hot sun for days while they waited to be checked and stamped. When each man's turn came, he was told to write his name. Some men wrote their names in Chinese, some wrote in English. The Japanese were at war with both the British and with mainland China. If you wrote your name in English, you were stamped as pro-British. If you had a tattoo mark on your arm, you were stamped as a member of the Triad, the Chinese secret society, whose members remained loyal to mainland China. If you forgot to apologize to the Kempei Tai either for having a tattoo mark or for writing your name in English, you were detained and later you would be taken to the seaside, where you and other detainees would be told to walk into the water and then the Kempei Tai would begin firing from behind.

Operation Clean-up was planned by Lieutenant Colonel Tsuji of the 25th Imperial Army, but the order to put it into action was signed by the commander in chief, General Yamashita. Six thousand Chinese died during that operation. Li Shin said that this was written in the books, and that we ought to remember it, there was no excuse for forgetting. We ought to remember it could happen again if we did not let other countries know they could not just walk in and take over. He said the next time someone tried to do this, we Singaporeans would have our own national defense. We would have our own army, our own navy, and our own air force. We would not have to rely on the British. The British were not as bad as Grandma seemed to think, but still, they were not Singapore people. In World War Two, when they fought to defend Singapore against the Japanese, they did it because Singapore was a British colony, which was also why the Japanese decided to attack us. But, Li Shin said, fighting for a colony was not the same as fighting for your own country. This was why we needed our own soldiers.

In Great-Grandfather's house, no one who could remember it would talk about the Japanese Occupation, which lasted three years, till the day the Americans dropped the atomic bomb on Nagasaki. What Li Shin knew he found out from reading books that our youngest uncle, Uncle Tien, would borrow from the adult section of the National Library downtown. Uncle Tien had been born after the Occupation. He was nineteen years old the year that I was eight. My cousins remembered that he used to play games with them, but I knew him as a quiet young uncle who smiled at us often but did not talk very much. I knew that he liked to draw pictures. He would draw pictures of Great-Grandfather's house, catching it from different angles. Sometimes he would sit outside all after-noon, underneath a coconut tree, and we would sit around him and watch his hands. Later when we were going back into the house he would let us carry his drawing pad with the thick red cover, his blue, red, and yellow pencils, and his small gray box of charcoal.

I knew that since August, Uncle Tien had not drawn

many pictures, that he had stopped spending time at home. On weekday evenings he would return from work with the other grown-ups, but soon after dinner Grandma would be asking, "Where is Yu Tien? Has he gone out again?" During the weekends, he would go out all day, till finally one October night the other grown-ups decided to tease him about the girlfriend that he must be hiding from Grandma.

"What?" they said. "You are afraid she won't approve?"

"I don't have a girlfriend," Uncle Tien answered.

"Must be one kind of girlfriend you don't want anyone to find out about," they said. "What is her job?"

"I don't have a girlfriend." Uncle Tien was soft-spoken, and his voice was almost like Li Shin's voice.

"Hmm, where do you go, you don't have a girlfriend?" they said.

"You know where I go," he said. "To the library."

"Oh, that again," they said.

They stopped teasing him, but later that night, Uncle Kuan took him aside and told him that he'd better be careful, that these days the government was suspicious of everyone, especially students who hurried off to meetings at night. Uncle Tien said, why should the government suspect students studying in the library? How could anyone prove it was not a study group? Uncle Kuan told him not to be so stupid. He said to Uncle Tien, "You don't know about spies? All governments have spies." He asked if Uncle Tien didn't remember what had happened last year, when the government announced its plan to reorganize Nanyang, a Chinese university, into an English university like the University of Singapore. The goal was

to eliminate competition by making Nanyang a branch of
the University of Singapore. Also, it was important for
all citizens to speak a common language, and what better place to start than within a university? Already too
much tension had been allowed to grow between Chinese-
speaking students and English-speaking students. A fledg-
ling nation like Singapore could not afford such tension.
Absolute unity among all citizens was essential. But the
students at Nanyang had decided to protest the government's plan anyway. They organized class boycotts and
picketed lecture rooms. So it seemed to the government
that they had divided loyalties, that they were holding on
too tightly to ancestral ties. "So remember what the government did," said Uncle Kuan. Uncle Tien said yes, he
remembered. He remembered that the government arrested the students for giving in to Communist influences,
and ignored the real issue, which was academic freedom.
Uncle Kuan said yes, maybe so. But if you were accused
of being a Communist, anything could happen to you. He
told Uncle Tien not to forget that.

In early November we heard that another demonstra-
tion for academic freedom had been reported in the newspaper. This time, students from various Chinese schools
as well as from the University of Singapore and the Singapore Polytechnic were involved. They called themselves
the Singapore National Action Front. The government
arrested all of them for giving in to Communist influences,
and expelled them from their schools. Noncitizens were
deported.

In Great-Grandfather's house the grown-ups argued
over the Internal Security Act. Uncle Tien kept insisting
that it was undemocratic. I asked Li Shin, what was the

Internal Security Act? He said, "Arrest and detention without trial." I asked him, what did that mean? He said it meant that the government did not need solid proof that someone was a Communist. If the government suspected someone of being a Communist, that person could be arrested and sent to jail. I asked him, why would the government do that? He said the government wouldn't arrest someone without having a good reason.

I did not have to ask why the government wanted to arrest Communists. Sister Adeline, who taught my class ethics and ballet in school, had told us that most Communists were not Singapore people. They were Malaysians and Indonesians who were entering our country illegally, and they were trying to brainwash our citizens into turning against the government. They wanted our citizens to vote against PAP in the next elections, so they spread the propaganda that although Singapore had stopped being a British colony since 1963, when we joined the Federation of Malaysia, PAP continued to be a puppet of British imperialism. PAP stood for People's Action Party. Our government leaders were all PAP members. When I told Li Shin what Sister Adeline had told us, he said that Communists did not understand the difference between imperialism and a guided democracy.

"What is a guided democracy?" I asked.

He said this meant we were guided by the Prime Minister, who was head of PAP. We were not like America. America was a free democracy, he said, because American people did not like being guided.

"How come we don't want a free democracy?" I asked.

"Because we're Asians," he said. "We don't always believe the same things as Americans."

"Do the Communists want a free democracy?" I asked.

No, he said, Communists did not believe in democracy at all. Communists believed that any kind of democracy was actually imperialism.

I was getting confused. "What's imperialism?"

"Imperialism is when you have to do what a foreign government wants."

I was still confused because I did not understand how a free democracy could be imperialist. But America was not my country. I was worried about my country. My country was the one the Communists wanted. And if they succeeded in brainwashing our citizens against PAP, what would happen?

"PAP will have to step down from office."

Then we would have a new government, a Communist government. We would have a leader like Chairman Mao. Chairman Mao sent teachers and doctors into rice fields and made them work as farmers, and now China had become backward. The same thing would happen to us. We would become uneducated. Westerners would not be allowed to enter Singapore. We would lose touch with the modern world, and all our citizens would be wearing old-fashioned dark blue Chinese shirts and trousers, and riding around on bicycles.

I had seen such pictures in Auntie Daisy's magazines, so I knew. Auntie Daisy was our youngest auntie. She was three years older than Uncle Tien, and she did not spend much time at home, either. But on the evenings that I would follow my cousins to her room, she would be lying on her bed, reading colorful shiny magazines. Some magazines Auntie Daisy had bought off the black market. She would not let us look at those, pushing them underneath a pillow as soon as she saw us. She said we were too young. But she would show us the magazines with pictures of China taken by American journalists. "See how lucky you are?" she had told us one evening. "Imagine being born at the wrong time in the wrong place. Imagine what you might be doing now."

On that evening I was lying on my stomach with my eyes closed, listening to Li Shin turn pages next to my face. The pages in Auntie Daisy's magazines were making a crisp clean sound, like paper kites fighting in the wind. "What's this?" I heard Li Shin say. I could hear him lifting the magazine from the bed, the edges of the magazine cover scraping the cotton sheet. I opened my eyes. Li Shin was holding up the magazine so that Auntie Daisy could see. The mattress dipped on my other side, Li Yuen stretching himself so that he could see, too. He knelt on the bed, leaning forward, balancing on the palms of his hands. I heard him read the caption: "Old women waiting in line behind a milk truck."

"Look at their feet," said Auntie Daisy. "When they were little girls, their mothers would tie up their feet in bandages every day, to crush the growing bones. Old-fashioned high-class Chinese men wanted their wives to have small dainty feet."

"Grandma has small feet," Li Yuen said.

"Not that small," Li Shin told him.

"Your grandma's father, your great-grandfather on that side of the family, was a farmer," said Auntie Daisy. "Daughters born to farmers had to work in the fields. They could not afford to have bound feet. You see those women in the magazine? They're from the city. That photograph was taken in Peking. A farmer's daughter didn't have much chance of marrying into a high-class family, anyway."

"Did it hurt?" Li Shin asked.

"Having your bones crushed every day?" said Auntie Daisy. "Yes, it hurt."

"Did the little girls cry?"

"Yes, they cried."

"And the mothers still tied up their feet?"

"Women were unlucky in those days. They had to look and behave exactly as men wanted. Otherwise, no one would marry them. And if no one married you, you had to stay with your parents until they died. And when they died, you were left all to yourself." Auntie Daisy paused. "What a life, huh?"

I could hear her small metal fan rotating on the windowsill. It turned slowly, side to side, sweeping in cool air from the trees outside. The motor knob was set on low so that the pages in her magazines would not flap about, out of control. In the whole room, talcum powder danced on the fan breeze, and I could smell also secret perfume and Raspberry Red nail polish. Auntie Daisy kept a row of nail polish bottles with white caps underneath the glass top of her dressing table, but Raspberry Red was her favorite.

"Chief, don't you want to see?" Li Shin was stroking the back of my head. He slid the magazine in front of me, and I looked at the old Chinese women dressed in blue shirts and black trousers lining up one behind the other on a gray road at five o'clock in the morning. The women carried metal pails in their hands. A man in the back of the truck was pouring bubbly white milk from a big wooden bucket into a metal pail sitting on the floor, and the first old woman in line watched him with her hands folded neatly in front of her. On the opposite page, there was a crowd of men and women and schoolchildren all poised on bicycles, waiting at a traffic light for the light to turn green. They also wore blue shirts and black trousers, and stood with one foot on the road, the other on the pedal, ready.

I pushed the magazine away so that I could put my head down and close my eyes. Li Shin laughed. "Chief's not interested," he said. "Grandma never tried to tie up her feet. Singapore girls can't afford to have bound feet, either. Everyone here must work. Singapore has only one natural resource, the people."

"Yes," said Auntie Daisy. "But you know, even in Singapore, men get better treatment than women."

"Like Malays and Chinese?" Li Yuen asked.

"Yes," said Auntie Daisy.

"It'll change," Li Shin said. "The Prime Minister has promised, everyone a first-class citizen. The Malays have to trust him, that's all, and do what he says. They have to get educated. And the Chinese students have to speak English. That's the language of the future."

"And the women?" said Auntie Daisy.

"The Prime Minister says women have different kinds of work from men," Li Shin said. "But they'll still get equal treatment."

"Equal treatment means equal opportunity," said Auntie Daisy. "That means equal opportunity at everything."

I listened to the fan turning in the window, showering talcum powder and Raspberry Red nail polish and that light mysterious perfume over our heads. I knew that I was lucky I did not have bound feet, and lucky I had not been born in China. Still, Grandma told me that Chinese girls were to be raised differently from the boys, no matter where we lived. I could not play in the rain. I could not stay out in the sun too long, otherwise I would get spots on my skin. And when I sat down in a skirt, I had to keep my knees together, not let them spread open so that everyone could see what color panties I was wearing.

But Singapore was different from China. I knew it, breathing in the sweet soft smells in Auntie Daisy's room.

Behind Great-Grandfather's house there was a path, a narrow footpath that ran from the last wood step of the back porch out across the grass towards the frangipani tree. Past the frangipani tree the path disappeared into the tall grass, which also grew behind the kindergarten playground at St. Catherine. I had heard the older girls call it love-grass. It grew bending a little to the side and had long feathery heads.

From the love-grass the footpath entered the cemetery, where it ran twisting between the thick old trees. When December came and a saltwater wind began to blow, drifting low, we heard it like someone sweeping dead leaves off the path. If we were sitting on the back porch, we would see it, the saltwater wind. It would blow out of the trees, brush through the love-grass, and make dust in the footpath rise. The dust rose brownish red, moving over the ground like a slow dance.

On the back porch we would sit on the steps to watch evening slip over the grass and smell that saltwater wind. Li Shin said you could always tell when the monsoon arrived. You could tell when the heavy rains were about to start, because of that saltwater wind blowing in from the sea. He said that Grandfather had taught him that. When Grandfather was alive, he used to call Li Shin out to the porch after dinner, and they would have their man-to-man talks. Li Shin said he wished he could remember what they had talked about, but he couldn't, it was so long ago.

Did he remember our parents? I would ask him sometimes, while we were sitting on the steps, watching the saltwater wind. This was when we were younger, before I had begun attending school. It was Li Shin who had told me about the accident. Our fathers had both worked for the government, and traveled all the time. Our mothers would go with them on their trips, and this was how all four of them got killed together, in the middle of the night on a highway in Malaya.

"I remember them a little," he would say.

"Do you miss your father and mother?" I would ask.

"They weren't home very much, Chief," he would reply. "Why? Do you miss yours?"

"No."

I had not known my parents. All I knew now was that my mother had chosen my English name, Esha. Grandma had not liked it and so had given me a Chinese name, Su Yen, which she said if it was pronounced the proper way meant Fair Cloud. This was what she had always called me. This, I knew.

During the first two weeks of that December in 1966, I would lie on the porch floor all afternoon,

while my cousins sat at the round wooden kitchen table,
studying. Since Li Yuen was in Primary Six, he had to
take the PSLE, the Primary School Leaving Examination.
He had to pass the PSLE in order to attend secondary
school. Li Shin would sit at the table with him until three
o'clock, and help him study. I would lie outside the kitchen
door, smelling coolness rise from underneath Great-
Grandfather's house, while I listened to them talking
about fractions, decimals, binomials, matrices. Mathematics was Li Yuen's weakest subject. Sometimes I would
hear Li Shin scolding him for not paying attention. Once
I heard a book fly across the room, pages fluttering. It
landed hard against the refrigerator and slid straight down
to the floor. Li Yuen hurriedly went to pick it up.

The coolness that was underneath Great-Grandfather's
house was the kind you had to lie down on the floor to
catch. You had to lie there with your cheek pressed to the
floorboards, and wait. Then it would come. It came as a
dark breeze between the cracks, and was safe like old
things. When I smelled it, I would never want to get up.
I would not want to get my uniform ready for school, or
do homework, or grow big, but want to stay there forever,
with the sun changing on the grass and light moving in
the shadows, and my cousins' voices inside the kitchen
doorway, saying, "Sets, subsets."

Then came the last afternoon before the examination.
Li Yuen stopped studying at four o'clock, when usually
he would sit at the kitchen table until dinnertime, even
with our amahs moving around him, chopping onions,
slicing lean pork and vegetables, boiling rice. But on that
last afternoon I heard him snapping his books shut, and
then he stepped out of the kitchen. He was carrying his

black toy rifle, and he hurried down to the grass. I watched him down there poking his gun into Grandma's lime bushes. He was pretending to check for Communists. When he glanced up and saw me watching, he stopped. He ran back up the porch steps and walked over.

"Are you a Communist?" he said, standing right above me. He held the rifle to my throat. "Tell the truth and shame the devil."

"I'm not a Communist," I said.

"Are you telling the truth? If you lie, twenty-five push-ups," he warned, pushing the rifle a little harder against my throat.

I was holding in my hand a twig that I used to loosen dried earth caught in cracks between the floorboards, and Li Yuen was standing so close I could see up his shorts and notice that he was not wearing underpants. Sometimes he did that when he had to sit down and study. He would take off his underpants and wear only his black running shorts. I raised my arm and jabbed him.

"What!" He stepped back, surprised. I got up at once. He said, "I'll kill you," and I watched him slide his hand into his shorts. He started feeling around, gently. I was nervous because I did not know how hard I had jabbed.

We did not hear Auntie Lily coming across the kitchen floor, so we did not notice when she stopped suddenly in the doorway. Then I saw her standing there watching us with her hands on her hips and her mouth open. "What are you doing?" she said, sounding horrified. Li Yuen yanked his hand out of his shorts. I grinned at Auntie Lily. "Aya," she said, shaking her head, the look on her face matching her voice. "What is happening in this house?"

Li Yuen pointed at me. "She jabbed my birdie," he said, trying to shame me with his eyes.

"He did it first," I said. "He tried to choke me."

Auntie Lily stared hard at both of us, and then her eyes narrowed down, picking me out, making me think of a huge bird that I had seen in one of Li Shin's books, which he said was the American bald eagle. "You have sand on your face, Esha." Her eyes were cold and knowing. "Go ahead," she said. "Lie on the floor some more. You want to have skin like sandpaper? You will never get a husband. Grow up and be an old maid."

I only half believed her. I could not ask for proof. Talking back to grown-ups was rude and I could get slapped hard for it.

"We're going to have visitors this afternoon," Auntie Lily said. "You children are to stay outside. See if you can behave yourselves."

"Who's coming?" Li Yuen asked. He stood up straight, swinging his rifle onto his shoulder as if he were about to begin guard duty.

"Government men," said Auntie Lily. "Be careful they don't haul you both off to jail for being juvenile delinquents."

"Why are they coming here?" Li Yuen asked.

"That's not your business," she said. As she stepped into the kitchen, her dress with white and green polka dots clung to her bum like sticky rice paper. She was very rounded all over. She had round hips, a round bum, and what I had heard the older girls in school call round boobies.

As soon as we could hear that Auntie Lily had left the

kitchen, Li Yuen turned to me. "It's all your fault," he said. "Now she'll tell Grandma we're perverts."

"Pervert" was his new word from school. His classmate Charlie Tan was a pervert. Charlie Tan hid a small mirror in his shoelace when he talked to girls. He would stand close to them, and the foot with the mirror would be moving about slyly, trying to get in the right position to reflect someone's panties. Charlie Tan's best friend, Lim Koh Swee, was also a pervert. Lim Koh Swee always walked into the girls' bathroom during an interschool swimming competition, pretending to take a wrong turn. Brother Dennis, who was Li Yuen's school principal, called them birds of a feather, and said no wonder their exam results were so low, their heads were never in their books.

A small breeze rose over the grass, and I listened to it smacking the bedsheets hanging out there on hollow bamboo poles. The poles were balanced on two metal stands. The tops of the stands had little semicircle curves for the poles to fit into and not roll off. The breeze smacked the corners of the sheets, making them flip tiny curtsies the way Sister Adeline in ballet class taught us to curtsy, all of us holding out the corners of our skirts and dropping down on one knee.

I could hear Li Shin walking quietly inside the kitchen. I knew it was him before I turned around and saw him standing in the doorway. He had a certain kind of walk, almost gentle. If he wanted to, he could walk so quietly no one could hear him.

"Catch," he said, throwing a white T-shirt at Li Yuen.

Li Yuen caught it with one hand. He put his gun down and slipped the T-shirt over his head.

When Li Shin stepped onto the porch, I could smell

that he had taken a shower. He was all soap and Johnson's baby powder. He rubbed my head and took my hand, and I saw Li Yuen pick up the rifle.

We walked down to the grass. We passed the mango tree and then Li Shin turned the corner, and Li Yuen and I followed him up the side of Great-Grandfather's house. Here the trees grew close to the wall and the ground was covered with dead leaves. The leaves broke apart as we stepped on them, making a sound like dry wood burning, a sound not like paper, since paper burned quietly. We were walking single-file. I walked behind Li Shin, and Li Yuen came after me. Li Shin always walked ahead, because he was the eldest. He had a duty to protect us. We passed one window after another, most of them opening into bedrooms where the grownups slept. I could not reach the windows, since the ground sloped away, sinking into the trees, but I could hear that all the rooms were empty.

The government men had already arrived. At the front of the house we saw a black car parked near the trees across the road. The driver was sitting behind the steering wheel. He wore a black songkok, a Malay man's hat. He seemed to be asleep. I could see his head leaning sideways on the back of his seat. But as soon as we had crossed over the grass and Li Shin was lifting the iron latch to open the gate, the driver sat up. The door on his side swung open, and we saw his legs sliding out of the car. He did not step out. He simply left the car door open and sat there with his feet on the road. He wore plain black shoes, black socks, black trousers, and a short-sleeved white shirt. He could have been a government man himself, except he did not wear a tie.

"*Selamat petang,*" he said, wishing us good afternoon.

"*Selamat petang,*" we wished him back. Then we strolled around the car, Li Shin keeping one hand on my shoulder to guide me along the edge of the monsoon drain. The smell of wet leaves rose from the bottom of the drain. We stopped and peered through the car windows, but the maroon leather seats inside were empty. There was not even a slightly wrinkled handkerchief, or a folded newspaper, or a yellow pencil or some coins that might have dropped out of someone's pocket. We circled around the bumper of the car and arrived again at the driver's door.

The driver had pretended not to watch us. Every time I looked at him, he would be staring towards Great-Grandfather's house, as if that was his job, what he was paid to do. But as soon as I turned away, I could feel his eyes fixed on our backs.

"Are you thirsty?" Li Shin asked him. "You want some iced water?"

The driver shook his head. "No need," he said, smiling. He thanked us, "*Terima kaseh,*" and looked us over, shifting his eyes from Li Shin to Li Yuen to me. Then he reached behind him, feeling for the glove compartment. When his fingers found the knob, he gave it a sharp twist and the small rectangular door popped open. We watched his hand groping around inside. It came back out with a chocolate bar wrapped in silver paper.

"*Satu sahaja,*" the driver said, meaning that there was only one bar and we had to share it. He held it out to us.

We looked at the chocolate bar for a while, and then Li Shin took it. He said "*Terima kaseh*" to the driver, who was leaning back to snap the glove compartment shut.

The driver turned back to us, looked at Li Yuen, and asked, "You are a soldier boy?"

Li Yuen held up the rifle in his hand. "It's just a toy,"
he said. He waved the rifle at Li Shin. "My brother's the
soldier. Li Shin's a marksman."

The driver looked puzzled. "You are a soldier?" he said
to Li Shin. "You are a schoolboy."

"I'm a National Cadet," Li Shin told him, and the driver
smiled, nodding, "Ah."

"He's a marksman," Li Yuen repeated. "He can aim at
things other boys can't even see."

"*Betul 'tak?*" the driver said, asking if it was true.

Li Shin shrugged his shoulders, looking uncomfortable.
He glanced around, afraid that someone might hear and
tell Grandma, who did not even know that Li Shin had
joined the National Cadets. I knew, but I had been sworn
to secrecy. I had crossed my heart and hoped to die. National Cadets were schoolboy soldiers and Grandma might
not approve, but Li Shin said he had to do what he had
to do. One day soon he was going to tell Grandma. He
was waiting for the right time.

Men's voices came drifting across the grass, and the
driver sat up straight. We turned and saw Grandma standing in the living-room doorway. She was looking at us
over the heads of the government men, who were bending
and putting on their shoes on the veranda. The men said
something to her before turning to leave. She raised her
hand and waved at us to come back to the house.

We crossed the road and walked back on the grass. There
were five government men coming down the path. They
all wore black ties, white shirts with short sleeves, and
black trousers. They carried black leather briefcases.
When they passed us, one of them glanced quickly at Li
Shin, as if he thought he had seen Li Shin somewhere.

Then he seemed to change his mind. He walked on with the other men, who were talking quietly among themselves. I saw how their black shoes left no marks along the path, where the sand was packed and hard.

There were two words that we could hear when we passed the government men: Barisan Socialis. They were Malay words splitting apart the men's English conversation, because Malay was so different from English to hear. When my Malay classmates spoke to one another, they spoke like singing or humming. Smooth pebbles rolling down a slope; Barisan Socialis was like that to hear.

I looked up at Li Shin, who was walking on the grass beside me, and I asked him, "What is Barisan Socialis?"

He shook his head. "Workers' Party," he said. "Don't say it in front of Grandma."

We stood on the veranda steps and watched the black car pulling out from the shade of the trees. It drove off smoothly, the dust on the road floating up after it and hanging a moment in the air before settling. Grandma had gone back into the living room, and now we could hear her in the corridor; the floorboards creaking soft sounds that disappeared further and further into the house.

Li Shin unwrapped the chocolate carefully. It had melted on the outside and small white nuts were sticking out of it. He tore it into three pieces and gave me the biggest piece because I was youngest. We sat down to eat, looking at the road where the government men's car had been parked. Li Shin said it was because that black car was so solid that it made us notice it when it was gone. It was so solid, he said. Li Yuen and I looked at the road again. It lay beyond the fence, shady gray and hushed, the late-afternoon sun seeping slowly through the patterns of leaves.

We were sitting there, chewing on our pieces of chocolate, when we saw the Malay boy walking along the fence. He wore khaki trousers and a white T-shirt. He stopped outside the gate and put his hands together in front of him. Then he raised his arms. He was carrying two small white flags on sticks. He moved them about in the air, signaling a message to Li Shin. Li Yuen and I had seen the same kind of flags in our bedroom cupboard, where Li Shin hid them in a cardboard box with his broken teddy bear. The flags were laid carefully at the bottom of the box, then covered with three layers of white tissue. The teddy bear lay on top of the white tissue, with its head crooked.

When the Malay boy had completed his signal, he dropped his arms and walked off.

"Are you going to the meeting?" Li Yuen said. Only a year ago he had not been able to read the white flags, but now Li Shin had taught him how. When I was older, he was going to teach me, too.

"No." Li Shin rubbed his toes against the wooden step. He looked disappointed. This was the third time that Malay boy had come to Great-Grandfather's house. Each time there had been a cadet meeting, and Li Shin had missed it, because he could not tell Grandma where he was going.

I wanted to ask him if his meetings were the same kind as Uncle Tien's. So I said, "Is your meeting in the library?"

He shook his head. "It's not the same thing at all," he said, reading my mind. He said his meetings were for survival training, meant only for National Cadets. A real army captain came and talked to the boys about how to survive in the jungle during wartime. Then the boys would practice by playing a game.

"What kind of game?" I asked.

"Just a survival game," he said.

We saw our uncles walking on the road, their white shirts misty in the evening light. Our twin aunties walked behind them, wearing red and yellow dresses.

"What kind of meeting does Uncle Tien go to?" I asked, and Li Yuen said suddenly, "Barisan Socialis."

Li Shin frowned at him. "We don't know that," he said. "Don't go spreading rumors."

"Grandma thinks so," Li Yuen said.

"Thinks so what?" I said.

"Never mind," Li Shin said. "Just don't say Barisan Socialis in front of Grandma. You don't want to make her angry for nothing." He was talking to me but looking hard at Li Yuen, so Li Yuen kept quiet.

Our twin aunties had no voices. Just before they were born, when they were babies curled up inside Grandma's womb, a monkey had jumped onto Grandma's back and frightened them. Grandma had been strolling through the Botanical Gardens, where monkeys swung from tree to tree, and you could throw them peanuts to make them climb down to you. Usually, the monkeys stayed away from people, but the monkey that jumped on Grandma was an odd one. Grandma said later that she should not have been strolling through the Botanical Gardens, she being a pregnant mother. With those monkeys around, anything could have happened to her unborn babies. Luckily our twin aunties were not born with monkey faces. Grandma said that babies in the womb that were shock-scared by an animal often turned out looking like the animal.

I watched our twin aunties ambling up the path, their red and yellow dresses swishing bright into the fast-falling night. Our uncles had stopped outside the gate to talk among themselves. Our twin aunties approached the veranda steps, smiling at us. We greeted them, "Hello, Auntie San One, Auntie San Two." Although their names were Chen San and Chen Lin, only Grandma called everyone by their birth names. The grown-ups referred to our twin aunties as San and Lin.

They nodded at us as they passed us on the steps, light fragrance hidden in the folds of their skirts. They shared a room a few doors away from Auntie Daisy, and their room too floated perfumy as if the air were crossed by silver threads, all spun from an invisible perfume wheel. In the afternoon when sunlight threw dusty rays across our twin aunties' beds, I would imagine a fairy circle in the middle of their floor, a circle where a Chinese Rumpelstiltskin sat spinning perfume the way he had once spun gold out of straw in exchange for the Emperor's firstborn child.

But our twin aunties did not have boyfriends, not like Auntie Daisy, whose boyfriends were slender young men whom she had met at the university. I had seen them outside the house late on some afternoons. They were quite handsome, the way they would drive up the road in their secondhand cars and park nonchalantly under the trees. "Don't worry," Auntie Daisy would tell Grandma. "They come from good families." To us, she would say, "They're students. They have so much studying to do.

Once in a while they need to relax." Her boyfriends wore faded American Levi's and white cotton shirts with sleeves rolled up to their elbows. They would stand under the trees with their hands in their hip pockets, looking stylish while they waited for Auntie Daisy. We always knew when they were out there. We would have heard them coming up the road, the sound of their engines shifting gears as they approached our gate, then purring as their wheels slid halfway off the asphalt onto the roadside grass.

Sometimes when the boyfriends came, Auntie Daisy would stay out on the road with them until evening. She did not work part-time at the office the way Uncle Tien did, so on days when she did not have classes, she did not have to go anywhere in particular. We would watch her through the hanging leaves of the coconut trees while she sat on someone's car and chatted and told jokes. She would be wearing Bermuda shorts and one of Uncle Tien's shirts, always a size too big so that it hung loosely about her shoulders and made her arms look even smaller-boned than they were. Auntie Daisy reminded us of lemongrass, springy and stalky. We would watch her until from across the road, over the tops of the other parked cars, the sun began to set, sending its long light slivers into the coconut trees. Then Auntie Daisy would slide off the hood of the car onto the road. The boyfriends would watch her flip open our gate. They would hope for one last careless thing that she might say, and sometimes she would give it to them, tossing it over her shoulder, a single word, a private joke, a name perhaps. They would laugh again, suddenly and always surprised. From the veranda we would hear them, young men's voices hardening in the warm closed shimmers of gold behind the coconut trees. Something taboo had been spoken, but Auntie Daisy would be walking back to the house, swinging her arms as if not caring what anyone might think. Still laughing, softly now, the men would move away from each other and return to their own cars.

Men did not wait under the trees for our twin aunties to go outside and join them. Perhaps at the office there was a man who would smile at them, who would lift his head whenever he caught a whiff of their perfume. Perhaps there was more than just one man, brain-tired and weary-eyed from poring over pages of names and numbers and dollar signs, who would sit back in his chair once in a while, and gaze in the direction of our twin aunties, and let himself admit that while our twin aunties had no voices, they certainly had curves. But perhaps there was no one. At night, when one of Auntie Daisy's boyfriends drove by and took her to a picture show, our twin aunties sat in their silent room, in the bright stewing light of seven lamps, and embroidered cushion covers and white pillowcases for the Little Sisters of the Poor.

The Little Sisters of the Poor were nuns who ran an old-age home near Mount Alvernia Hospital, which was the Catholic hospital where my mother had given birth to me. Most of the men and women in the old-age home had no families, or were bedridden and so their families could not afford the time to take care of them. On Saturdays our twin aunties took their embroidery baskets to the old-age home so that they could keep some of the old women company while they sewed. They sewed green-and-orange lovebirds snuggling on leafy branches along the borders of the white pillowcases, or they sewed baby birds just learning to fly. On the cushion covers they sewed butterflies balancing on the edges of flowers. Sometimes they sewed bees stinging the centers of the flowers, or simply plain flowers shooting up straight like grass on a hot still day. Once in a while, they sewed thin brown-skinned Chinese men wearing large straw hats. Coolie hats. The men would be walking behind water buffaloes in a padi field, or standing up in wooden boats, fishing.

It seemed to me that on that evening we were watching our uncles discussing something private at the gate I understood a little why Auntie Lily did not want me to end up an old maid. She herself was not to be called an old maid, for I knew that she had been married once. When Auntie Lily was a schoolgirl, she had met a boy named Bartholomew Sim, who had married her as soon as she had finished her schooling. A year later, that boy Bartholomew Sim had entered the seminary to become a priest, and he was now Father Bartholomew at St. Ignatius's Church in the Bukit Timah district. My cousins had heard it said that Bartholomew Sim had had no family and so had willed all his worldly possessions to Auntie Lily, which she had traded in for cash. But we never knew if this was true, since grown-ups did not discuss their affairs with us, and Auntie Lily especially did not talk about herself.

An evening breeze passed through the veranda. It whispered into the bougainvillea flowers hanging soft shades of pink over the white rail, into the hard brown vines, half hidden, that wound themselves around the white posts to climb up to the roof. I could hear our twin aunties' footsteps fade slowly into Great-Grandfather's house. Our uncles were still talking at the gate. The sun had long since dropped behind the trees, the road now hushed like a river in blue-green twilight. Soon it would be nighttime. Soon the frogs and crickets would begin their cry. I watched Uncle Tien reach over the gate to lift the iron latch. He held the gate open for our two older uncles to pass through. They walked past him and continued walking. Uncle Tien shut the gate and hurried up the path to catch up.

In that blue-green twilight, smooth-skinned and narrow-hipped, our uncles came towards the house, and I could see why the older girls in school called boys and men cucumbers. Even Uncle Kuan, who was related to us by marriage, not by blood, vaguely resembled one of those cucumbers I had seen cupped in the palm of a nun, once when I had seen the nun buying vegetables from the peddler who set up his stall in front of St. Catherine every Tuesday morning.

Our uncles paused at the bottom of the steps. Uncle Wilfred loosened his tie and stared at Li Yuen, who was sitting on the last step, hugging his knees. "You are ready for your exam?" Uncle Wilfred asked him. Li Yuen shrugged his shoulders and said, "So-so." Uncle Wilfred pulled off his tie from around his shirt collar. He rolled it into a neat black ball. Uncle Kuan and Uncle Tien also loosened their ties, but they did not take them off. "So-so is not good enough," Uncle Wilfred said. Li Yuen glanced up, and Uncle Kuan and Uncle Tien smiled at him. He smiled back, a brief quick smile. Then he got up and ran over to the trees, and we could see him over there hunting the ground for snails.

Uncle Wilfred frowned. He looked up the steps to where Li Shin stood leaning on a wooden post.

"He's ready," Li Shin said.

"You think so," Uncle Wilfred said. He glanced over his shoulder and shook his head. At the trees, Li Yuen was squatting down to play with the snails. We could see him reaching out slowly and touching each snail with the tip of his finger, making the snail slide its head back into its shell.

"Does he know what will happen to him if he fails?" Uncle Wilfred said.

"He knows," Li Shin replied. "He won't fail."

Uncle Kuan moved past Uncle Wilfred. He came up the steps to the veranda and put his hand on Li Shin's head. "When did you grow so tall?" he said. "Only last week you were like that." He dropped his hand, spreading his fingers three feet above the floor.

Li Shin smiled. He watched the trees where Li Yuen was playing, and then he told our uncles about the government men. Our uncles nodded their heads as if they had been expecting this for a long time and now it had finally happened. They sent one another silent glances. Uncle Wilfred wanted to know how many government men we had seen and whether they had arrived in one car or two. When Li Shin mentioned that the government men had been driven by a chauffeur, Uncle Tien turned and looked for a moment at the road, and I remembered that black car sitting parked under the trees in the afternoon, how we had not even heard it coming up the road. Uncle Tien turned back to us. He walked thoughtfully up the steps. Uncle Kuan put a hand on his shoulder when he passed him on the top step.

"Ma is going to chop my head off," Uncle Tien said in a low voice.

"Don't say we didn't warn you," said Uncle Wilfred. He sounded a little angry, but mostly worried.

Uncle Tien let out a soft sigh. He took off his tennis shoes and walked into the house without another word.

I heard Li Shin ask Uncle Kuan, "Is he going to get arrested?"

It was Uncle Wilfred who answered. "Not if he keeps his mouth shut from now on," he said, coming up the steps. "Not if he stops going to those meetings."

"They would have arrested him by now," Uncle Kuan explained, "if they wanted to do that."

"This afternoon's visit was just a warning," said Uncle Wilfred. "The government is giving us a second chance. A favor to your parents." He gazed over to where Li Yuen was now sprawled on his stomach, with his arms stretched out on the grass and his head turned to the side. Li Yuen was lying very still. "What is the matter with that boy?" Uncle Wilfred murmured. He shook his head and looked puzzled.

"He's playing," Li Shin said.

"Playing what?" Uncle Wilfred said. "He's already twelve years old. Time for him to act more serious. Look at him. Big exam tomorrow and he's not even worried."

"He's worried," Li Shin said.

Uncle Wilfred bent to take off his shoes. He wore modern European shoes, the kind with a curved lip across the front and two fringed tassels. All he had to do was grab hold of the heel of each shoe and it slipped off easily. "We'll be lucky if that boy doesn't end up washing people's cars for a living," he said, as the second shoe came off.

Uncle Kuan laughed suddenly. He wore ordinary men's shoes, with thin black laces that he had to kneel down and untie before the shoes could be taken off. "Why do you worry so much?" he said, standing up with his shoes in

73

his left hand. He stepped into the house after Uncle Wilfred. "Li Yuen is a good boy," I heard him say.

Uncle Wilfred muttered something back, and then their conversation shifted to Uncle Tien, and their voices became serious again. I could hear them in the corridor, drifting further and further away, almost like the echoes of the older girls calling softly to each other in the narrow stairwell that led from the chapel to the bell tower jutting from the rooftop of St. Catherine. We younger girls were not allowed in the stairwell. The nuns were afraid that we would fall clumsily and break our necks. Even among the older girls, only the bell ringers were really allowed. The bell ringers rang the bell for General Assembly, and for the start and end of class periods. On Holy Days of Obligation they rang the bell at noon for Mass, which the whole school attended downstairs in the courtyard. They also rang the bell whenever a funeral Mass was about to begin. But I had seen other older girls entering the stairwell, too. They went there during recess. They would take turns climbing up the spiral staircase to the bell tower, and someone was always left at the chapel door to keep watch.

"Wait here," I heard Li Shin say. I was still watching the doorway into the living room, and when I turned around, he had already left the veranda and was walking across the grass to Li Yuen.

I saw Li Yuen get up from the grass. He said something to Li Shin, and Li Shin said something back, their voices soft murmurs in the blackening green of the nearby trees. Now early nighttime had arrived. The grass sent crisp jagged sounds into the dark as my cousins came walking back to the veranda.

I thought about what I had heard said in school, that from the bell tower you could look down into the grounds of St. Peter's, into that part near the side wall that was thick with bushes, where at certain times of the day there would be certain boys who went there. It was a game they played, said the older girls, who had seen the boys pull down their pants. In the game the boys would rub their birdies until they squirted seed onto the grass. That was what the older girls called it. Seed. It was not pee-pee, they said. They said don't go and ask the nuns, otherwise you'll get smacked. We were not supposed to know about this yet. We were not supposed to know that if a boy's seed touched a girl's bottom, it could make a baby. This was something reserved for that time when we were older.

"Dinnertime, Chief," Li Shin said, coming up the veranda steps with Li Yuen behind him.

I wondered if my cousins played that game that the boys at St. Peter's played. I thought of Li Shin marching around his school courtyard with his platoon. He would be carrying a rifle on his shoulder, a real one, not the toy one that Li Yuen had but one that was steel-black and heavy and could shoot real bullets. I could not imagine him putting his rifle down to play with his birdie. As for Li Yuen, Li Yuen was a runner. I imagined him practicing on the asphalt track, his brown legs cutting sunlight the way I knew flamingos must when they got ready to fly. There were flamingos in my geography textbook, pinkish-red and wild. I could not imagine Li Yuen hiding behind bushes among a circle of boys, all of them most likely perverts.

From inside the living room the grandfather clock began

to chime. I took off my sandals and followed my cousins into the house.

Grandma was in Uncle Tien's room that night, and they were arguing. They spoke in hushed tones and the door was closed, so we could not hear what was being said. But we could hear urgency in the sound of their conversation, in the ebb-and-flow rhythm of their fight. Grandma would say something, and Uncle Tien would say something back. Then Grandma would say something, and Uncle Tien would say something back. Grandma's voice was more rushed than Uncle Tien's, more certain, less compromising. She was the flow, the high tide. She attacked. Uncle Tien was always low tide. His voice would sound as if he were about to give in, but he never did.

We stood in the corridor with our faces pressed to the pale green wall, and listened until we could hear Grandma coming towards the door. Then Li Shin grabbed my hand, and he and Li Yuen and I walked away quickly.

Later, after everyone had gone to bed, we heard neighbors knocking on the front door. It was after midnight. Rain was falling in the trees outside, slashing gray-white down the dark air. The air everywhere was thick with seaweed. During the monsoon it seeped through the windows and made our room smell like salt water, and that night I could smell it. I sat up in my bed and listened to the rain drumming softly on the leaves, the lighter, less common kind of rain that sometimes came in between the heavy downpours. My cousins were watching our bedroom door, which stood half-open and showed the corridor outside, where a light had come on and doors were opening and we could hear the grown-ups stepping out of their rooms to look at each other while one of the amahs shuffled into the living room in her soft black slippers to find out who was at the door.

"Mr. Fong's sons," we heard the amah say, when she came back.

"Are they waiting in the living room?" asked Grandma, who had put on her red housecoat and was standing just outside our door. We heard the amah say, "Yes," and then Grandma looked into the room and saw us listening. "Your souls are not finished playing," she said to us. "Go back to sleep." Grandma believed that while we were asleep our souls left our bodies and floated outside to play. She would say to us that children's souls needed more time to play than adult souls, and this was why children must go to bed early.

We could hear our aunties and uncles following Grandma to the front of the house, to Mr. Fong's sons, who sat waiting in the living room. Mr. Fong was Grandma's old friend the police inspector, who lived a mile up the road and who had sat next to Grandma at our grandfather's funeral and held her elbow to steady her when she got up to leave. His sons would have left their raincoats and wet rubber boots out on the veranda when they entered the living room. Now they would be sitting in their socks, with their feet together and their hands in their laps. There were four of them. The eldest one would be the one to tell Grandma about the riot that had just been reported on the other side of the Causeway, which was a three-quarter-mile bridge that now lay across the Straits of Johore. In the past, before the Causeway was built, there had been a ferryman to take people across the Straits, where if we thought back far enough into the past, there would be the ferryman who had rowed young Malaysian girls down to Singapore so that they could find work as amahs here and look for husbands.

It was a race riot, said Mr. Fong's son. We had followed the grown-ups to the living room without their noticing us, and now as we hid in the corridor, we heard Mr. Fong's son telling Grandma how Malay bandits armed with parangs had broken into the homes of several Chinese families, and how some of the Chinese men who had stayed behind to fight back with kitchen knives had been slaughtered. Family members who had escaped into the jungle reported that the Malaysian police had taken their own sweet time arriving, and that by then the bandits had set everything on fire and had disappeared. No one could identify any faces, because the bandits had covered their faces with scarves like American outlaws in the Wild Wild West. But all police stations in Singapore were on Red Alert to watch out for Malaysians attempting to come across the Causeway. It was suspected that some of the bandits had already escaped, and were hiding among relatives in Singapore. What the Singapore government did not want was for the escaped Malaysians to instigate riots against the Chinese here.

Mr. Fong's son spoke just loud enough for all the grown-ups in the room to hear. His words were very clear. He had been educated in England, and spoke English like a newscaster, pronouncing each syllable just right. His brothers could not speak like him. They had been locally educated only, and spoke colloquial English the way ordinary Singaporeans did. This was because they were Mr.

Fong's ordinary sons, having arrived second, third, and fourth. Mr. Fong's first son was the favored one. Also, he was the one who had to lead. Grandma said that our family did not follow the same tradition as Mr. Fong exactly. All of us were favored, she said, no matter when we arrived. But Li Shin, being eldest, still had to lead. That part of the tradition did not change.

While Mr. Fong's eldest son was talking, the youngest son kept looking at Uncle Tien. He was the same age as Uncle Tien, and the two of them had been friends since they were in primary school. Uncle Tien noticed him looking, and when all the brothers got up to leave, he followed them out to the veranda.

The grown-ups were turning around. They began moving towards the corridor, where we were still standing in the shadows, and there was no time for us to return to our room. They would have seen or heard us running away, and then we would have received a good scolding and even a few slaps. Li Shin pushed me and Li Yuen into the red room, and we hid in there until all the grown-ups had walked past the door and were going up the corridor, except for Uncle Tien, who was still outside. When we could hear that the living room was empty, we went over to the windows. It was still drizzling outside and we could hear the rain on the veranda roof. Uncle Tien was standing out on the road with Mr. Fong's sons. He was not wearing a raincoat, nor was he carrying an umbrella, and we wondered why Grandma had not stopped him, why she had not made him cover his head, because otherwise he might catch cold. Night air especially was dangerous. Grandma was always scolding Auntie Daisy for forgetting to carry an umbrella. "You will get rheumatism," she would say, when Auntie Daisy came home again in wet clothes. "You can't feel it now, but wait. When you are forty years old and your bones start to ache every time it rains, then you will say, How I wish I had listened to my mother."

Mr. Fong's sons were walking off, and Uncle Tien latched the gate shut and came running back to the house. He leapt up the veranda steps two at a time. When he stopped to slide his feet out of his wet shoes, we could hear the shoes squishing water. He left them out on the veranda, stepped into the house, and closed the door. We heard him turn off a lamp in the living room. Then he entered the corridor, and we saw him pass by the red room. He was rubbing his hands together and shivering a little, and later, when we were walking in the corridor back to our room, we could feel damp spots on the wood where he had stepped.

It was on the next night that he disappeared, along with Mr. Fong's youngest son, and some other young men whose names we did not recognize when Uncle Wilfred read aloud the list given in the newspaper. For a few days after that, we heard a rumor that all the missing men had been brainwashed into joining an underground Communist party, and that they had been shipped to Indonesia for further indoctrination. The young men were all university students who were known to have "radical ideas." Then a letter appeared in the newspaper. It was from some of the young men's fathers. The fathers insisted that their sons were good sons who would never have betrayed Singapore, and that, instead, they had probably gone to China, to work on the farms and help with the Great Proletarian Cultural Revolution. Young men were prone to acting on impulse, said the fathers. Their sons might have been a little misguided in their radical thinking, but they were not traitors. Don't blacken our son's names, the fathers pleaded.

Grandma did not participate in the letter-writing. When Mr. Fong came to ask if she wanted to sign her name, she told him that she had the rest of her family to think about. "Yu Tien left this house of his own free will," she said. "He is still my son, but he is in the care of the gods now." She said that Uncle Tien had put our whole family at enough risk, and she warned Mr. Fong that he himself had better move cautiously. No one escaped the government's eye.

Around half-past four one morning we heard the grown-ups outside our bedroom windows. A light rain was falling again, late-January rain that brushed past the trees and skimmed gently off the porch roof. Uncle Tien had been gone three weeks. The New Year according to the English calendar had begun, and the PSLE results had been announced. Li Yuen had passed with flying colors, which surprised everyone. "So there's more inside your head than coconut water," Uncle Wilfred had said. And when Li Yuen's eyes turned a little red, Auntie Daisy had rubbed his shoulder and told him, "Your uncle is teasing you." On the morning that their voices woke us up, we saw lights moving over the grass, and Li Shin slipped out of bed and went to look. He leaned on the curtain, using it to hide himself. When I tiptoed over, he put a hand on my shoulder to remind me to stay quiet. Then Li Yuen came and stood behind us. Through the leaves of the mango tree we saw the grown-ups moving about the grass. They wore raincoats and hats and they were carrying flashlights, the beams from the flashlights washing pale white over tree leaves, showing up the dark spaces in between. Li Shin tapped my shoulder and pointed to the door. We left the windows, tiptoed out into the corridor, and went to Uncle Tien's room.

Uncle Tien's radio was on, and a man's voice speaking Malay slid and crackled in the darkness as we stepped inside. Li Shin closed the door after us, and I looked around the room. The curtain was drawn across the window, where a narrow bed was pushed into the corner and faced the door so that no one could have entered the room while Uncle Tien was asleep without waking him up. The light from the corridor would have fallen on his face as soon as the door was opened. Next to the bed was a wooden crate turned upside down. Uncle Tien had used it as a nightstand. On it he had a small alarm clock and a small lamp, and usually there would be one or two library books. The radio man's voice was coming from somewhere near the wooden crate. I watched Li Shin walk over. He knelt down and reached underneath the bed and pulled out the radio. Then he dusted off the top and lifted the radio to his ear.

Li Yuen was standing at the window, peeking around the edge of the curtain. "They're still outside," he whispered over his shoulder. "I'll keep watch." I could see in front of him the desk where Uncle Tien used to work at his drawings sometimes. It was a high light-wood desk with a tilted top, and Uncle Tien would sit there on a high light-wood stool. I knew that the light wood was called pine, and that it came from overseas.

Years back, when I was four or five years old, Li Shin

used to lift me onto his shoulders and I would sit there and watch Uncle Tien's hands moving over the smooth white paper that he would clip onto that light-wood desk. The drawings that Uncle Tien would be making were not charcoal drawings. They would be drawings that he made for school, for classes that he took in what was called technical drawing. They would be full of lines and circles and semicircles. In technical drawing you were not supposed to see people's bodies, or faces. You were not supposed to see shadows. You could draw thinner or darker lines, but they all had to be definite and sharp. There were different kinds of pencils that you could use. A 2H pencil drew a light, thin line that unless you were looking closely at the paper you could not easily see. An HB drew ordinary black lines. A 2B drew a slightly darker line, and a 4B drew a darker, thicker line.

It was usually morning when we would go to Uncle Tien's room, and he would be sitting at his desk, drawing quietly, with only the sound of pencil lead skating across the paper, and from time to time the sound of his steel rule knocking on the giant plastic set squares. The curtain would be pulled far back from the window so that while he worked, sunlight came through and fell on his hands. His window, like ours, looked out the back of the house and faced the cemetery, where the sun rose. Outside the grass would be warm and bright and Uncle Tien would work until noon, using a giant plastic protractor to measure out angles and a pair of silver dividers to mark off distances without leaving pencil dots. My favorite moment would be when he picked up his silver two-legged compass with the pencil lead sticking out of one leg. There was a slim knob at the top where the two legs were joined.

Uncle Tien would hold the compass there, grip the knob between his thumb and forefinger. He would point one leg to the paper. Then, as he twisted the knob, the other leg would swing around, its leaded tip drawing out a perfect circle that met slowly, end to end.

Once I had heard him say to Li Shin that he did not enjoy technical drawing as much as he enjoyed drawing with charcoal. Charcoal drawing was freehand, he said, and it gave you more satisfaction. But you could not study it in school. It served no purpose here, "here" meaning Singapore, meaning that a developing nation like ours needed engineers and technicians and the government had already explained that we could not afford to waste our skills on luxurious endeavors pursued by bourgeois citizens in the richer countries like America. It was rumored that America was so rich, the American government threw leftover food into the sea. In Singapore there was no such thing as leftover food.

Still, Uncle Tien had once said something about going to America, because in America, he said, there was artistic freedom. He said that technical drawing was his duty, but that truthfully, he was a charcoal artist. This was how I knew, that night in his room, that there was a third place where he could have gone, besides China or Indonesia. I remembered the drawings that he used to make of my cousins and me sitting on Grandma's bed on Saturday nights, the year Grandfather died. That year Grandma would call my cousins to her room after she had bathed me and helped me put on my pajamas, and the three of us would watch while she knelt at the foot of her wardrobe and tried to pull open the last bottom drawer that never slid out easily. The drawer had two porcelain knobs decorated with blue flowers and tiny green leaves. Grandma would hold on to the knobs and shake the drawer from side to side. She would pull it out a little, shake it again, and pull it out some more. Inside the drawer there was a soft brown envelope packed full with old photographs. When Grandma showed them to us, the people in the photographs stared back at us with solemn coppery faces. Here are my brothers and sisters, Grandma would say. We would look at the boy standing in the corner of a photograph, smiling, with his hands hanging freely at his sides. He was Grandma's youngest brother, the friendly but stubborn one. His name was Sha Yong. When Grandma pointed to the other faces we would speak their names too, and hear our voices reciting Mandarin sounds like a poem. For us, the sounds were only sounds. Not knowing Mandarin, we could not translate them into the word-meanings of English. Even so, after we had spoken the names, Grandma's room would feel thick with things finished, and soft too, because there were other things that were only whispered and wished.

In the lamplight the walls in her room would stand so still, breakable as rice paper. We would look into the corridor and Uncle Tien would be sitting on the floor with his drawing pad balanced on his thighs, its red cover flipped over his knees. He would be watching us through the doorway. Sometimes in his drawings he would trace thin gray stripes onto the plain cotton pajamas that we wore. Grandma had looked at the striped pajamas once, and said to him that he had better show more respect for our ancestors. She had told him he was putting himself in danger of losing their protection.

When the radio man stopped talking and a tune began

to play, Li Shin switched it off. He put the radio back underneath the bed. Then he walked to the door. He did not say who might have switched the radio on, or whether it could have been on since Uncle Tien left and perhaps no one had noticed. He was worried about something, I could tell from the way he stared straight ahead and reached for the doorknob without looking at it. I looked at Li Yuen. Li Yuen was watching too, and then he left the window, and both of us followed Li Shin out into the corridor.

In the kitchen, which that morning floated like a dream in shadows, Grandma stood at the altar, praying. Her back was to us as we entered, but we could see the smoke rising from the joss sticks that she clasped in front of her, and we could smell its incense smell. The back door was open and we could see the grown-ups standing on the porch in their wet raincoats.

Above Grandma's head two candles burned off fierce white flames in the center of the red altar box, where a white porcelain Kwan Yin, Goddess of Mercy, sat cross-legged on a rosewood platform and smiled down upon all human beings. Even in the shadowed light we could see her kind round face and gentle eyes. She made the photograph of our grandfather, which sat beside her in the box, somber and disapproving. The photograph had been taken on Grandfather's wedding day. He wore a white shirt and black bow tie, and his hair looked as if he had combed it carefully in olive oil. But he was not smiling. I had believed that all bridegrooms smiled. When I was younger, Li Shin had read me the stories—the Beast when he discovered that Beauty loved him, the Frog when the Princess kissed him, Prince Charming holding the glass slipper in his trembling hand as Cinderella slipped her foot in.

"The police will catch them," Uncle Wilfred's voice floated in from the porch.

Someone else responded, "That's right. The curfew has started. They are sure to be seen, running around with their parangs. *Gila Melayu.*"

The last two words meant "crazy Malays." They were Malay words but when spoken together they became a Chinese curse.

"Why must they hate us so much?"

"They're tired of us taking over their property." That was Auntie Daisy. She spoke in a soft sad voice, which my cousins and I had never heard before.

"Now you sound like your brother Tien," we heard Uncle Wilfred say.

"Tien was not completely wrong, you know. The Malays were here long before us. And now the government wants to take full control of their lives."

"We Chinese are more organized." That was Auntie Lily. "Is it our fault? When the Malays had the island to themselves, what did they do? They went fishing."

"The government treats them like second-class citizens. How can you command people to move out of their homes and go live in a flat?"

"It has already been explained to them. Atap roofs are a fire hazard. These Malays are so uneducated they can't understand a simple thing."

"It's we who don't understand them. We don't even have the decency to try."

The darkness outside swayed softly in the still falling rain, and I could hear water tapping like ghost fingers on the wooden steps. I watched Li Shin as he walked over to the altar.

When we were younger he used to come across our room to me. When the heavy rains came and slashed through the trees, and rattled the porch roof like the sound of people beating drums, I would see him standing by my bed, the outline of his body in the dark. He would climb into the bed and put his face close to mine, and say, Chief, don't be scared, it's only rain. But outside the wet leaves would go on rasping, and I would know the earth was softening. I would lie there listening to his warm soft body fall asleep, while I waited for our dead relatives to push up through their graves and come flying back into Great-Grandfather's house. I had not yet been told they were no longer there, their spirits had returned to China.

At the altar Li Shin lifted his hand to touch Grandma's elbow. She turned when she felt him. Then she looked over the top of his head to where Li Yuen and I were standing near the corridor. We were hoping to be told to go back to bed, that it was too early in the morning for children to be up wandering around. Instead, she waved us over to her. I saw her reaching for the unlit joss sticks that sat in a silver cup in the back of the altar.

In the front of the altar were sacred oranges arranged on two oval plates of violet porcelain, our family's offering to the Goddess, who interceded for us with the other gods so that we could have long life and prosperity. I wondered that morning what Great-Grandfather's house must look like to the other gods. A dimly lit space in the middle of darkness, without roof or walls or trees. A place for candles, where the altar light was always burning, because before the flames of the old candles could go out, new candles would be taken from a kitchen drawer and held up to the old candles to be torched. We had seen our amahs carry out this duty. The altar light came from the first candles ever lit in Great-Grandfather's house and it was not to go out. It had to be kept, passed on, just as it had been all these years, traveling from candle to candle, every now and then held up by a different hand. It kept us visible to the gods.

I wondered, too, if the gods were partially blind, needing candlelight to see. Grandma plucked three joss sticks out of the silver cup, and I watched her push them in a bunch into the flaring candle flame. The tips of the joss sticks caught fire, sizzling red-gold as she dragged them away. Blowing lightly on them, she passed the joss sticks down, one to each of us. "Pray a safe journey for your Uncle Yu Tien's soul," she whispered. "Close your eyes."

Li Shin stared at the joss sticks, and then at Grandma. "Close your eyes," she said again. He bowed his head and closed his eyes, and Li Yuen and I did the same. Outside the rain was getting heavier. We could hear our aunties and uncles leaving the porch and slipping quietly into the kitchen. Over the strong-smelling incense smoke Grandma's voice began to chant. She was singing the water prayer, a prayer for the newly dead. Someone closed the back door. Grandma went on chanting, the slow un-English notes riding the dark morning air like a string of yellow floats on seawater.

I knew then that Uncle Tien would never return. He would never be allowed.

Four

The path that ran out from behind the house, that ran into the love-grass where in December the sand dust floated in the saltwater wind, was hot when the noon sun fell on it, and then we had to walk on the grass. We would pass under the frangipani tree and walk through the love-grass and then we would be in the cemetery. In the cemetery, where the sunlight rarely fell, the ground was thick and soft with leaves and Li Shin would say, Don't step on the graves. He would say to me, Come here, Chief, walk where I walk. I would go to him and step exactly where he stepped, because I did not want to walk over a grave. Grandma said that sometimes souls came back to visit and if you walked over a soul lying in its grave, dead people would stand beside your bed at night and you would dream strange things.

There was a green light in the cemetery that was greener than the light of the rubber trees. It was that clean underwater green that came from trees grown older than the plantation, rain trees many of them were, named for the fibery earth-brown root-vines hanging off their branches like monsoon rain. Sometimes walking in the green light we had to cross patches of lalang that grew amidst the rain trees. The lalang was not soft like love-grass. It was loose sharp grass where if we stood still we could hear the breeze scratching. We would walk through it to get to the place where green moss clung to tombstones. The green moss was like fur to touch. When we ran our palms over it, we could feel underneath to the rough hard stone.

Some of the tombstones in the cemetery were cracked. We would stand looking at the cracks running across names, and Li Shin would point and say, That used to be his papa, and that was his mama. But now they lay under the leaves, where light trickling down through treetops made small pools on the ground, a pale yellow softness dabbed to dry leaves half sunk into the red-brown earth. The earth that covered the graves was crisscrossed with twigs. We would pick up the twigs and snap them, not because we wanted to but just to do it, the way sometimes you do something just to do it. You might be walking past a row of waste cans one night and want suddenly to topple them over, topple all of them over, break up their smug, taunting line of order. But you walk quickly so that soon they will be behind you and you will be saved from yourself. Or you might stop outside a brightly lit City Hall window, someone inside working late. You might bend to pick up a stone, even though you know you will never throw it. You go on standing there. You roll that rough grainy stone in your palm and think how much it could tear loose, hurtling into the back of someone's head. You have heard of another child doing it. It sounds to you so fine and brave, because you know when you are a child that you can do very little that would tell enough. Still, you roll that stone in your palm, knowing that you will not throw it, knowing that if you did, it would not be because you wanted to. It would be just to do it.

In the cemetery we would snap twigs and that was how to do it, to do it without thinking, do it just for the doing. The twig breaks, you drop the broken pieces. We did that, too, without thinking.

You might snap a twig while listening to the lalang scratching wind, or you might snap one when you stop on the sand path to look ahead of you. From where you stand you might watch how the path winds its way between the trees, running like a crooked dry stream in the green light. That's the way it's been forever. You will remember it that way. That's the way it is. The sand path runs like a crooked dry stream in the green light. It winds its way between the trees. The green light is cool because it must sift through the layers and layers of overhanging leaves, big and small leaves that often come floating down upon the sand. You watch them float, thinking they are so pretty when they do that, the big and small leaves, and around you lie all the twigs that you have broken ever since you were old enough to walk in the cemetery with your cousins, who were walking there before you, and you have done it all without thinking and you are without guilt until you realize that you have done it all without thinking, snapping twigs not for the wanting, breaking things just out of the sin of careless unthinking, doing acts just for the sake of that. Grandma would say this was how the gods did things sometimes, that sometimes we must not look for reason in an act because the gods might have done it just for the sake of that. But it was not a sin for them because they were the gods. A time was coming when she would sit in her room, saying that, when she would sit in her rocking chair and rock to and fro in quiet even rhythm, how she sat all day beside her window, and when evening came and her room grew dim in the last minutes of daylight she would stare out the window saying that. She never used to be that way. Grandma was a slow-moving woman, but she moved. She walked softly and never stepped on anything in a hard heavy way. She had very small feet. She was actually a small-built woman, but until you are becoming a woman yourself that never occurs to you, because until then, she is your grandma. It is an undeniable impossibility that your grandma could be small, or quietly yearning, or ordinary. You are a child. Your eyes cannot see what your heart cannot believe.

Five

I could hear them, somewhere out there, young men's voices, restless, wakeful, hungry in the promise-heavy evening light that dripped wet through the coconut leaves and splintered the shadows on the ground. The road lay silent, empty behind the coconut trees and the fence. Auntie Daisy's boyfriends had stopped coming to the house, because I was eleven and Grandma had told Auntie Daisy that it was time she set me a good example. It was time she stopped lying on top of young men's cars. But I could hear the jungle trees twitching in the heat, growing so close to the house, bringing back the sounds of those past afternoons, sweaty teasing sounds of young men laughing.

When Grandma came into the red room to turn on a lamp, I watched her bend towards the porcelain man sitting on a table near the door. She reached into the lampshade and pulled the chain switch, and I heard the light click on, bright yellow instant light that fell on the porcelain man like a blessing. The porcelain man, an old Chinese sage, sat staring happily at the world with his hands folded neatly over his hard round belly. He had tiny eyes filled with glass. In the sudden light the eyes shone like mirrors, seeing nothing.

"Su Yen," Grandma said, when she noticed me standing at the windows. "What have you been doing in here in the dark?"

"I was watching the road," I said.

She came over to me and pushed my hair behind my ears. "What are you thinking about?" she wanted to know, while I stood looking at her spectacles, two round circles of glass balanced gently on her nose. Her hair sat in a bun pinned to the back of her head. It always looked neat, because she wore a black hairnet held in place with bobby pins.

"Is it boys?"

I walked my finger up the side of the curtain, watching the heavy red silk dimple beneath my fingernail. Something had happened that morning at St. Catherine and I was trying not to think about it too much, afraid of the strangeness that seemed to flow, bubbly cold inside me, when I dared to think about it even a little.

"Do not think about boys yet," I heard Grandma say. "You are too young. Boys are trouble for you, you understand?" She slipped her hand under my chin and turned my face to make me look at her. "I will let you know when the right time comes for you to think about boys." She dropped her hand. "Concentrate on your studies." I looked outside the window.

During recess that morning my classmates and I had

noticed a kite caught on a branch near the back wall at St. Catherine. It had been a fighting kite, the kind that Malay boys made by hand using stripped-down, carefully weighed bamboo splints and brightly dyed tracing paper, the kind they attached to a spool of thin cord coated in crushed beer-bottle glass for knife sharpness in kite wars fought among the neighborhood gangs. My classmate Patricia Wee had noticed it first. She had pointed to where the kite was quivering blue, green, yellow, and red, up there among the leaves. Then as she began climbing up the tree to get it, my other classmates and I had cheered her on, hanging back at the edge of the love-grass and shouting out, Be careful. Don't fall.

"Do you like this room, Su Yen?"

"Yes." In my head I could still hear the loud clapping that had broken out as soon as Patricia had reached out to disentangle the kite from the branch.

"It was your grandfather's favorite room."

There must have been at least twenty St. Peter's boys waiting on the other side of the wall, crouching down on the grass. In the midst of their wolf-whistling I had heard a camera snapping frantically. Patricia had hurried back down, sliding and crawling as fast as she could, leaving the kite still in the tree. Marching red-faced through the love-grass, she had yelled over her shoulder, Bloody bastards. While my other classmates were trying not to laugh, I had wondered how much a Catholic schoolboy would pay for a photograph of Patricia's panties.

"He liked the sun." Grandma's hand was on the back of my head, stroking me. "You know, how it comes in here in the afternoon."

Out there along the road the sun had begun to set, and I watched the long raggedy rays pierce the leaves of the

coconut trees. The coconut leaves hung down long and
spiked, like the fringes that Li Shin had shown me how
to cut along the edges of sheets of old newspapers the
grown-ups would give to us to play with when we were
small. We had used the fringed newspapers to make hats,
which we never wore.

Slowly, the sun dropped behind the rubber trees. I saw
again nearby on the veranda steps two shapes moving,
where I had seen them late one night after waking up
from a dream. In my dream an accident had happened on
the road outside Great-Grandfather's house, and when I
woke up I had gone to the red room to look out the
windows, but when I saw the road I could not remember
any more of the dream. Instead, I had heard a man's voice
teasing softly in the dark, Daisy, let me see your daisy.

"Do you miss him, Grandma?" I asked. "Grandfather,
I mean."

She was staring out the window, a misty look in her
eyes. I had seen it before. It would slip in whenever she
was seeing something far away, long ago. "It's life," she
said, although the misty look was still there. Then it faded.

I touched the bougainvillea growing along the window
frame, its sugary pink petals cupped open, gathering twilight. Over by the veranda steps the two shapes met, the
sound of cloth scratching on cloth. I could hear her skirt
ruffling as his hand moved over her thigh. No more talking
now, just whispering, and then not even that. I closed my
eyes, hearing the elastic turning down, something sliding
down her legs. He put his hand back inside her skirt, up
between her thighs, and rubbed her where she was wet,
the squeaky sounds of her wetness pumping softly into
the dark, dark night.

"You do not remember your grandfather."

I opened my eyes. "No, Grandma."

"When you were a baby, I used to bring you in here after your bath. Your grandfather would be sitting over there, in that chair." I turned to look. Grandma was pointing to a chair near the bookshelves. "I would put you on a towel in my lap, and spray powder over your tummy, and your grandfather would come over to us, and he would bend down and tickle your tummy with his nose." She smiled. "You liked that."

I tried to imagine her at eighteen, leaving her home and her family to come to Singapore so that she could be married to a man thirty years older than herself. Li Shin had asked her once, You didn't mind, Grandma? She had smiled that misty smile, and touched his cheek, gently, with one finger. She had looked off into the distance, and when she spoke again, it was about something else. Li Shin had watched her face closely, and he had told us later that while Grandma was staring off at the sky she was seeing her village in China. She was seeing how her father's house looked and how the street in front of it looked, all cracked with dried mud the way village streets were in China back in olden days, and the neighbors' houses standing along that street with the dusty trees behind and the hills farther away, and right in front of Grandma's father's house were the footprints that her friends had left in the dried mud when they came to see her that day she went away. While Li Shin was telling us this, Li Yuen had wrinkled up his face in disbelief. Grandma saw all that? he said. Li Shin said, Yes, that was what Grandma was doing. He would never ask her his question again.

I touched the bougainvillea, and squeezed its petals lightly. "Did you have bougainvillea in China,

Grandma?" I asked. Her voice beside me answered, "No, no bougainvillea in China." I dipped my finger into a tiny flower cup and bent the petals back, one by one.

"But the other flowers, they grow there."

I leaned my head against her. I could hear her heartbeat. "Other kinds," her voice murmured, and I felt her hand brushing my hair back from my face. "Do you know which was the prettiest flower I ever saw, Su Yen? It was a long time ago." I stood still, smelling eau de cologne faintly through her blouse, a few drops from the blue glass bottle on her nightstand, a few drops dabbed carefully to the underside of her breasts. Two weeks ago I had seen her naked breasts for the first time. I had walked into her room to tell her about the new grasscutter, who on that day had stood waiting at the gate, not wanting to step onto our property until he had formally introduced himself. I had gone to get Grandma, and had found her studying herself in the full-length mirror in her room, her blouse and brassiere laid out neatly on the bed. And I had seen her breasts, bare and huge, flopped down on her belly like overripe papayas with nipples.

"I was still a little girl, such a long time ago."

"What kind of flower?"

"It was in a big field. I found it in a big field full of wild grass and weeds. It was the only flower in that field."

"What kind of flower was it, Grandma?"

"No kind." She turned to me. "If you dig up a flower, Su Yen, and you plant it in a garden with many different flowers, then you must give all your flowers names."

"Didn't you dig up your flower to take home?"

"It was hot that day. The field was far away from my father's house." She turned back to the window. "Such a beautiful flower. So many flowers die when you move them to another place."

"Why do they die?"

"Because people forget," she said solemnly. "They forget to watch over their flowers."

She was telling me something that I was not expected to understand yet. I was expected only to pay attention, and to keep what I had heard in a safe place. Someday all that I had kept of hers, all that she had passed to me, would be taken out, unraveled, and given away, and it would become useful. How this was to happen, I did not know. It occurred to me that evening that there was much I did not know. Until then I had believed that the thing called sex was a thing only grown-ups understood, a thing only grown-ups could feel.

But that morning while the St. Peter's boys were still whistling and clapping, Patricia's best friend, Anna Lin, had reached underneath her pinafore skirt and pulled down her panties. Are you crazy, I had heard one of my classmates say. Just watch, Anna had told her. We were all watching. We saw Anna step out of her panties. Then she had picked them off the grass and, very calmly, stuffed them into her pocket. We had looked over our shoulders, scanning the surrounding field for nuns. At ten o'clock in the morning the sun had melted the field yellowish green, and where a game of rounders was going on, someone leapt over the home baseline and we had heard a cheer soar into the bright clean air. Over by the side wall, where casuarina trees stood shading the ground with needles, we had noticed girls kneeling in circles, playing Five Stones. They had looked up for a moment, then gone back to their own game.

That evening I tried to grasp what it was that I had witnessed.

The whole field had been noisy, flashing blue and white with girls, and the only nun I had seen had been sitting far away at a picnic table with the detention girls. She had to make sure the detention girls did not have any fun. I had turned and joined my classmates in watching Anna, who was grinning as she made her way through the love-grass.

The St. Peter's boys had been whistling when Anna's head appeared above the wall. Then, abruptly, the whistling had stopped. I had heard from across the field the girls in the tower ringing the bell for the end of recess. Anna had reached for the kite, grabbed it, and shaken it loose. Then, with only one free hand, she had started to climb back down. All the while staying calm, she had reached the lowest branch, her light easy body swinging from it with one hand. Awed, I had watched her land, thump, onto the ground.

I closed my eyes, imagining Anna back up in the tree. Again I heard the silence that had fallen across the wall. In that silence a crowd of uniformed teenage boys had knelt, paralyzed-shocked and prayerful, their soft lips drooping open. Some budding thing had raced unstoppable through their hearts while they were watching Anna crawl from branch to branch with no panties on. I opened my eyes and moved closer to Grandma.

"It is not healthy," she said, brushing my hair back from my face again. "Staying inside the house the whole day. Li Shin is outside, on the porch. Go now, it will be dark soon."

❀

When I stepped onto the porch, Li Shin was bending over the rail with his elbows on the wood, his face cupped in his hands. He turned his head and saw me, and he said, "Hey you."

The grasscutter was leaning on the wooden post near the top of the steps. He smiled at me as I crossed the floor. Around the porch the trees were turning blue-black, and somewhere a bird was hopping from branch to branch, rustling the leaves.

"So you are sure about this," the grasscutter said, turning to Li Shin. "You want to be a soldier." He shook his head. "Why?"

Li Shin reached into his pocket and took out a piece of chalk. "This country needs soldiers," he said, looking at me as he walked to the middle of the porch. "The Prime Minister says we don't have enough."

The grasscutter shook his head again. "You think these are your people?" he asked.

"My country, my people," said Li Shin. He bent down on one knee and drew a white line across the boards.

"You are Chinese," said the grasscutter.

A smell of seaweed came with the night wind passing through the cemetery trees, and the air on the porch smelled like sweat. Li Shin continued to draw, marking out three squares, one on top of the other, and then two big squares side by side, and then one more, and then two again.

"Our soldiers are Chinese," he said, standing up. He slipped the chalk into his pocket and wiped his hands on his shorts. "Why are you against them? You and Grandma, why are you like that?"

"Chinese?" said the grasscutter. "Ya, ya, they look Chinese, but they speak Malay, they give commands in Malay. Am I right or not?"

Li Shin pulled out a roll of thick red string wound several times around itself. It was one of the things a cadet always carried in his pocket, for emergencies. He gave it to me. "You don't understand," he was saying. "We have to do this, we want peace with the Malays. The Prime Minister says—"

"Ya, ya, I know what the Prime Minister says, one nation, one people." The grasscutter shook his finger at us. "But let me tell you something. The Malays will never become Chinese."

I dropped the red string in the first square so that we could play Hopscotch.

"You are talking like a Communist," said Li Shin.

The grasscutter smiled and shook his head. "No," he said patiently. "I am not a Communist. But I am Chinese."

I skipped through the squares, then swung around and skipped back, balancing myself to pick up the string when I reached the first square again.

"Your grandma," said the grasscutter, "she is going to let you join the army?"

I passed the string over to Li Shin, because it was his turn. He dropped it and started skipping through the squares. "I'm not a small boy anymore," he answered, when he reached the last two squares. He swung around and skipped back.

The grasscutter sighed. "You don't even dare to tell her you are a cadet."

Li Shin looked up a moment. "Tonight," he said suddenly. "Tonight I will tell her." He gave me the string and I tossed it into the second square.

"Many boys become National Cadets. They like the uniform."

"It's not like that with me."

Someone walked into the kitchen to turn on the lamps. I swung around at the last two squares and a yellow beam fell through the doorway, hitting one side of the grasscutter's face. In the light I could see dirt smeared across his cheek, where he must have rubbed it with the back of his hand.

I skipped back and picked up the string.

"You should think of your grandma," he said, stamping out an ant on the floor. "She is your grandma."

I stepped out of the square, and Li Shin pulled me against him. He started to play with my hair. "She thinks one of these days we're all going back to China," he said.

"She is your grandma."

We could hear our amahs walking around in the kitchen, taking the dinner plates out of the cupboard, turning on faucets, running water.

"I know she's my grandma," I heard Li Shin say, and his voice was sad. He continued to play with my hair.

The blue-black light had begun to melt over the grass like thick water, mixing all the trees and making leaves and branches disappear.

"You want to shoot Japanese soldiers?" the grasscutter asked.

"If they come again," Li Shin answered.

"They will not come again," said the grasscutter.
"What if they are not Japanese?"

Li Shin kept his hands on my shoulders, but he was
staring across the grass into the cemetery trees. The grasscutter put on his hat. "It won't matter," I heard Li Shin
say.

The grasscutter walked down the steps and paused on
the grass. "You should not go out tonight," he said, looking up at us. "You have to go to school on Monday, am
I right? So, you should study. Do your homework. When
you grow up, then you can be a soldier."

He went around the corner, and we could hear him
walking on the leaves.

"Are you going somewhere?" I asked.

Li Shin was still looking at the trees. "No," he said.
"Not tonight. The grasscutter's right. It's time I told the
truth." He picked up his red string and shoved it into his
pocket, and I looked around, knowing now how we must
not trust the trees at night. Out there was where shapes
collapsed, lines fell to dust, and anything far enough away
was lost. "Let's go in," I heard him say. And we stepped
into the house.

It was May 1969. That year I was getting
old enough to notice how fast our country had grown,
faster than anyone had imagined possible. Where once
there had been kampongs, now there were high-rise flats,
long white blocks of buildings layered with balconies.
Some of the blocks stood twenty-two stories high, and
were surrounded with walkways and playgrounds, sloping
lawns, cement steps. The playgrounds shone off bright

red climbing bars and swings, yellow and blue tunnels, giant sandboxes loosely packed with pale clean sand. The government had begun to take care of everything. Government workers tended the grass, trimmed the trees, swept the walkways and steps, picked up crumpled candy wrappers and plastic parts of broken toys left behind. We had peace now. We had progress. Not only Malays lived in the high-rise flats. These flats were also the homes of the once-poor Chinese, citizens whose immigrant ancestors had not done quite so well financially in the British colonial regime. These Chinese were the descendants of coolies. There was to be no more poverty in Singapore, no more slums. Slums affected everyone, the government said. It was fair for taxpayers' money to go into building homes for the less fortunate. Now there would be fewer diseases, and healthier people, and everyone could go to work and we could all build a better Singapore.

The mass transit system was being improved that year so that no one had to be late for work. New roads kept appearing, smooth and black, smelling of fresh tar. There were new buses, clean, with bright yellow and orange seats. There were bus stops with rain shelters, each stop marked clearly with a tall silver pole carrying a stiff blue metal flag, on which was stenciled the white frame of a bus.

Outside St. Catherine two trucks and seven or eight men began to show up every weekday morning. They came to widen the road and build sidewalks, the new cement sidewalks that were appearing all over the island, five feet wide and bright white in the sun. We knew that when the men were done with their work, there would be squares of soft dark earth cut into each sidewalk and spaced evenly apart, and that overnight there would be a young tree transplanted into each square. The tree would have a slender gray-white trunk. It would have soft green leaves that flicked about the sunlight, and whispered the rain instead of thrashing it the way the jungle trees used to that had once stood there. It would be like all the other young trees springing up along the new roads, a sign from Prime Minister Lee that he intended to keep his promise. Singapore would industrialize, and become modern, but there would be no concrete city like New York or Hong Kong. Singapore would remain green. Prime Minister Lee had told us that he was building for us a garden city, an island state where workers walking to their offices every morning could walk past flowers, in and out of the shade of trees. In a few years Prime Minister Lee would prove himself. In a few years tourists and commercial investors arriving in jet planes would look down at us, and from the air they would see only the green, green canopy of our overnight-grown equatorial trees.

It had been three years since Uncle Tien had disappeared, and for a while, the government men had continued to come to the house, arriving silently in their shiny black car. One of our amahs would hurry out and meet them at the gate and accompany them back up the path to the veranda, where the men would take off their shoes before they entered the living room. They would walk to the four straight-backed chairs lined up along the wall and they would sit down with their brief-cases in their laps. One of them would snap his briefcase open and take out papers for Grandma to sign. Grandma would be sitting on the sofa nearby, which had fierce dragons carved into its back. She would study the papers

carefully, tracing out sentences with her fingers. When
the amah reentered the room, carrying glasses of iced
water on a bamboo tray, the men would stand up, then
sit down again holding the glasses gingerly in their hands.

When we asked Grandma why the men kept coming,
she said that the papers they handed her contained police
reports on arrests that continued to be made at meetings
held by local citizens, who were suspected of being in
league with the Malaysian Communists. She said that she
had to put her signature on the papers to swear that she
did not know any of the people who had been arrested.
In school we were told that the government was just taking
precautions. Government men were going to everybody's
house. Everybody was being asked to sign sworn statements. Sworn statements had to be read carefully before
they were signed, Sister Katherine said. If you lied on a
sworn statement, even if it was out of carelessness or
ignorance, your lie could send you to jail.

In the first year that Uncle Tien was not with us I would
hide in the corridor with my cousins whenever the government men came. From the corridor we would listen to
the living room turn stiff and hard, until even the lamplight seemed to glow in a hard yellow way. There would
be only the sound of papers shifting hands in the room,
then long silent moments in between, and once in a while
a soft sigh that we recognized because it was Grandma's.
She had told us to stay out of the room. From the corridor
we would watch the sun on the veranda. You could see
the veranda through the living-room doorway, the white
wooden rail with its design of squares, the bleached planks
in the floor. Sometimes it would be four o'clock in the
afternoon and the sun would be sloping through the
wooden squares, making boxed shadows on the floor. Past

the veranda you could see the path running out to the gate. We would notice the gate standing half-open, and the road with the trees shading parts of it, and light flickering in the leaves. Light would be flickering, too, along the side doors of the shiny black car that belonged to the men, and then we would know that there must be a breeze outside, and that when the men were gone we would hear it, and hear all the other sounds again.

We never went out to talk to the Malay driver again. With Uncle Tien gone and no one knowing where, it was not safe. We had to keep our mouths shut.

Sometimes after the men were gone I would stand in the small dark alcove that opened off one corner of the living room. I would stand there facing the grandfather clock that stood against the wall with its white face raised high above the floor. The grandfather clock told time in large neat numbers. It had two dark hands that stayed joined to a point like the slim silver compass in Uncle Tien's room. The two hands marked off big slow circles and the circles were time.

Next to the grandfather clock was a narrow glass pane that you could look through to see if anything was happening outside, and sometimes I would look through it and someone from the market would be passing by on the road—a man would be cycling by with a box of apples, or oranges, or bananas. The glass pane was so narrow, no one looking at you from the road could see you. It was there mostly for the grown-ups, who often used it late at night, after the doors were locked. Usually our uncles would be the ones to go into the alcove. They would take turns getting up at one or two o'clock in the morning, and whosoever's turn it was, he would walk into the living room and step into the alcove and look outside. In that

first year my cousins and I would sometimes follow which-
ever uncle it was into the living room. We could do it
quietly enough not to be noticed. But all we would see
would be that uncle standing in front of the glass pane,
peering out at the road.

On the afternoons that I spent standing in the alcove
by myself, my cousins would be at school. Grandma never
wondered why, because in the morning my cousins would
have told her that they had to stay after school for track
practice. Actually, it was only Li Yuen who had track
practice. He had joined the school track team, which had
been Li Shin's idea. Li Shin had told us one day that one
of his classmates, another cadet, had offered to let him
keep his uniform at the classmate's house. Now, he said,
all he needed was an alibi. Both Li Yuen and I had volunteered. And Li Shin had thought about it, and then
decided that Li Yuen should join the track team and I
should stay at home as decoy and spy.

Even on days when Li Yuen did not have track practice
he would stay after school. Then, in the evening, he and
Li Shin would come home together. Li Yuen had probably
volunteered for the same reason that I did. Li Shin was
being called away from us. A voice had summoned him,
which we could not hear. But volunteering to lie for him—
even though Grandma had warned us to never, never lie—
allowed us to keep Li Shin within sight, at least for a little
while.

On those evenings while I was waiting for
them to come home, I would go into the red room and
stand at the windows, and sometimes, to pass the time, I

would pretend that it was 1958, a year only my cousins could remember, but even they remembered it vaguely. I would imagine that blue-green November morning that now I sometimes heard them talk about. It had been around half-past five, when my cousins had huddled together at the window, hiding behind the bougainvillea while our parents paced up and down the veranda outside. Our parents were leaving for the airport. They were waiting for a government chauffeur to drive by and pick them up. I could imagine how they must have looked, straight thin shadows in the still dark light, their suitcases lined up and ready at the bottom of the steps. Grandma had been out there, too. I had heard Li Shin say that she had asked our fathers if they were ever going to stay home for more than two weeks at a time. I had heard him say that his father had answered, "In our line of work, you can't tell, Ma." Li Shin could remember his mother looking at his father, and my mother turning to look at my father. Our mothers did not work for the government, but they always accompanied our fathers on these "business trips" so that they could act as decoys while our fathers attended underground meetings, in Thailand, Japan, the Philippines, Malaya.

I would imagine the black car that Li Shin said had pulled up in front of our gate. I would imagine our parents stepping off the veranda and picking up their suitcases. I saw Li Shin's father looking back at Grandma, and telling her, gently, that he was sorry. I saw my own father and mother walking out to the road, where the driver of the car had stepped out. He had left the car engine running, and I saw him standing by the gate, holding it open.

❀

On that night he decided to tell Grandma, riots had just broken out in Kuala Lumpur, the capital city of Malaya. We had heard the news in school, and even Li Yuen and I knew that this was what the grown-ups must have been waiting for, what they had sensed would appear, sooner or later, a sign that old trouble was still around.

We were in our bedroom when we heard Grandma talking to Li Shin out on the porch. He had stepped out after dinner, knowing that if he stayed out there long enough, Grandma would come looking for him to make him step back inside.

"What is this?" we heard her asking, and we tiptoed over to the window.

Li Shin stood by the steps, with his back against a wooden post. He kept his hands folded behind him. Grandma was holding up something small in front of his face. "What is this, Li Shin?" she asked again. He looked at the thing in her hand. Then he looked at her. Silence hung between them, weighted like that moment after the sounding of a bell.

"My beret, Grandma," we heard him say.

"Your beret." Grandma's voice in the dark had a cut in it, a clear, clean cut. "Is this the truth? You are telling me the truth?"

"Yes."

"When did you join?"

Again, there was silence.

"Li Shin? When?"

"Three years ago."

"All this time you have been lying to me?"

"I'm sorry, Grandma."

"This is how I have brought you up? To be a liar to your own grandmother?"

"No, Grandma."

"Liar." She shook the beret in his face, then threw it on the floor and went to sit down in her rattan chair, where she always sat with the red cushions to bring her good luck.

"I was afraid," said Li Shin, softly. He bent over and picked up the beret. "Grandma, I didn't want you to stop me."

"And now," she answered, "now you are almost grown up. You see that I am just an old woman, nothing to be afraid of. A superstitious old woman, isn't that what you call me, Li Shin? You laugh at me now."

"No, Grandma."

"Yes. That's the truth."

Li Shin walked over to her and knelt down. "Grandma, don't be like that," he pleaded, looking into her face. "This is important to me."

We heard her sigh. "Why, Li Shin? Why do you go against me?"

"Grandma," he said gently. "The Communists keep trying to take over. It's my duty to protect us. I was meant to be a soldier, I can feel it."

"You will get yourself killed."

"I have to risk it."

"That was what your father said. And where has he been, all these years, while you were growing up? Tell me, Li Shin, do you believe that was his duty, to leave his children without parents?"

Li Shin stood up and walked over to the rail. "My father did his duty as a Singapore citizen," he said, but his voice had weakened, the sound of a flower wilting in an unexpected drought.

"It's a dangerous thing," said Grandma. "Being a Singapore citizen."

"The government needed him."

Grandma sat up in her chair. Holding on to its arms, she leaned into the dark. "Listen to me, Li Shin. You are not the government's son. I'm your grandmother. I tell you the truth, who you are."

Li Shin went on standing at the rail with his back to her. He twisted his beret over and over in his hands. Finally, he put it on.

"So," we heard Grandma murmur, "I am too late."

Li Shin turned around as she got up from her chair. He slipped his hands into his pockets, and watched her as she stepped into the house. Then, for a few minutes longer, he just stood there. And Li Yuen and I could see now the line that had always been there, scratched into the ground in front of him wherever he had tried to walk, a test for his freedom. Li Shin had just stepped over it. But we saw, too, that it was a line which once you had crossed, you could never step back over.

A little shaken, we left the window without calling out to him, and went to bed.

After lunch the next day Li Shin put on his cadet uniform and stepped out on the porch in his socks. He had to return to school for a cadet meeting. His uniform was all green, army green it was called, the green of leaves growing in the middle of the jungle. This was so that a cadet who was wearing his uniform could hide in the jungle if he was being followed. The jungle leaves were supposed to protect him, camouflage him out of the sun.

Grandma was sitting in her rattan chair. "You will come home for dinner on time?" I heard her ask. I was kneeling on the floor, practicing a few rounds of Five Stones with the tiny triangular beanbags that our twin aunties had made for me. I tossed two beanbags, caught them, and glanced up in time to catch the frown that appeared briefly on Li Shin's face. He had crossed over to stand at the rail. "I'll try, Grandma," he said.

She said again, "You will come home on time, yes?"

"We're going to have shooting practice today," he said, staring at the trees. "And we have some new recruits coming in. I'll have to help them."

"You practice during the day," she said. "At night you come home."

I looked at the grass around us lying green and still in the sun, so still I could almost hear light banging on the blades.

"Tell your teacher, if he wants you to stay late, come and talk to me."

Li Shin pushed his hands into his pockets. "Grandma," he said, turning around, "I can't do that."

"Why you can't do that?"

"Grandma, I'm a captain."

A breeze ruffled the tops of the bushes near the rail, and at the bottom of the steps the blue periwinkles shivered in the bright sun. I put my beanbags aside and swept together some sand scattered over the floorboards. I made a small pile, then flattened it with my palm the way I had seen the amahs flattening dough for Chinese New Year cakes. I wrote the letter C with my finger. Then I wrote an H. I gathered more sand and spelled my name. CHIEF. The name my cousins had given to me when we were small and played the Founding of Singapore game, in which I had been the Temenggong, ruler of the island. The name no one at St. Catherine knew. At St. Catherine they thought my name was Esha. Esha, Sister Adeline would say. Raise your arms, Esha, light, like a butterfly. I was in Primary Five and had to attend ballet class. On the first day Sister Adeline had told us to raise our arms, we were going to fly, and sway, sway like branches tossing in a monsoon wind. Remember, Sister Adeline would say, elephants do not fly, so we're not going to be elephants, are we. Sister Adeline wanted me to dance with some grace. Dance with some grace, Esha, she would say. She would plant her hands on her hips and shake her head, How can such a small girl be so clumsy? Tadadaboomdeeye. Tadadaboomdeeye. In that room where girls danced I had sat in a corner watching sunbeams cut through windows, the four-o'clock light tilting. While the gramophone played old scratchy Italian records, girls flitted over the polished parquet floor, skipping lightly away, twirling and skipping back again, girls like butterflies. On the first day I had been made to stay for extra practice after school. Watch them, Esha, learn. When Li Shin arrived to take me home, the girls dancing had turned their heads. They smiled at him, their faces interested, their rhythm broken. Sister Adeline had to clap her hands, shaking her head from side to side as she tried to get back their attention. Girls, girls, she called.

I looked at Li Shin, now standing close to me with his

hand on the rail. For the first time I realized that he was handsome. He looked a little like Wang Yu, the Hong Kong movie star who always played the part of the gentle country boy in martial-arts films. Wang Yu never entered a fight unless he was continually provoked. He never attacked, he only defended. This was the oath that all martial-arts black belts had to take when they passed their final sparring test, although not all of them kept it. Many black belts went astray. Wang Yu would have to fight those who had gone astray. He always won in the end, because his soul was good, because he had kept the oath.

Out of the corner of my eye I could see a yellow butterfly skipping about the periwinkles. When I turned my head, it leapt up and winged away into a bush. A slow afternoon wind passed through the trees. Leaves were rustling along the left side of the porch, where Grandma sat. I heard Li Shin say into the quiet, "I'll come home on time," and then Grandma got up from her chair and stepped into the kitchen, satisfied.

Li Shin was looking down at his hand. It sat on the red wood like a fish the amahs had put there to dry. After a while he lifted his eyes and saw me watching, and he winked. "You have a dictation test tomorrow?" he asked, and I said, "Yes."

"Spell Hopscotch," he said.

I spelled Hopscotch.

"That's good, Chief," he said.

"Give me another word," I said. "A long word this time."

"A long word," he said, looking around, searching the trees.

I waited.

"Hiroshima."

I followed him into the kitchen, spelling Hiroshima.

          The shoe rack sat against the wall, just inside the door. Li Shin's boots were on the bottom shelf. He picked them up and sat down on a small square stool beside the rack. I leaned on the refrigerator nearby and watched while he loosened the laces. "What time you going to come home today?" I asked, listening to the refrigerator hum.

"Same as always," he answered, pulling on a boot.

"Last Friday you were late," I reminded him.

"We had shooting practice, Chief." He tucked his trouser leg into his boot and hooked up the thick black lace.

I liked watching his fingers work the lace. Li Shin had long, slender, quick fingers. They were strong, stronger than anyone would have imagined, seeing how pale and fragile-looking they appeared. Auntie Mei had once told Grandma that she ought to find a piano teacher to come and teach Li Shin to play the piano. Auntie Mei said that children with long fingers were often gifted to play the piano. But Li Shin had turned himself into a sharpshooter instead. A boy had to have strong fingers to be a sharpshooter, I knew that. Rifles were heavy, and the trigger on a rifle was always tight, difficult to pull.

"We have to practice, Chief," he said, pulling his bootlace tight from one side to the other and back again. "It's important." He yanked once at the lace. Then he twisted the two ends in and under, and tied a double knot at the top of the boot.

"Sister Katherine says we're not in any war."

He sat up straight, looked at me, and said, "Some countries are having war. Did she tell you that?"

I listened to the refrigerator humming against my head.

Li Shin cupped his hands over his knees. "Take, for example, Vietnam," he said, letting his fingers spread over one knee like a spider. "You know Vietnam?"

Only a week ago he had unfolded his pocket map and pointed out Vietnam, a pink country with a river. I nodded. "Are we going to be in a war soon?" I asked, thinking about the riots in Kuala Lumpur.

"It's just good to be prepared," he said, pulling on his other boot.

"Do you think we're going to have riots?"

He finished lacing his boot. Then he stood up, pressing his hands over his thighs to make his trousers look neat. "Not like before," he said. "Things aren't as bad here as in Malaya. But it's still dangerous."

"What is still dangerous?"

He smiled. When he smiled his eyes lit up as if he had just spotted one of the grown-ups walking into the house with vanilla ice cream, his favorite. "Life," he said, throwing up his hands. "Life is still dangerous."

That evening six of his cadet friends came home with him. They were all in uniform, with their trouser legs tucked inside their black boots and their berets tipped up smartly above their foreheads. I stood in the living-room doorway and watched them walk single-file along the fence, all of them the same height, all of them moving with the same shy, loosely excited walk that told the world they had just turned seventeen and were ready to register for National Service. They were ready to stop being children and, on their eighteenth birthday, enter boot camp.

Li Shin reached the gate and lifted the iron latch. He stepped aside, holding the gate open while the other cadets passed through.

Li Yuen was sitting on the veranda steps with his back to me, and he did not know I was behind him. He spun around when I stepped onto the veranda floor. Then he saw that it was only me. "Don't creep up on people like that," he said. He went back to watching Li Shin and the other cadets. I walked over and sat beside him on the steps.

Out by the road the cadets were taking off their berets and hanging them on the fence, all except for Li Shin, who kept his beret on. He was crouching on the grass with another cadet. I could hear them fiddling with the knob of a transistor radio, turning it different ways, trying to hit some station. Static came fizzing across the grass and evaporated, sputtering, into the stillness.

The sun had just begun to set. It was too early in the night for frogs or crickets, and the trees were silent, the air in them filled with gold light. Li Yuen was holding in his hand a branch he had broken off a bush, and he began to pluck off all its leaves. I knew that the heats for the interschool sports competition had begun. "Which schools you going to run against tomorrow?" I asked.

"St. Joseph's, Catholic High, Tanjong Katong."

"Are they fast?"

"Tanjong Katong has good runners."

"You scared?"

"I'm faster." He sat there plucking off the last few

leaves. Then he held up his bare branch like a sword and
whipped the air back and forth in front of him. The leaves
he dropped lay scattered over the steps below us, and a
breeze came and blew them down to the grass.

I watched the gold light move over the grass, where it
disappeared into the trees. At the fence Li Shin was standing with his right foot crossed over his left, his right hand
on the gate. He stood facing the cadet with the transistor
radio. I could hear a man's voice coming from the transistor radio like someone speaking in a locked, dusty room
many rooms away. The other cadets were leaning with
their backs against the coconut trees, their hands in their
pockets.

"Can you hear what the radio man's saying?" I asked
Li Yuen. He shook his head, glancing over his shoulder
at the sound of someone coming towards us from inside
the living room.

"We're not supposed to hear," he said quietly, as he
turned back to the road.

Grandma appeared in the living-room doorway, and I
looked across the grass to see if Li Shin had noticed. He
had. He was signaling to the cadet with the transistor
radio, and the other cadets were picking up their berets
from the fence. The cadet with the transistor radio turned
it off, stood up, and moved towards the gate. The other
cadets followed.

They stood outside the gate awhile, watching Li Shin
as he came up the path towards us. Then they turned and
started walking away.

"Didn't you tell your friends not to stay so late?"
Grandma said, when Li Shin reached the veranda
steps.

"It's not that late, Grandma," he said, with one foot on the bottom step.

"It is already sunset," she said. "It is not safe for anyone to be walking out on the road."

By now the cadets were gone. Li Shin took my hand and pulled me up from my seat. "Hi, Chief," he said.

"Hi." I looked at the road, at the rubber trees on the other side where we were not allowed to play anymore because two years ago some metal signs had been put up. Government Property. No Trespassing. I looked at the wooden fence that separated our family's property from the rest of the country. I could hear insects scuffling in the jungle trees near the veranda. Perhaps our grandfather should have put up a No Trespassing sign. I was beginning to feel afraid. Whatever had pulled Uncle Tien out of the house three years ago was still out there, waiting. And no one had ever said how long it had been there.

"Come on, Chief." Li Shin was pulling lightly at my hand. Grandma and Li Yuen had already stepped into the house. I looked up at Li Shin. He smiled and squeezed my hand, and then we went inside, too.

The riots in Kuala Lumpur lasted six days. In Singapore we heard that more than three hundred Chinese had been reported dead, slaughtered like cows in a meat factory, the newspapers said. The rumor was that some reporters visiting the sites of the riots had seen bloodstains on the streets, which could not be washed off. The newspapers would never print such a detail, because it would interfere with objectivity, said people in Singapore. But our aunties and uncles said, "Objectivity, bull."

Evenings after dinner they would gather in someone's bedroom and argue over disguised harmony and not taking risks. Their questions thickened the night air while we slept, left us tuned to their voices awake behind the walls. They spoke in hushed tones, their grown-up worries spidery on the ceiling, making us wish for morning. Sometimes we heard the name Sukarno. Sukarno, a name whispered on the streets that year, a name I had heard in school. "Sister Katherine," I had heard some girls calling across the field one day. "Sister Katherine, tell us, who is Sukarno?" Answer: Indonesia's President, Supreme Commander, pro-Communist. "Is Sukarno good or bad?" asked the girls. Answer: Misunderstood. "What does that mean, misunderstood?" Means: Communists in one country aren't necessarily like Communists in another country. Means: Depends on the country and on people in that country. Means: Many Indonesians are currently unhappy because they don't understand. "Sister Katherine," asked the girls, "what's happening in Indonesia?" Answer: The army might take over. They asked, "How bad will it be?" Answer: It will be bad. Indonesia will become a police state. They asked, "What does that mean, police state?" Answer: Enough questions.

Some nights, while our aunties and uncles were inside a room talking among themselves, Grandma would be out on the back porch with the grasscutter. They seemed to have fallen in as great friends since that first afternoon he arrived, as if they had known each other from another time, when both of them were younger perhaps, perhaps when they were children. But Grandma had told us no, no, the grasscutter was not an old friend from her past. No, the grasscutter was not someone she had known before she married our grandfather. These were questions that Li Shin had put to her, and she had assured him that he was not to be so concerned. Just because the grasscutter came often did not mean there was some funny business going on. It had made Li Shin blush when she said this, and he had apologized. Grandma told him it was all right, that the grasscutter was a good friend, and she hoped we would all be polite to him. We were. Afternoons we would come home from school to find him squatting on the grass in the back, where he would be digging out weeds with a red metal spade. He would wave to us and we would wave back. Sometimes our amahs would be out there talking to him while he worked. They would be standing on the grass, hands on their hips, laughing while they told him witty stories to make him laugh, too. The grasscutter had a shy laugh. He seemed to be that kind of man, tall and shy, who watched the ground as he walked and always wore a straw hat to shade his face from the sun. The straw hat was yellow, watered-down yellow, like padi at harvest time, our amahs liked to say.

On the nights that he came up to the porch to talk to Grandma, the grasscutter would hold his straw hat in his hands. It was the only time we ever saw him take it off. He would hold his hat in his hands and lean on the rail close to her rattan chair, and from inside our bedroom we would hear their voices strangely happy on the night air, like an old-fashioned ballroom dance. My cousins would stand in the dark with their hands on the windowsill. They would try to listen. But what Grandma and the grasscutter said to each other rolled up round and formless in the heat, and only the sounds of their voices passed by our room, the dips and rises in their conversation, and the punctuating lulls.

Then one night the grasscutter came later than usual. It was after eleven o'clock and we were in the red room. We were watching the road for the army trucks that often passed by at a quarter past the hour. Li Shin had turned off all the lights. He always did that. Sometimes we would watch for half an hour and if no trucks came, he would turn the lights back on and then we would go to bed. But usually there would be trucks, two or three of them at least. They would rumble by slowly, packed with recruits wearing black blindfolds. The blindfolds, together with the late-night traveling, were meant to disorient the recruits, to confuse them so that they could not know which camp they were going to or even which direction they were moving. It was part of their training. It was to stop them from thinking that they could go home anytime. It would make them tough, not let them become mama's boys. Make the children grow up tough, Prime Minister Lee had said in his speech on Children's Day. Prime Minister Lee was nineteen years old when the Japanese arrived in World War II. He had watched eighty thousand British troops surrender when our water supply ran out. He had taken an oath. There would be no more foreign domination when he became Prime Minister. All boys must register for National Service. We must build a rugged society.

On the night that the grasscutter came late, the army trucks did not pass by. At half-past eleven Li Shin was about to turn on the lamps when Li Yuen pointed out the window, and we saw the grasscutter wheeling his bicycle along the fence. He stopped at the gate, reached over to lift the iron latch, then swung the gate open and pushed his bicycle through. We watched him shut the gate behind him. He wheeled his bicycle over to a coconut tree and leaned it against the trunk. Then he walked quickly up the path. He was wearing his straw hat, tilted at the usual angle over his face even though it was nighttime, and we could not tell what expression his eyes carried, if he had come to pass on bad news, or good news, or if this was just an ordinary visit and some business had kept him from arriving sooner.

Just before the grasscutter reached the veranda steps he turned and cut across the grass to the corner. We heard him disappear around the side of the house, and Li Shin quickly turned on the lamps.

"Let's go," he said, walking to the door.

Li Yuen and I left the windows at once.

On our way to the kitchen we saw Auntie Mei stepping out of Uncle Wilfred's room. She held a folded newspaper in one hand and a blue ballpoint pen in the other. She was dressed in blue-green floral shorts and a white T-shirt, and her hair hung loose and silky down her back. Auntie Mei was a schoolteacher, and usually she wore her hair in a single plait to keep it neat, and so that she could mark her pupils' compositions without distractions, she would say. But every night she would sit at her dressing table and brush her hair out, and then she would toss her head back and stand up, and when she walked her hair would shift subtly across her buttocks. She had used to let her hair grow until it reached the backs of her knees. But she had been a schoolgirl then. Now she was a married woman, and an English teacher, and such long hair would not look appropriate, I had heard Auntie Lily say to her. They were in Auntie Daisy's room at the time, with the door half-closed, and from out in the corridor I had heard Auntie Daisy jump in, laughing: What's wrong with a woman looking sexy for as long as she can? Auntie Mei did not respond, but the next day when she came home from teaching, her hair no longer reached the backs of her knees. At dinnertime Auntie Lily had watched her walk into the dining room, and as Auntie Mei was sitting down, Auntie Lily said, I thought you were going to cut it short, pageboy-style. Auntie Mei shrugged her shoulders lightly and said, Compromise. She was looking across the table at Uncle Kuan, who always sat in the chair opposite hers because he was her husband. Uncle Kuan had a wide smile on his face, which made Auntie Mei smile too, although she tried to hide it.

Now as we approached her outside Uncle Wilfred's room and she lifted a hand to stop us, I saw how with us she was always serious, what the nuns at St. Catherine would call dignified. She was not playful with us the way I had heard her playful with Uncle Kuan, giggling when he called to her, Chin Mei, come here, you delicious pear. I had heard them on my way to the bathroom one morning just before sunrise. In the darkness their voices seeping out from underneath their bedroom door sounded so fresh and private, I had walked away embarrassed.

"Did you see your Auntie Daisy anywhere?" Auntie Mei asked us now.

"No," said Li Shin.

Auntie Mei tapped the ballpoint pen against her thigh, looking worried. "Where are you going?" she said. Li Shin told her we were going to the kitchen for a drink of cold water. Auntie Mei looked at him sharply. "Is the grasscutter here?" she asked.

"Yes."

She shook her head. "You children should give him

and your Grandma some time to themselves. Must be they have something to talk about, if he's come here so late."

Li Shin was rubbing his right cheek with the base of his palm. He always did that if he was not sure about something he was about to do.

"If you see your Auntie Daisy, tell her I'm looking for her," said Auntie Mei as she walked off. She added, looking over her shoulder, "People get lonely, Li Shin. Old people, too."

I watched her glide down to her room, the soft ends of her hair licking the curve in her hips. As she stepped into her bedroom, I heard her say something to Uncle Kuan. Then their door swung closed, landing with a firm click into the wooden doorframe like a pat on someone's buttocks.

"Come on," Li Shin said, and we continued on to the kitchen.

When Auntie Mei was growing up she had been Grandfather's favorite child. This was why when Uncle Kuan married her, instead of her moving in to live with his family, he had moved in to live with us. This was in 1955, before I was born. Li Shin was three years old at the time, and he remembered that two priests had arrived at the house. The younger one had driven up in a blue Volkswagen Beetle. He was from the Church of the Holy Family, where Auntie Mei had been baptized when she was fifteen years old. Auntie Mei and Uncle Kuan were the only baptized Catholics in our family. The rest of us were supposed to be Buddhists, like Grandma. It was she who had invited the other priest, the not-so-young one, to the wedding. He was from the Chinese temple. Li Shin remembered that he had arrived on a bicycle, and that he had walked up to the house carrying a brown package under his arm. An amah had led him into a room, and when he came out later he was wearing an orange robe. He did not look like a Catholic priest. His head was shaven smooth, and his orange robe smelled of incense.

Grandma had never taken Li Yuen or me to a Chinese temple. She herself would take the bus downtown once a month, to pray in a temple where Li Shin said there was a giant Buddha sitting on a platform facing a huge empty marble floor. He had been to the temple with Grandma a few times when he was four or five years old. There were no pews in the temple, he said. Not like in a Catholic church. And instead of dipping your fingers in the holy water and making the Sign of the Cross on your forehead when you entered, you had to bend down and take off your shoes. You had to walk barefoot on the marble floor because that was the praying ground.

Perhaps Grandma knew that if she had asked us, Li Yuen and I would not have wanted to go. Li Shin had stopped going since the day he started primary school. Not even our aunties and uncles went to pray in the temple, he said. They were too modern for that. When they wanted to pray, they stopped by the Cathedral of the Good Shepherd after work. The Cathedral of the Good Shepherd stood at the corner of Victoria Street and Bras Basah Road, one block away from the National Library, where Uncle Tien used to go to borrow books. It was a big old church with stained-glass windows and dark wooden pews, and stone statues of all the saints. The doors stayed open from early in the morning until late at night, and our aunties and uncles, like us, were familiar with it, with the feeling inside, which was that feeling of intense silence. The nuns at St. Catherine called it residue of the Holy Spirit's work. They said that troubled people who entered a church in faith never left without finding the peace they had come for. That was the Holy Spirit's work, to soothe suffering, which the nuns said felt like a deep cut far inside your soul.

Our aunties and uncles, too, had studied at Catholic mission schools when they were children, because Grandma believed the education here was better than in the government-aided schools. Government-aided schools did not teach you ethics. Also, Grandma said, the pupils did not learn enough discipline. She had seen them on the streets. They were usually rowdy and loud, with their uniforms all untidy. Pupils from mission schools, on the other hand, always looked neat and well-mannered, and always queued up when waiting to get on a bus. So we were all to attend mission schools. Besides, Grandma said, Catholic religion was not so different from Buddhist religion. Both taught us to make prayer a way of life. As long as we learned to pray, it did not matter how. What mattered was that we would be kept safe.

I thought about Uncle Tien as I followed my cousins across the kitchen floor. Grandma had not spoken his name in three years. No one had. I thought about Uncle Tien roaming around outside with only Grandma's water prayer for company, a prayer he could probably feel when the darkness surrounded him at night, a lantern waiting for him to die. It could not protect him while he was alive, but at the moment of his death, it would burst into light. It would shine a path for his soul to follow, and ward off the hungry ghosts that came chasing after the newly dead.

At the moment of his death Uncle Tien would know Grandma was still taking care of him.

We stopped at the back door, which was open just a crack. It was dark outside on the porch. We could hear Grandma's voice coming from her chair. We could not see her, but we could see the grasscutter half-sitting on the porch rail close to her. He sat with his legs stretched out and his feet crossed, his long thin body leaning slightly towards her, his hands holding on to his hat.

Grandma was talking to him in Mandarin. We listened for a while and then we would have left, except that Auntie Mei came walking into the kitchen. She looked at us but said nothing. She opened the back door wide, and stepped outside.

"Daisy went to the pictures by herself again," we heard her say to Grandma.

The grasscutter uncrossed his feet. He looked up a moment, then looked down and crossed them again. He sat there like a schoolboy who could not sit still for very long and was always ready to jump up and move around.

"What time show?" Grandma asked Auntie Mei.

"We're not sure," Auntie Mei replied. "San and Lin saw her leave around nine o'clock. Probably she went to the Odeon. There's a Gary Cooper film showing there."

"Gary Cooper?" said Grandma.

"The American actor," said Auntie Mei. "Very handsome. The one Daisy likes."

"When will she stop this nonsense?" said Grandma. "Twenty-five years old and still chasing after film stars. Are you sure she went by herself?"

Auntie Mei looked at the grasscutter. The grasscutter sat looking down at the floor.

"Was she meeting a man?" Grandma said. "Another new boyfriend?"

The grasscutter continued to look at the floor, and Auntie Mei stood there saying nothing. We could hear the heat in the trees crackling with insects. Then the grasscutter uncrossed his feet and looked up. "They were announcing on the radio that there might be curfew tonight," he said, glancing towards Auntie Mei.

Auntie Mei nodded. "I just heard another announcement," she said, turning to Grandma. "It's not official yet, but chances are there will be a curfew."

For a moment they seemed to have forgotten Auntie Daisy.

"The government is going mad," said Grandma. "Every few years they announce a curfew. In 1966 it was necessary, but the trouble is not so serious anymore."

"Ma, it's a different thing now," said Auntie Mei. "Remember there's a rumor about that ship from China coming in."

"Mao's people," said Grandma. "They are Chinese, like family."

"Communists," said Auntie Mei. "You know they're in contact with PKI and Barisan? Both PKI and Barisan have Malay members, you know."

PKI stood for Partai Kommunist Indonesia. Sukarno's people.

"I do not believe that," said Grandma. "That is a lie the Malays tell us, to break us up."

The grasscutter turned his hat over slowly in his hands. "It's not a lie," he said softly. "We're all mixed up now. There are Malays in Barisan, and Malays in the government." He looked at Grandma. "This country has changed since 1966, Shu Wan."

"Have you become anti-Chinese too?" she asked him.

"You know what I feel," he said.

"Then why do you talk like that?"

"I am saying that things are different. I don't like it, but they are different. What to do?"

We could hear Grandma rising from her chair. "When Daisy comes home," she was saying, "I will give her a good scolding. Leaving the house without telling anyone where she's going. So careless."

We tiptoed quickly towards the corridor, so that by the time Grandma entered the kitchen, we were already gone.

It was after two o'clock in the morning when Auntie Daisy came home. I had fallen asleep, but the sound of our bedroom door opening woke me up. It was Li Shin about to step out into the corridor. When he turned and saw that he had woken me up, he put a finger to his lips.

I slipped out of bed and ran over to him. "Where are you going?" I whispered. He whispered back that he had heard something coming from the front of the house.

"Want to play soldiers?" he asked.

I nodded.

"Get your gun."

Ever since Uncle Tien disappeared we had kept our black toy guns next to our beds. It was a game that Li Shin had made up for us to play, but it was also practice. We would be like the recruits in boot camp, who slept with their guns close by in case they had to get up in the middle of the night. Li Shin said that in boot camp often a bell would ring in the middle of the night, and then all the recruits would have to jump out of bed and put on their uniforms and run downstairs to line up in the courtyard. They would have ten minutes to do all of that. With just ten minutes you could not afford to waste time looking for your gun. If you arrived at the courtyard late, the officers would make you do fifty push-ups and then you would have to run ten laps around the camp. Li Shin said that sometimes a recruit would put on his uniform inside out, and the officers would put him on extra guard duty. There were always recruits who put on their uniforms inside out during their first midnight drill because they were not used to dressing in the dark. Li Shin said there was no time to turn on the lights. Also, in case of war, turning on the lights could give you away to the enemy.

I picked up my gun and met him back at the door. Li Yuen had joined us by now. He too was carrying his gun. "Take the rear," Li Shin whispered to him. Li Yuen nodded and moved into position behind me.

"Chief, keep your head down."

I nodded and followed him out into the corridor, looking both ways for a sign of the enemy.

We made our way quietly to the red room, tiptoeing past the closed doors where our aunties and uncles were asleep. I could hear Uncle Wilfred snoring when we passed by his room. As we walked safely into the red room, Li Shin leaned his gun on the edge of the table near the door. Then he crossed over to the windows and stood there with his hands behind his back. Li Yuen and I put down our guns and went to stand beside him.

There was a police car parked outside our gate. The siren on its roof was flashing, and I could see the red light soundlessly searching the trees, then swooping down and combing the grass. A policeman was standing beside the car, holding open the door to the backseat, and Grandma was standing at the gate, watching. Auntie Daisy climbed out slowly. The policeman held her arm as she stepped onto the road. She stood up straight, still for a moment.

I had expected her to be laughing, or leaning sideways on the car door and tilting up her face to flirt with the policeman. But she only stood there and stared at Great-Grandfather's house.

The policeman bent down and spoke to the driver through the front window. Then he straightened up and took Auntie Daisy's arm again. He led her to the gate, which Grandma was holding open. Auntie Daisy walked as if she did not recognize where she was, as if she did not know the sound of the iron latch snapping loose from the wood, or the sound of the rusted hinges swinging the gate open, then closed. She let the policeman guide her towards the house. Nothing was familiar to her, not even the path leading them to the veranda, the ground worn bare by all our relatives who had walked across the grass since our great-grandfather's time. I watched her come up the veranda steps, numbed and deaf.

On afternoons long ago, she had sat on those steps with us, telling us that a wind was coming soon which was going to blow on the fence just hard enough to topple the fence over. We were still small then, and only Li Shin was attending school. Auntie Daisy told us that Grandfather himself had put up that fence while she was still a child. He had hammered wooden posts into the earth and knotted them together with wire. It had been a firm little fence back then, marking out the property that our great-grandfather had passed down to Grandfather, property that would be passed down to us, someday in the future.

But over the years the fence had aged. It had become a shaky wooden thing, said Auntie Daisy. The wire had rusted in the rain and sunshine, and now the fence needed fixing. Any day now, a wind was coming. Auntie Daisy told us that when it came, that fence would rip itself out of the ground.

We used to run out and walk along the fence, where the grass grew raw and thin, riddled with small stones. We would walk dipping our fingers into the narrow spaces between the posts. And Auntie Daisy, watching us from the veranda steps, would call out, Careful, don't cut your feet on the stones.

I watched the policeman hand her over to Grandma. I could hear him saying something in a low voice. Then Grandma took Auntie Daisy's arm and walked with her into the house. The policeman turned back to the road. His voice had sounded very young, light and easygoing the way Uncle Tien's voice had been, and he walked very straight. I watched him walk towards the gate. The path shivered watery white in the dark behind him, and as he reached the fence, I remembered where I had once pushed on the wooden posts to make them shift deep in the soil.

We stayed in the red room until we heard Grandma and Auntie Daisy pass by the door. Then Li Shin picked up his gun. He waited a few minutes. Then he stepped softly into the corridor, and Li Yuen and I followed.

In the months ahead we would watch our aunties and uncles when they visited Auntie Daisy in her room. They took turns. Auntie Daisy would receive one or two visitors every day. No one spoke a word to us about that night. The door to Auntie Daisy's room stayed shut all the time, except when someone was entering or leaving the room. We were told not to go there anymore. Auntie Daisy needed to rest, we were told. We must not disturb her. She was not well. We did not ask what it was that had made her sick. Not even Li Shin wanted to ask. On some mornings as we were leaving for school, we would hear Auntie Daisy in the bathroom, splashing water and singing to herself. She sang hymns. Ave Ave Ave Maria, the long sweet notes dropped like casuarina needles, moist in the steamy perfumed air that we could get on our palms if we bent down and stuck our fingers in the crack beneath the bathroom door. Then, one morning as we were about to leave the house, Li Yuen realized that he had forgotten to pack a book. He hurried back to our room to get it, and that was when he saw Auntie Daisy just as she was closing the bathroom door. That was how we found out she was pregnant.

Six

February arrived, a time of warm steady rains and the smell of wet grass. At St. Catherine the flowers that had been planted by the older nuns who had grown too tired to teach were blooming crazily all along the school walls. I was in Primary Six A, in a classroom on the second floor of the back building. The room had lemon-yellow walls and big square windows. Since my desk was near a window, I could hear the rain when it fell, the light tapping on the ground, and after each heavy shower I could smell the flowers and the soggy earth. When the sun was out I could look out into the field and watch different classes go through their PE rituals, girls in white T-shirts and blue shorts running through obstacle courses, doing jumping jacks and swaying their hips inside hula hoops. I could also see the wall where the St. Peter's boys had tricked us with their kite, and I would think about the side wall where they used to go. No one knew if they still did. Two years ago a nun had caught some girls coming out of the stairwell who were not supposed to be there, and that was the end of that. The door to the stairwell had been locked ever since, and only the bell ringers were allowed to get the key, which hung on an iron hook in the principal's office. My classmates sometimes spent whole recess sessions plotting out ways to steal the key, now that we were old enough to pay attention to boys in swimming trunks, now that we were curious. But no one was willing to tackle Mrs. Bhanu, the principal's secretary, who had a reputation for being Singapore's most dependable human lie detector. Mrs. Bhanu had once been overheard saying to a girl, Don't lie, it makes you smell bad.

So we remained curious as to what a boy's body might look like without clothes, until that day Patricia Wee brought to school some magazines she told us she had found at the bottom of her mother's wardrobe. There was no time to look at the magazines before General Assembly, so Patricia promised to show them to us during recess if we each paid her five cents. There were forty-two of us, and by the time the assembly bell rang, Patricia had collected two dollars and ten cents in loose change.

At nine o'clock that Friday morning Sister Calista sat at the teacher's desk marking our history tests, which we had just taken. We had Sister Calista for a double period that day, because she taught us two subjects, history and mathematics. The class was working on problem sets that she had written on the blackboard. Outside the window I could hear the kindergarten children down in the field.

Sister Magdalen was trying to teach them some simple exercises for good health, and I could hear her voice saying, Bend and touch your toes. Keep your knees straight. Then the kindergarten children would laugh, and she would laugh along with them. I glanced around the room, and that was when I noticed Patricia passing one of her mother's magazines to Anna. Anna flipped the magazine open to where a bookmark had been stuck between the pages. She grinned widely and looked up to wink at Shanta, who sat in the back row with her and Patricia, and was next in line.

Sister Calista continued to mark our tests, her nononsense black-rimmed spectacles perched firmly on her nose. She held a red ballpoint pen in her left hand, because she was left-handed, and there were two extra pens on the desk just in case.

The magazine switched from hand to hand down the back row, from Shanta to Geraldine, Geraldine to Kee Lai, Kee Lai to Monica. Later they would not be able to stop talking about the pictures they had seen, which were of naked British people chasing one another around a garden. I watched the magazine circle the corner. It moved up into the next row, and then, as I was turning back to my problem sets, someone whispered, "Look at his birdie." Now the whole class turned around.

Yew Ling and Pin Nyun sat rocking quietly in their seats, their hands pressed over their mouths.

Sister Calista put down her pen.

"Bring it to me," we heard her say.

A chair leg scraped the floor in the back. Someone dropped a pencil as Patricia walked to the front of the room with her mother's magazine rolled up in her hand.

We watched her hand it to Sister Calista. Then she looked down at the floor and waited while Sister Calista flipped through the pages quickly. I could hear Sister Magdalen's voice outside calling to the kindergarten children to start lining up two by two.

Sister Calista lay the magazine quietly on her desk. She closed her eyes, and for a full minute, she stood there fingering the black rosary beads that hung from her waist. Her crucifix banged softly on the white cloth of her habit, and a silent dread crept into all of us.

"Go stand in the corner," she said, opening her eyes.

I saw Patricia glance sideways at us as she walked over to the corner, where she stood between the blackboard and our classroom door.

"Take off your pinafore."

Patricia unhooked her belt. She pulled her pinafore over her head, folded it neatly, and left it on the small stepping stool that those of us who were assigned blackboard duty stood on when we were trying to reach the top of the board.

"Pull down your panties."

Patricia stood still. Then she bent forward and pulled down her panties, and we saw that she wore white cotton panties, the kind you could buy from a woman in the market, three for one dollar. They slid easily down her legs and caught around her ankles. She stood there covering herself with her hands. She was trying not to cry, but her face was already turning red.

Sister Calista slid open the top drawer of her desk and took out a wooden ruler. She walked over to Patricia. "Hold out your hands," she said, but Patricia just stood there and stared at her.

"Please, Sister," we heard Patricia whisper. "I'm sorry."

"Hold out your hands."

Patricia held out her right hand.

"Both hands," said Sister Calista.

Patricia stood there biting her lip as she pulled her other hand out from between her thighs.

Sister Calista's ruler whipped down hard, and we heard it crack twice. Around the cold brittle silence of us sitting there, watching, the air felt like glass, now broken forever. We watched Patricia snatch her hands away. Then we looked down at our books.

"Now you can turn and face the wall."

We looked up and watched Patricia turn. She took small jerky steps so that she would not trip. Her shoulders were shaking quietly.

"Go back to your problem sets." Sister Calista stood looking down the room at us, the wooden ruler clasped firmly in her fist. "Stop wasting time," she commanded. We picked up our pencils and bent over our books, avoiding one another's eyes.

For the rest of the morning whenever we looked up we could see Patricia's buttocks hanging out below her white blouse. When Sister Judith came to take over from Sister Calista, we watched the two of them talking softly out in the corridor. Once we heard Sister Judith say, Unfit punishment. Another time we caught the name St. Augustine. After about fifteen minutes, Sister Calista walked off and Sister Judith entered the room. She told us to take out our watercolors. She told Patricia to put her panties back on. But Patricia would not move. Sister Judith put an arm around her and told her again, gently, to put on her panties. Still, Patricia just stood there. Finally, Sister Judith hugged her and left her alone.

At recess when Sister Calista had ordered our whole class to stay in the classroom, Anna had brought Patricia's lunchbox to her. But Patricia would not take the lunchbox even from Anna. So Anna left it on the floor beside the stepping stool, and the lunchbox stayed there until twelve-thirty, when the last bell rang for dismissal. Then Patricia was allowed to leave the corner.

We had begun packing our schoolbags even before we heard the bell. For our last period we had Sister Katherine, who always ended her lesson three minutes early on Fridays. Anna had packed Patricia's bag for her, so as soon as Patricia had pulled on her pinafore and hooked up her belt we were ready. We lined up in twos in the corridor and marched downstairs, and then we ran out to where the school buses were waiting outside the convent gates.

❊

It was a warm dry afternoon, the sun bouncing hard stony green off the grass. Near one of the school buses some of the senior-class girls stood talking under the old mango tree. Sunlight filtering through the leaves played across their backs. I could hear their voices in the heat like bubbles. I stood outside the gates awhile, watching my classmates crowding up the steps of a school bus. I could not ride with them, because none of them lived anywhere near Great-Grandfather's house, and it would have taken the school bus too long to get me home.

A girl left the mango tree and came over. She wore her hair in a thick long plait, like Auntie Mei's except that Auntie Mei did not tie a silky black ribbon to the tail of her plait. But this girl did, and I recognized her as Susan, the fat man's daughter. Her father, the fat man, owned a small shop in the market near Great-Grandfather's house. He sold brooms, mops, dustpans, baskets, pails, and tubs in all sizes and colors. I had been to the shop a few times when I was very young, in the days when Grandma used to bathe me, and every once in a while she would take me to the market and buy me a new tub and I would choose my own color.

Susan came along the side of the bus and stopped in front of the folding doors, where Patricia was sitting on the bottom step, munching hungrily on a sandwich. She looked up at Susan, who reached into her pinafore pocket and took out a bar of chocolate wrapped in red-and-gold paper. I watched Susan give the chocolate to Patricia. Then she looked over at me and smiled.

"Hi, Esha," she said, coming towards the gates.

"Hi."

"Are you walking to the bus-stop? Want to walk with us?"

I nodded. I was old enough now to ride the street bus by myself, but lately I had grown lonely for company, now that Li Shin was occupied with cadet meetings and Li Yuen had track practice. Often they would stay back after school, and I rarely saw them at the bus stop.

As I walked towards the mango tree with Susan, I could see my classmates through the bus windows. They were pushing each other in the aisle and fighting for window seats. Someone yanked at Kee Lai's plaits, and I heard Kee Lai screaming out a swear word. At once Anna told her to shut up. Shut up, Anna said fiercely. You want all of us to have to stay back for detention? What if we get Sister Calista?

"How was your history test, Esha?" Susan asked.

"It wasn't so hard," I said, watching her friends step out from under the mango tree. They were four years older than I, and I knew, from the time the government nurse came to give all of us a physical checkup and I had seen the senior class girls undressing in the music hall, that they wore brassieres underneath their school blouses. Most of their brassieres were plain white, but I had seen some girls wearing lacy brassieres, with a tiny pink ribbon tucked between the two cups.

We had to walk to the bus stop near my cousins' school, because the one outside St. Catherine had been temporarily taken off the bus route. This was because the roads in the surrounding area were being repaved. The workmen had not reached St. Catherine yet, but as we walked on, I could smell fresh tar in the warm air and somewhere up ahead there were machines and a lorry was moving slowly. We passed through a neighborhood with white brick semi-detached houses, L-shaped lawns, and tall metal fences half-covered with hibiscus. It was a neighborhood where modern people lived. There were cars parked along the roadside, bright shiny modern cars with radio antennas sticking out in front of their side mirrors. When I looked at the rooftops of the houses, I saw that many of them had television aerials, some of which were probably connected to color television sets. Television was forbidden in Great-Grandfather's house. Grandma said that watching television would make us lazy and cross-eyed.

We turned a corner onto the road where men were working. A red lorry carrying hot tar was parked in the middle of the road, and behind it sat an orange tractor with giant roller-skating wheels. The men were on their coffee break, and the machine noise had stopped. I could see a few men squatting on the grass with their trousers rolled up, showing their black rubber boots. Their shirts were tossed over the lower branches of trees, where other men stood smoking cigarettes. I watched the men near the trees lifting their chins to blow thin blue smoke into the leaves.

"Did you answer all the questions about the flag, Esha?"

"Yes." I was walking behind Susan, and when I looked down I could see her thin white socks with the frail white lace that went around the edge.

"Did you get all of them correct?"

"I think so."

"Good for you." She smiled at me over her shoulder, and I looked over at her friends' socks, all trimmed with lace.

Someone whistled, and from the quiet shady grass the workmen began to laugh. Two of them left the trees and came to stand by the roadside to watch us. They dropped their cigarette butts, grinding them into the road with their boots.

"Esha, come here," said Susan, reaching over to take my hand.

We walked past the men slowly. When I looked behind us, their silent eyes were smiling into our backs. I saw that one of the men had stepped onto the road. He was thin and brown and his nipples were like two soft grape skins.

He waited until we were further away and then he called out, "Oh pretty girls, you like to eat banana?"

"Wait till I cut it off," said Susan.

Her friends giggled and answered back, "You'll go to jail."

A breeze moved through the trees, and I felt Susan's hand holding on to mine. Her hand was warm and tight. We kept walking, and slowly the men's laughter died in that smooth clean sound of leaves.

"I will, you know," she said after a while. She stopped walking, and I looked at her standing beside me with her free hand planted on her hip. "Don't think I'm carrying my scissors around for nothing." She sliced at the air with her fingers. "Snip here, snip there, that's all, very easy."

Her friends looked at me cautiously.

I jumped, trying to touch the leaves of branches that drooped over the road.

"How's Auntie Daisy, Esha?" I heard Susan ask. She started walking and pulled me along.

I told her, "Fine, thank you."

"How's Grandma?" she asked next.

I told her, "Fine, thank you."

She turned her head and smiled at me. I smiled back and then I jumped. I pushed my hand up through the sunny air, but when I hit the ground, the leaves were still hanging, dark green, limp in the rising February heat above our heads.

I heard one of Susan's friends say, "You're going to have a new cousin, Esha," and I answered, "Yes."

"Are you excited?"

I was not sure.

"I don't know," I said, and Susan's friend laughed. But she stopped when I looked at her. "You want a boy or a girl?" she asked.

I watched sunlight shimmering in the leaves above us. The leaves were so bright I almost stopped walking, but Susan dragged me along.

"A girl, right?" her friend was saying.

I jumped and felt the leaves slip between my fingers.

"Right, Esha? Don't you want a girl?"

I tore them off the branch. Then I tossed them up and they floated through the air like soft green dying birds. Susan was looking at me, so I said to her, "My Auntie Daisy doesn't have a husband." She looked at her friends.

"You know why?" I asked.

"No," she answered.

"You sure?"

She was still looking at her friends. Then she turned to me and said quietly, "You want to know why, Esha?"

I looked at her friends and they looked at me and then at Susan.

"Don't do it," they said.

Susan continued to look at me, as if she could not hear them. "Your Auntie Daisy was raped."

Her friends looked away. I put up my hand and jumped and made the leaves shiver. Bright green leaves. I could see through them to the sharp white dots of sun.

"You know what that word means, Esha, rape?"

One of her friends said, "Susan, enough."

"That means a man—"

I jumped again.

"A man tells you to take off your panties, Esha, and if you don't do it, he tears them off himself."

I crumpled the leaves and watched them flake away. We stopped walking. I held the last leaf up, against the light. A scratchy blue sky glinted through a tiny crack.

Susan pulled softly at my hand.

I let the leaf go, and then we were walking again.

❀

At the bus stop near St. Augustine's my
cousins were waiting underneath a flame of the forest tree
that grew there with its branches sprawled over the sidewalk. A patch of the sidewalk sat buried in bright red
flowers, and I could see that a wind had blown some of
the flowers off the white cement onto the road, where
they were wilting in the hot early-afternoon sun. I waved
to Li Yuen, who was kicking a stone about the sidewalk.
He waved back, then turned and called to Li Shin, who
was leaning on the tree trunk, reading in the shade. All
around them were trees where boys and girls wearing
different school uniforms were gathered in groups, waiting
for the bus. Above some treetops I could see an iron cross,
where St. Augustine's stood behind a yellow brick wall
and wrought-iron gates.

Li Shin walked out from under the flame of the forest
tree, closing his book. He came to meet us. "How was
your history test, Chief?" he called out.

"Easy." I waited for him to smile, for his eyes to curl
up and shine, bright black like promises.

"Tell me what the crescent on the flag stands for." He
took my schoolbag from me and slid it onto his shoulder.
It was a khaki cloth schoolbag with a wide shoulder strap,
the kind of schoolbag that many of us carried.

"A young country. A new nation."

He was smiling now. "How many stars around the
crescent?"

"Five."

"Tell me what the five stars stand for."

His dark eyes were watching me.

"You know the answer, Chief."

"Democracy, peace, justice, equality, and progress."

He winked at me and I laughed and he laughed back. Then we heard Susan's voice breaking in, asking, "You going to take the bus with us today, Li Shin?"

"You know I can't," he told her. "I have to meet with the other cadets."

She slipped the silky black ribbon off her hair. Then she tossed her head to the side and shook her hair loose, combing it out with her fingers. "Are you all going to practice shooting today?" she asked.

"No. We're going to talk."

A big yellow leaf dropped off a nearby tree as we passed it, going towards the bus stop. Li Shin walked next to me with one hand on my schoolbag and the other in his pocket.

"Did you hear what happened yesterday evening?" said Susan. "There was an accident, on Telok Kurau Road."

"I know," said Li Shin.

I looked at Susan's friends walking on her other side with their blue pinafores flapping against their knees. Suddenly they looked up and smiled at Li Shin. They never spoke to him.

"Someone's car blew up," Susan said. "They think it was a homemade bomb."

Li Shin nodded his head. "I know."

"You know anything else?" she asked.

He told her, "No, not yet, but I'll let you know. Maybe I'll stop by your house after the meeting, if there's time."

She tilted her head and smiled up at him from that angle.

He blushed. Then he looked away, facing the flame of

the forest tree where Li Yuen was chasing a stone around the flowers like a soccer ball. After a while he said, "Is it all right for me to stop by your house? If there's time?" He was still looking at the flame of the forest, and his voice was soft and not very sure.

"Yes, it's all right." Susan was looking down at her ribbon and playing with it. "What time will you stop by, do you think?"

"I might not have time." He glanced at her. "But if I do, you know?"

She smiled. "I know, your meetings always end late."

"Not always," he said, shaking his head.

"Most of the time."

Li Yuen was bending to pick up his schoolbag. We waited for him on the road. He straightened up and ran towards us, swinging his schoolbag and his water bottle over his shoulder.

"You going to win the one-hundred-meter race this year?" Susan asked him when he reached us.

He squinted at her. She laughed and waved her hand over his hair. He was a little shorter than she was, though not by much, and sunlight danced between her fingers. Then Li Shin tapped my shoulder and I turned to take my schoolbag from him. That was when I saw the bus. It was coming slowly from down the road, a green metal bus with a sleepy quiet sound that was so quiet I might not have heard it if I had not turned to take my schoolbag.

A breeze shook in the trees. We were all of us watching the bus now. As it came closer, we could see the soldiers inside. They wore their green uniforms and little green caps and they sat neatly along the windows. Not one soldier was turning his head to look outside.

As the bus slipped past us I felt a soft wind.

"Don't they look like Boy Scouts?" said Susan. "They look just like Boy Scouts."

Li Shin was frowning when he turned to her. "Recruits," he said. "You're supposed to call them recruits."

The bus reached the curve in the road. It followed the curve and disappeared behind the trees, slapping up dust underneath its tires.

"I'm late for my meeting," said Li Shin. "I have to go."

I turned to him, but he was already walking away. When he stopped for a moment beside the flame of the forest, I waved to him. He waved back, then swung around and ran into the trees, towards St. Augustine's iron cross.

The bus that we rode back to Great-Grandfather's house was Number 21, an ordinary street bus that rumbled noisily along the road and screeched when it came to a halt. That afternoon it arrived a few minutes after Li Shin left, so we did not have long to wait. When we got on, I paid my fare of ten cents and sat down in the first empty seat I saw, which was near a window, while Li Yuen walked on to the back of the bus with Susan and her friends.

As it moved away from St. Augustine's the Number 21 entered the downtown district, where the trees thinned out into rows of small dim shops. All the shops looked the same to me, a series of small square fronts packed side to side, each with a dark open doorway and two dark open windows. They had two stories, so that shopkeepers and their families could sleep on the second story. Downstairs those families sold boys' running shorts, Made in China, 100 percent cotton. They sold white T-shirts, Made in China too. They sold sports trophies and stainless-steel platters, car tires, bicycle tires, small silver bicycle bells, locks, pumps, Japanese sandals, American tennis shoes, antique bedscreens smuggled out of Hong Kong. Some shopkeepers had small back rooms where they engraved names into the metal of slim expensive fountain pens, Made in Germany. The modern shopkeepers used shrill-sounding machines, but the old-fashioned ones still engraved by hand.

Outside some of the shops sat old people gathered around wooden tables. They sat underneath canvas canopies, holding coffee cups in their hands while they chatted. I knew from Li Shin that instead of Mandarin, these old people spoke the dialects, Hokkien or Cantonese or Teochew, even Hakka. They had arrived in Singapore in the early 1900s, among the second wave of immigrants, who were mostly blue-collar workers. In China they had been peasant farmers. Those from the cities had been coolies. They had never been inside the Forbidden City, and Li Shin said that their only dream now was to save enough money for tickets to Peking. Every day they spoke of passing through the gates of the Forbidden City, of walking where the Emperors had lived. Singapore would never be a real country to them, Li Shin said, because they had never considered themselves citizens here. They saw themselves as visitors, waiting for things back home to get better. Their radios were always tuned to stations that aired Chinese opera music. They never listened to the news or talked about the riots in Malaya and Indonesia. For a while they had been interested in the League of Common Alliance founded by Dr. Sun Yat Sen, who had set up a branch in Kuala Lumpur in 1906. That was when the league became known as the Kuomintang. But in 1911, the Kuala Lumpur branch was outlawed by the Malayan government because the Kuomintang was said to have been involved in anti-British activities. In 1911, the British still had the final say in Southeast Asia, which the old people said was a sign that Southeast Asian governments were small fry.

I had seen old people gathered, too, in the market near Great-Grandfather's house, where some of them owned food stalls. I had seen them sitting in jagged circles outside the stalls, sipping coffee where the hot steamed smell of noodles rose from big black pots and filled the air. They would be talking to one another about mahjong games and horses to bet on at the weekend races. Sometimes, if it was early enough in the morning, their grandchildren would be there, helping out before they left for school. The grandchildren would be dressed in their school uniforms. They would walk about quietly, unfolding wooden chairs and tables and arranging them neatly around their families' stalls. And Grandma would say to me, See how lucky you are, Su Yen. See how much work some children have to do.

When we got off at the stop near Great-Grandfather's house, Li Yuen wrapped his water bottle around his wrist, twisting the blue plastic strap around and around.

Susan and her friends walked in front of us without talking. Above us the sky burned like blue fire and eter-

nity, the kind of sky that closed your eyes if you dared
to look at it straight. It sent heat through the trees the
way we knew the rain must have come when Noah built
his ark, that we had learned about in Catechism, how the
different animals climbed on board, two by two. I could
see a silver line tracing the edge of the treetops. When a
tree leaf wafted off a branch, I picked it up and threw it
up again.

Li Yuen swung his water bottle around in the air, cutting plastic blue circles first one way, and then the other.
"You know where the soldiers are by now?" he said after
a while.

"Where?"

"At the army camp." He slapped the water bottle
against my legs. "You know, the one near the market."
The water bottle hit my legs again, and I tried to move
away. Li Yuen grabbed my arm. "Did you know there's
barbed wire all around the camp?" he said.

"To keep out Communists," I said, looking at Susan.

She looked over her shoulder at me but said nothing.
I watched her as she pulled her hair into a ponytail. She
tossed the silky black ribbon in and out between her fingers, tying a knot.

"No," said Li Yuen. "To keep the recruits in."

Then he saw a small stone lying near the edge of the
road, and he ran over and kicked it. The stone bounced
silently into the grass. He walked back to us, slinging his
water bottle over his shoulder.

We left the main road, and as we turned onto the other
road, the one that ran past Great-Grandfather's house, Li
Yuen pointed up ahead to a man walking near the trees.
The man wore a white singlet, baggy shorts, and a straw

hat, and we knew it was the grasscutter. Actually the grasscutter was a tall man but he did not look so tall walking under the trees. We could see the road stretching long and gray in front of him and behind him. He was like a small thin shadow, and the trees on both sides of him like tall leafy guards winking sun off the sky. I saw him stop at our gate. He opened it, walked through it, and closed it behind him.

"He's going to cut grass again," I said.

But Li Yuen said, "Don't be silly, he cut grass on Wednesday. Nobody cuts grass every two days." He started running and I followed him, leaving Susan and her friends staring after us on the road.

We saw him in the back, underneath the frangipani tree at the edge of the cemetery. He was sitting on a wooden crate turned upside down on the grass, the kind of wooden crate that oranges came in. Sometimes a boy would deliver the oranges to Great-Grandfather's house. Sometimes his father did. The boy and his father owned a fruit stall in the market up the road. Sometimes they would come to Great-Grandfather's house together, on bicycles, each with the wooden crate strapped to the rack in the back and the oranges packed in soft purple paper.

Li Yuen dropped his schoolbag and water bottle on the porch steps. He pulled off his shirt. "Here, Chief," he said, giving me the shirt. "Throw this into the basket when you go inside."

I was halfway up the steps. I looked at the shirt he held out. It smelled like him, the sleeves showing black streaks where he had wiped his face. "Do it yourself," I said. "I'm not your coolie."

"Don't be like that, Chief," he said. "You're going in anyway."

"I'm not going in," I said.

"It's your turn to get the shoes," he said.

I looked at the grasscutter, who sat up very straight under the frangipani tree. He was watching the ground, with his hands cupped over his knees. Around us the heat was rising fast, and I could see the sky glowing whitish blue. Somewhere in the trees a bird was calling, a lone single cry.

Li Yuen came up the steps past me and walked to the rocking chair in the corner. He grabbed one arm of the rocking chair, tilted it towards the floor, and let go. The rocking chair swung back at once and began to rock. I watched Li Yuen as he stepped over to the rail. "Chief," he said, speaking to me over his shoulder, "go get the shoes."

I turned to the kitchen, and at the frangipani tree the grasscutter stood up. He was looking at the sky. He swung around and walked into the cemetery.

"Maybe he's going to pee," said Li Yuen, before I could say anything. "Now will you get the shoes or not? We'd better wash them before it gets too late."

When I stepped out with the shoes, the grasscutter was still in the cemetery. But as we walked down to the shed, he walked out of the trees carrying a pile of branches in his arms. They were long thin branches and they still had leaves on them. The grasscutter dropped the branches under the frangipani tree. Some of them rolled away, and he knelt down to gather them back. Then he stood up and looked towards the shed, where Li Yuen and I were getting ready to wash our shoes.

At the shed there was a water pipe two feet tall coming out of the ground. It stood against the wall, and it had a tap that was connected to a red plastic hose, which when nobody was using it was rolled up and hung over the tap. The walls of the shed were blue, and inside the shed there were brushes and a big blue pail that were used for washing shoes only.

Li Yuen walked into the shed and came out with the blue pail. He turned on the tap, leaving his hand there until the pail was full. Then he turned off the tap. I watched his hand bounce a shadow off the wall, a pale shadow like a small ball hitting the light blue wood. The pail was on the ground next to his feet, and I bent to see my face in the cool water. But I could not tell if it was a pretty face or an ugly face. It had very short hair, though not short enough for me to look like my cousins, Grandma not wanting me to look like a boy or a soldier. I dragged my fingers through the water and made the face in the pail disappear.

The grasscutter was still looking at us when I looked up. He stood between the pile of branches and the wooden crate and seemed quite tall with the flowers in the frangipani tree hanging just above his head. He stood there with his singlet pressed limp against his chest. It was an old singlet, worn many times, stretched soft with washing.

"Don't think I'm going to wash your shoes for you," said Li Yuen. He was kneeling on the other side of the pail, with his three pairs of shoes lined up neatly on the grass. He had pulled out the laces of one pair, and was dropping them in the pail.

I turned back to the grasscutter. He pulled out a pocket knife, flicking it open with one hand. It had the kind of blade that slid in and out of the handle, depending on which direction you pushed the control button. The grass-cutter picked up a branch as he sat down on the wooden crate. First he skinned the branch, peeling off half its leaves. Then, keeping the branch balanced across his thighs, he started sharpening it at the tip.

"Do you see what the grasscutter's doing?" I said, picking up one of my two pairs of shoes. I owned two pairs instead of three, because I could keep them clean longer than Li Yuen could. They did not have laces. They were girl's shoes, the kind you buckled on the side.

"Yes, I see what he's doing," he said.

I dipped my brush into the pail and let the water drip over the shoes. The dripping made a sound like sudden rain. The white canvas soaked up the water, and turned wet gray. I put down my brush and looked up. The grass-cutter had two piles of branches now, one on either side of him. The new pile was still small and was made up of the branches that had been sharpened and that were only half-covered with leaves.

I picked up the soap powder. It came packed in a fat blue box that was already cut open at the upper right corner. "Why's he doing that, you think?" I said, pushing in the cardboard flap.

Li Yuen handed me a blue plastic spoon.

"Ha?" I said. "Why's he doing that?"

"That's too much powder, Chief," he said, watching my right hand.

I held the spoon near the hole and tipped some powder back into the box.

"All right, that's enough."

I picked up a shoe with my left hand.

"Now shake it evenly, don't let it clump."

I tried to look annoyed.

"Last time you let it clump," he said. Then he picked up the box and shook out some powder without even measuring it with the spoon. He added, without looking at me, "I can do it this way because I know how." He kept his head bent and I could see his hair, cut so short it stood up like grass. I looked past him, at the frangipani tree and the grasscutter sitting underneath. A wind shook the tree and a dry white flower floated off a branch. It floated past the grasscutter's shoulder, and he swatted at the air behind him as if it were a fly or a mosquito that had bothered him.

Li Yuen spread the soap powder over all his shoes. Then he put down the box, picked up his brush, and started scrubbing. So I picked up my brush and started scrubbing too.

When our shoes were almost clean and we were getting ready to lay them in the sun, Grandma stepped out of the kitchen and came down the porch steps and walked across the grass to the frangipani tree. She stood in the shade, and seemed to be discussing some greatly important matter with the grasscutter. He was standing too. As soon as he had seen Grandma coming towards him across the grass he had stood up, leaving his knife on the wooden crate. Now he listened while she talked, and from time to time he would nod or shake his head. Then she stopped talking. They stepped out of the shade into the sun and stood looking at each other. After a while he said something, and she said something, and they were talking again.

Their voices sounded thin, fading into the static-crisp trees. The grass shone bright around their feet and I wondered if they were hot standing in the sun so long.

Li Yuen began to rinse his shoes, dipping them into the water and pulling them out, dipping them in and pulling them out. He held them upside down, letting the water stream back into the pail. Suddenly he looked up. He pointed at the house and said, "Chief, look at Auntie Daisy."

I turned around to look.

Auntie Daisy's room was in the far left corner of the house. Even if you were not trying to find it you noticed it easily because the window was barred with vertical iron rods, which we were told Auntie Daisy herself had asked for. It was a tall window, like most of the other windows except for the rods, and also for the white lace curtains, sewn by our twin aunties a few weeks after that night the police car brought Auntie Daisy home.

Auntie Daisy was standing at her window, staring up at the sky. I could see that her hair had grown. It used to reach her shoulders but now it hung down to her waist. Since the windowsill was at a level halfway up her thighs, I could also see that she was wearing nothing but a pair of black panties.

Grandma and the grasscutter were still talking on the grass. I saw the grasscutter glance at the house. He was saying something, but he stopped suddenly and Grandma turned around.

Someone pulled Auntie Daisy away from the window,

but Grandma was already hurrying back to the house. The grasscutter watched from the frangipani tree. He stood there with his hands on his hips. I looked at Li Yuen, who shrugged his shoulders and tipped the blue pail over. He shivered as the cold sudsy water ran across his feet. "Aunty Daisy's not well," he said, repeating what Grandma had told us to say if strangers came up to us and asked about Auntie Daisy.

The ground darkened near our shoes, and the soap bubbles burst slowly on the grass. I gathered up the shoes. Then I carried them over to the porch and arranged them along the bottom step. After Li Yuen had collected our washing things and put them back inside the shed, he came and sat on the steps with me.

A bird flew out of the treetops above the cemetery. I watched it fade into the sun. Under the frangipani tree, the grasscutter picked up his knife from the top of the wooden crate and sat down.

Li Yuen turned to me. "I heard something today," he said. "The Malay boys told us."

"Told you what?" I said, picturing Chinese and Malay boys eating together at a wooden table in the tuck-shop.

"Told us this island is haunted."

"Haunted," I said. "The whole island?"

Li Yuen looked at the trees. "Her name's Pontianak," he said. "She's a woman devil."

"The devil is a man," I said.

"The Malay boys told us she hides in banana trees."

We watched two birds fly towards us, slanting down from the sky. They landed on a flowerpot that was sitting underneath the mango tree. The flowerpot was half filled with water, and one of the birds started to skip in and out. We saw the water splash the other bird, which was walking around the edge.

"We don't have banana trees," I said.

Li Yuen traced circles on his right knee with his second finger. "One of the boys, his name's Amin, told us near his house they have a banana tree. Every evening, before sunset, his father goes outside and ties a red string around a banana. If you do that, and Pontianak's in the tree, she must stay there." He dropped his hand and sat there hugging his knees. "Amin told us some nights you can hear someone crying outside his house."

I turned to watch the grasscutter. He was aiming his knife at the tip of a branch. He shaved it down, and a chip of wood fell softly to the grass.

When the grasscutter got up and walked about, it was already past four o'clock. The light slanted on the grass the way it always did after four o'clock, and we could see the slight shadows. The grasscutter pushed his hands into his pockets. He walked past the frangipani tree one way, then turned around and walked past it again, and then he sat down. He shifted on his seat to get comfortable. We could tell he was doing it to get comfortable, because the grasscutter was that kind of person, the kind who was not going to do anything unless he could get comfortable doing it, not walk or sit or stand up if he could not get comfortable doing it but just lie down, just lie down for the rest of his life.

When Auntie Daisy screamed, he looked up slowly, as if he had been expecting to hear it, as if all afternoon he had been waiting.

❀

Li Yuen got up. He walked down the steps and broke a branch off a bush. He knelt beside the path. First he drew a square in the sand. Then he drew watchtowers at the corners of the square. An ant crawled out from under the bush and he shot it down, saying, "Nobody gets into my camp."

Auntie Daisy was still screaming. She screamed as if Grandma had tied her to the bed with barbed wire. But the amahs said that sometimes crazy people screamed when they saw ghosts moving around the room. The voices of other grown-ups drifted out of the window, and Li Yuen looked up for a moment. Then he drove his branch into the ground like a spear and stood up. He turned and began to walk towards the cemetery.

I got up and hurried down the steps, knocking off a shoe. I stopped to pick it up, but Li Yuen was already approaching the trees. "Wait for me," I called out. He kept walking. I dropped the shoe and ran after him, and the grasscutter looked up to watch.

I caught up with Li Yuen inside the cemetery. I grabbed his wrist from behind, pinching it hard. He swung around. "Let go," he said, pulling away. I let go. He rubbed his wrist, and I could see my finger marks on his skin. "You're crazy," he said. "Just like her." I kicked at the sand between us. A thread of dust rose and shivered and sank back into the path.

"I want to go with you," I said, looking up.

"No," he said.

The sun was coming through a crack in the treetops. Li Yuen stood in the pale white light, and I thought suddenly that he looked like Li Shin, with Li Shin's pointed

face and Li Shin's dark, dark eyes. Then a cloud passed
overhead and the treetops dimmed. The light disappeared.
"I want to go with you," I said again.
Li Yuen bent towards me, his hands clasped over his
knees. "Scared of Auntie Daisy?" he said, peering into
my face.

"No," I said.

"Yes, you are," he said. "You're scared. Chicken." He
straightened up and flapped his arms. "Paaak-puck-puck-
puck-puck."

A breeze dragged through the trees. The ground around
us shifted with the dry sound of fallen leaves, leaves that
had been lying there for hundreds of years.

Li Yuen stopped flapping his arms. He put his hands
into his pockets and turned away and started walking
again. I put my hands in my pockets and walked behind
him. We walked like that for a while, he pretending not
to know that I was there. Sometimes he stepped off the
path and walked along the edge instead, and I heard the
dry old leaves that gathered around tree roots ripple and
crack under his feet. Once he bent to pick up a long twig.
He continued to walk, dragging the twig beside him, and
it made a thin line in the sand. Then the light around us
became greener. We passed the middle of the cemetery,
and I touched the hanging roots of the giant rain trees.
They felt hard like wire. Li Yuen kept on walking, his
feet leaving small dips in the softer sand.

Then from far away came the sound of grasses moving
in a slow wind. "Where are we going?" I called out.

Li Yuen spun around and rushed back to me through
the trees. "You dummy," he whispered, "talking so
loudly."

He grabbed my shoulders and shook me, then yanked

me to the ground. I slipped, my right foot shooting out
and slamming into his foot. Our ankles locked. He fell
over backwards and I heard the leaves scatter when he
rammed his elbows into a thick tree root.

The cemetery was very quiet after that. "You're bleeding," I said, and he sat up slowly, looking surprised. I
pointed to his elbow. He bent his arm, scraped the sand
off his elbow, and squeezed the skin around it. It was a
deep cut. I watched the blood drip onto his knee.

"You have to get the dirt out," he said, looking up and
catching the fear on my face. Then he stood up.

"Are we going back now?" I asked.

"Not yet." He turned and began to walk. We were
already deeper inside the cemetery than we had ever been,
and this time Li Shin was not with us.

We walked until we could see daylight
coming through the trees ahead. Then we stopped and Li
Yuen told me, "Chief, listen," and when I listened I could
hear that in the trees where daylight was coming there
were birds. They made soft sounds, and the light moved
very slow. It came through the trees in short thin lines.
I could hear the leaves silent and slow around us. To our
right, to our left, and behind our backs, the air was thick
with them, and I looked up and saw more leaves closing
over us. I looked behind us again, where the sand path
curved a short way into the trees. Then it disappeared,
lost in the cool moist green.

"Let's go," I heard Li Yuen say.

We walked slowly now, pretending we were soldiers.
Li Yuen watched the ground and stepped carefully, and

sometimes he would stop and look ahead to the trees where the daylight came. He would look before he continued to walk. I followed, stepping in the places where he stepped. I thought he was looking out for graves, even though all the graves had been dug farther away from the path. But actually he was looking for footprints.

The trees began to thin, and the daylight came through in stronger streams, passing over our feet so that we had to move into the shadows. But I did not move at first, because already I could see through the trees to the other side. I could see patches of pale sand and green seawater, and I stood there until Li Yuen pulled me behind a tree. "Are you an idiot?" he said. "Standing in the light like that."

"That's the beach," I said. "We live so close to the beach?"

He looked at me, surprised that I never knew.

"How come we live so close to the beach and we never go there?" I asked.

He grabbed my hand and pulled me towards the light, but making sure that we stayed in the shadows. "Look," he said when we stopped. "Do you see anyone on this beach?"

I stared through the trees. We were standing close to the edge now and I could see how the sand ran into some high rocks far away. The beach stretched whitish-brown and empty except for some trees that had crashed near the edge, their sides looking burned from a lightning storm. I watched the water from the sea slide up where the sand was dark, then slide back down. Sometimes a wave would leave dark green seaweed along the shore. The next wave would come, break, slide up, slide down, sometimes taking the seaweed back, but sometimes when that wave broke and was gone the seaweed was still there.

The sea looked shiny blue in that light of late afternoon. Along the horizon four or five gray ships sat lined up against the sky like old people waiting, not moving. Then I saw something in the water close to shore and I watched it for a while, and then I knew two people were swimming over there. I pointed them out to Li Yuen. He stared, saying softly, "They're not supposed to swim there." We could not see the swimmers very well. They were too far away and swimming close together. I heard Li Yuen say again, "They're not supposed to," and I asked him why.

"This is army beach," he said, pointing to the high rocks. "No one's supposed to swim in the water. You can't play here."

I looked towards the high rocks.

"You know what's behind them?" he said, still speaking softly. "Patrol squads."

I looked for the swimmers. They were swimming towards the beach now. The sky turned soft dark gray behind the ships, and Li Yuen whispered, "There's a storm coming." But the sea was still calm, and I watched the clouds gather behind the ships until the sky was like the sides of the fallen trees that had fallen from lightning. The swimmers reached shallow water and stood up and began to walk. One of them looked like a girl with long hair tied back into a ponytail, but she was not wearing anything on top. She was not wearing a girl's swimsuit.

I turned to Li Yuen. "You think that's a girl?" I asked him. He was standing very straight, as straight as if somewhere the national anthem were playing.

"Yes," he said. But there was a funny look on his face, and I knew that he was hiding something from me.

The swimmers stood in the water, facing each other. The water was only as high as their knees now, and we could see that both of them did not wear swimsuits. They held each other's hands and leaned close, kissing. Then they pulled back to look at each other. They leaned close and kissed again. The water moved around them slow like lost-somewhere dreams, and the gray ships were still. There was no one else on the beach, but I could see the quiet high rocks hiding patrol squads behind them, and I looked at the swimmers again. They were holding each other now, their skin brown and wet in the paling light. I thought that they were so beautiful in the water. It was the most beautiful thing I had ever seen, and Li Yuen must have thought that, too, because he stood there and did not say anything about walking back.

I could see the boy moving his hand up and down the girl's back. He moved his hand slowly up and down, up and down, a few times, and then the last time he reached down further. He rubbed soft slow circles over her buttocks, and I saw the girl drop her hands and then she was doing the same to him.

Li Yuen watched beside me, leaning forward on a tree with his hands behind his back. I glanced at him a few times, but he would not look at me. When I turned back to the swimmers, the boy was kneeling in the water. He slid his hands over her legs. She was looking at the sky, bending over backwards so much I thought she would break. When he pressed his face to her where she held him they rocked, and rocked, and did not fall into the water.

"We'd better go back now," I heard Li Yuen say.

He had stepped away from me and now he stood on the path, looking the other way. Somewhere behind the trees a breeze shook the grasses, and we heard it like small fingers slapping the grasses side to side. I plucked a branch off a bush and gave it to him. It was full of soft leaves. He swept sand over our footprints and tossed the branch into the trees. We began to walk, he walking in front of me as before. We walked without talking until we had passed the rain trees. Then he turned around and whispered, "Chief, did you hear something?"

"What?"

"I think someone's following us."

"I don't want to play anymore."

"I'm not playing," he said, looking at the trees. "Just listen."

The wind was blowing in the tall grass. I wondered if the swimmers were still in the water. Li Yuen stood still, looking at the trees and listening. "It's only the wind," he said softly. Then we were walking again and he did not stop anymore.

Outside the cemetery it was not as late as we had thought. The grasscutter, still working underneath the frangipani tree, looked up as we passed him. The ground was strewn with frangipani flowers. We crossed over the grass to the porch steps, where Li Shin was waiting for us in the kitchen doorway.

"Where did you go?" he asked.

"We saw the beach," I said, still shocked that no one had ever talked about it.

"You're not supposed to go there," he said, looking past us at the cemetery.

"We didn't really go there," Li Yuen told him. "We stayed in the trees. We didn't even walk on the sand."

Li Shin was watching the grasscutter at the frangipani tree. "You shouldn't have gone that far," he said, glancing at Li Yuen. "You know that." Then, turning to me, he said, "Better go wash your hands, Chief. Dinner's almost ready."

Seven

In Great-Grandfather's house, just after sunset we would walk into the dining room for dinner. We would sit at the long table in the middle of the room, where there were many chairs. The table and chairs were made of blackwood, and there was no tablecloth. At St. Catherine, where I had seen Sister Magdalen taking the kindergarten children into the parlor to have milk and biscuits at the round marble table, there would be a tablecloth, a blue lace tablecloth that hung over the edges of the table. While Sister Magdalen talked, the children would play with the blue lace tablecloth, their fingers tracing all the tiny holes and curves. But in Great-Grandfather's house, no one did that. All of us sat at the blackwood table and looked at our faces looking back at us. The blackwood was always clean, and shone with polish. We would sit there in our own places, that were ours because they had always been. In Great-Grandfather's house things that had always been were as if they would always be, having no beginning and no end. I never asked if they would always be. It never occurred to me to ask.

When we walked into the dining room that night, the grown-ups were leaning on the table and talking to one another in low, serious voices. Then Auntie Mei glanced up and saw us and she tapped the table. The talking stopped.

After we sat down, she smiled at us and said, "Is the grasscutter still working outside?" When Li Shin told her he was, she said to Grandma, who was just then coming into the room, "We should invite him to eat with us."

"I don't think he wants to do that," said Uncle Wilfred. He looked at Grandma, and Grandma nodded as she sat down.

She said, "No, it will make him uncomfortable to eat with us."

"Is he going to eat with the amahs, Grandma?" I asked.

"Yes," she said.

"He likes to do that?"

"Yes, they have a nice time eating and talking."

Li Yuen picked up the soya sauce bottle and sprinkled soya sauce all over his carrots. As he was putting the bottle back down, he asked, "What are the branches for, Grandma?"

"They are just to have," she said. She looked at me, because I was pushing my carrots to one side of my plate. "Su Yen, people are starving in China," she said to me.

"Carrots taste funny," I said.

Li Yuen was looking at Grandma. "But what are the branches for?" he asked again.

"Just to have," Grandma said, dipping into the soup

bowl with a big wooden spoon. She scooped out stalks of wet green watercress and left them on his plate.

Uncle Wilfred was watching her, and then I saw him push his fork into the soup. When he pulled it out, the watercress was caught on it. He dragged the watercress onto his plate, twisting the stalks into his rice. Without looking up, he said, "Don't you think you should tell them?"

"This matter is not for children," said Grandma.

Uncle Wilfred looked at her and said, "What about Li Shin? I think he's old enough now."

I looked at Li Shin, who looked back at me and winked. "You'd better eat your carrots, Chief," he said.

Li Yuen turned to Uncle Wilfred. "Tell us what?" he asked.

Grandma shook her head. "Eat your dinner," she told Li Yuen.

I sat staring across the room, where wineglasses were kept in glass cupboards lining the wall on one side of the window. Nobody used them anymore, because visitors seldom came to the house, and yet the amahs kept the glasses washed and shiny just in case, standing them up on the glass shelves like rows of oleander flowers. I could hear the other grown-ups in their places all around the table, separate forks and spoons clinking on separate plates. They did not join in the conversation.

"It will be better for Daisy to go to the hospital," said Uncle Wilfred. I turned back to Grandma. She ran a slice of raw onion through the peanut sauce in front of her and said firmly, "No," and slipped the onion into her mouth.

"At the hospital they have equipment."

"No."

Sitting next to Uncle Wilfred, Auntie Lily picked up her spoon and waved it in the air. The silver spoon danced in the white fluorescent light. "I agree with Wilfred," she said, turning to him. "Wilfred, I agree with you."

Grandma picked up her napkin and dabbed at the corners of her mouth. "I have delivered three grandchildren," she said. "I can do it one more time."

Auntie Lily waved her spoon again. "What about Papa's dream?" she said, looking at Li Shin. Then, for some reason I did not understand yet, she looked at me.

I heard Uncle Wilfred say, "Just in case," and Auntie Mei joined in, "Ma, this one may be different."

Now our twin aunties were the only grown-ups still eating peacefully. Auntie Mei put out her hand and touched Grandma's elbow. "Ma," she said again, softly, "we don't know who the father is."

"Daisy should go to the hospital," said Uncle Wilfred, picking up a chicken leg. He peeled the meat off the bone with one stroke. "They have equipment," he added.

Auntie Lily rapped her spoon on the table, and even our twin aunties stopped eating to look at her.

I saw Uncle Kuan pick up his water glass. When he saw me watching, he winked. He took a sip, put down the glass, and burped, which made Auntie Mei stare hard at him. "Stop that," she said. Uncle Kuan nodded at her and then he burped again.

Auntie Lily rapped her spoon.

"You promised to try," said Auntie Mei.

Uncle Kuan patted his stomach and said to her, "I try, but the stomach will not try." He looked at me and winked again. "In olden days," he said, leaning across the table, "you had to burp after finishing your dinner. Otherwise the host thinks you didn't have enough to eat. That's an insult to the host, you see."

Auntie Lily rapped her spoon a third time, and Grandma snatched it out of her hand, saying, "You want me to slap you?"

Uncle Kuan burped once more. He covered his mouth with his hand and looked at Auntie Mei out of the corner of his eye, and she shook her head, and almost smiled. "You are not a guest in this house," she told him.

"It is bad luck," said Auntie Lily.

Auntie Mei and Uncle Kuan looked at her, and she went on, "Keeping a pregnant woman in the house under such circumstances." She slowed down on "such circumstances," pronouncing each syllable as if it were a favorite sound. Everyone seemed to know what she meant, but no one was saying a word. I heard Li Yuen put down his spoon.

"What happened in Grandfather's dream, Grandma?" he asked.

"Just before he died," said Auntie Lily.

"Grandfather had many dreams," said Li Shin. "They were just dreams, that's all."

"Yes," said Grandma, "just dreams."

"No," said Auntie Lily, looking around the table. "Papa himself told us this one's a warning."

Grandma looked at me. Everyone sat quietly for a while, and I listened to the ceiling fan whirring above our heads, the quick hard flat metal notes flying towards the window and out into the trees. Grandma was saying, "He was very sick that night." I followed the free metal notes out the window.

That was my place. Every night I would sit at the table

facing the window, and the neat dusted shelves of oleander wineglasses. The window sat alone in the wall, which was green not like jungle trees but like the color of apples. When we were younger we would run our palms over that wall, and feel the thickly painted-over wood grain. In the daytime we used to lean out of the window, which opened to the trees that grew along the side of the house, where if you leaned towards the branches you could see sunlight falling off the dark green leaves. You could look out into the layers of jungle trees and imagine them to go on forever. But at night there was nothing outside the window except blackness, which you could imagine creeping towards you from the forever into which the trees emptied. You could imagine it to creep up to that wall like a Japanese soldier. You have never met a Japanese soldier but you have heard the stories, and you know how they creep up to the walls of a house before they bang down its doors and capture its people. You know how they steal across the darkness and their footsteps fall so silent, you never hear them come.

"I remember that," I heard Li Yuen say. "Once Grandfather had a dream about an elephant. Some blind men came along and touched it and tried to decide what it was."

"That wasn't a dream," said Li Shin.

"But they couldn't agree," Li Yuen went on. "Because each of them was touching a different part of the elephant and they were all blind. So they had a big fight. And Grandfather said that in the kingdom of the blind, the one-eyed man is king."

"That wasn't a dream."

"Grandfather told it to us. I remember."

All the grown-ups were looking at Li Yuen. Then

Grandma said, "No, it was not a dream. But it was one of his favorite stories. I am sure it makes your grandfather happy to know you remember it."

I turned back to the window.

Sometimes while you were sitting there you could hear the leaves, even if you could not see them. Even if you could see only the blackness, that crept up to that wall like a Japanese soldier when he stole across the darkness and his footsteps were so silent you never heard them come, even if that was all that you saw, sometimes you could hear that soft familiar sound of leaves in a slow wind.

But I could not hear anything that night.

Then Li Shin was standing beside me, and I felt his face bending close. He said softly, "Chief, let's go." He pulled back my chair and I tried to slide off but my T-shirt caught on something in the back and I felt it move up, cooling my skin in that sudden way that happens when you take off your clothes on a hot day, because even on a hot day there is that moment when you take off your clothes and a quick sudden cooling brushes on your skin like water when you lie on top of it, floating.

Li Shin unhooked me and pulled my T-shirt back down.

All the grown-ups had finished eating by now and they were getting up from the table, pulling their chairs back softly against the floor. We stood by our chairs and watched them walk out of the room. For a while we could hear them talking in the corridor. Then they were gone and only Grandma and we were left.

Li Shin took my hand. We walked to the door, and Li Yuen followed behind. At the door we stopped to see if Grandma was coming too, but she was still sitting at the table. In the window I felt the blackness like a Japanese soldier pressing his face against the wooden frame, peering into the room. Grandma was very still, looking straight ahead. Sometimes she sat that way, keeping still and straight, with her hands folded in her lap, and it was her stillness that told us she was not looking at anything in front of her, that if she saw the things in front of her it was not because she was looking at them but only because they were there.

I looked at the plates and bowls laid out neatly in front of her. Then I looked at her face. Now that no one else was in the room, the fluorescent light became sudden and white, and I saw how she had wrinkles. They lined her forehead, pinching at her eyes, reminding me of the yellowed ceiling fan, and the old shaky wooden fence outside, and thick solid tree trunks that grew in the cemetery so deeply rooted we believed they would be there forever, that when we looked at them we saw strength in infinity unopposed, unchallenged.

"Let's go, Chief." I felt Li Shin pulling at my arm. We walked away, leaving Grandma to be by herself in the room and have some peace.

When we entered the kitchen with our schoolbags, we saw that the altar candles were about to burn out. Usually one of the amahs would replace them, but now Li Shin pulled open a drawer and took out two new ones. I walked up to the table. When I put down my schoolbag, the table shook. "It's time we fixed that," Li Shin said, coming over. He gave me the candles.

Li Yuen was at the window, looking out.

I watched Li Shin pull an exercise book out of his school-bag. He tore out a page and folded it in half. Then he folded it again, making it into a small rectangle. He folded it three more times, while I watched the yellow light from the table lamp shine over his shiny black head. Finally he ducked beneath the table with a fat tiny wedge of folded paper. I slid off my seat and knelt on the floor, laying the candles by the table legs. The legs were connected by two pieces of wood lying across each other about three inches off the floor. I could see their shadows slanting over the boards, mashing into our own shadows. Li Shin squeezed his wedge of folded paper underneath one of the table legs. Then he grabbed hold of the table edge and shook it. He let go, pulled out his wedge, and unfolded it once. He pressed it flat against the floor with his right thumb. He stuck it underneath the table leg again, screwing his lips together and looking like a hopeful bird. I thought how he would look like a bird when he was doing home-work, not when he was writing, but when he was staring down at an empty page.

When he stood up, I picked up the candles and stood up too. He touched the table edge lightly and pushed, testing it again. Then he said, "It's fixed, Chief. Sit down and do your homework." And he took the candles from me.

I unbuckled my schoolbag. There was a wide flap that closed over the top of the bag and buckled to the bottom of it. I flipped open the flap and took out my mathematics exercise book. Sister Calista had given us extra problem sets for homework. An idle mind is the devil's workshop, she had said to us that afternoon when she walked out of the classroom to talk to Sister Judith. On Monday she would make everyone exchange books, and then she would write the answers on the blackboard in blue chalk. You gave your book to the girl who sat on your right, and you marked the wrong answers with a red pencil. Sister Calista kept the red pencils in a gray cardboard shoe box, which would be passed silently up and down each row of desks while she was writing the answers on the blackboard.

I looked for the page where I had copied down the problem sets. Li Yuen was still at the window, and I heard Li Shin say to him, "Aren't you going to do your homework?" He was standing at the counter near the sink, holding a burning matchstick in his hand. I watched him light the altar candles one by one. Then he blew out the matchstick, ran its head under running water, and flicked it into the wastepaper basket on the floor. I waited while he carried the candles to the altar.

Li Yuen left the window and came to the table and sat down. He opened his exercise book, holding a blue pencil in his hand.

"What dream was Auntie Lily talking about?" I asked, when Li Shin turned from the altar.

"Grandfather had many dreams," he said, walking over. He pulled out a stool from under the table and sat down. "Don't worry about it."

"But she kept talking about it."

"Everyone gets dreams."

Li Yuen had started to write in his exercise book, and I leaned over and saw that he, too, had mathematics homework, except that his mathematics was more advanced, something called trigonometry. But I could see that he was not working on his problem sets. He was sketching. He had sketched a tank and two soldiers. The soldiers did not have guns yet, so he was giving them guns now. I knew why he had stood so long at the window. Mathematics was still his least favorite subject. He could not do it as well as he could run, even though he did it the same way, which was what Grandma had told him. Li Yuen ran like the wind and Grandma had told him once what a pity it was that he did mathematics the same way, with nothing but wind for a brain.

Li Shin was reading a book filled with small black words. I sat there and watched him for a while. His eyelashes were long enough so that when he was looking down like that, it was as if he might have closed his eyes. You might think he was asleep.

"What, Chief?" he asked, looking up.

"What kind of dreams did Grandfather have?" I asked.

"Dreams," he said, watching me. "You get dreams, don't you?"

"Yes."

"So did Grandfather."

"Were they scary dreams?"

"Sometimes," he said. "Everybody gets scary dreams sometimes."

"Was Grandfather scared?"

"No."

"He wasn't scared?"

"Grandfather was never scared."

Li Yuen looked up, his pencil suddenly holding still. Then he looked down again and continued drawing. There was a third soldier appearing in his exercise book now.

Li Shin turned and saw the third soldier. "You'd better do your homework," he said.

"I'll do it after this," Li Yuen answered without looking up.

"You'd better do it now."

The pencil stopped. "After this."

"Now."

They looked at each other. Then Li Yuen turned away slowly, and when I looked into his exercise book again, he was doing his problem sets.

❀

Later that night, when Auntie Lily came into the kitchen and saw Li Yuen and me sitting there, she stood still and looked at us as if we made her forget what she had come into the kitchen to do. Then she said, "Where is your grandma? Do you know where your grandma is?"

"Grandma's outside," Li Yuen answered.

"There?" Auntie Lily pointed a small dry finger at the back door.

"Yes," Li Yuen said. "Li Shin is out there too. I think they're talking."

Auntie Lily hurried across the floor like a mouse that knew where the cheese was kept. She put out her hand, reaching for the doorknob even before she was at the door. Li Yuen and I glanced at each other, but we did not say anything. We could hear her muttering to herself, "It's bad luck. Very bad luck." She opened the door and stepped outside and left it open behind her. I looked at Li Yuen. He placed a finger on his lips and stared at me, and I nodded.

"It's almost time," we heard Auntie Lily say, her voice coming in from outside on the porch.

"Is everybody ready?" came Grandma's voice.

"Wilfred says it is not too late to call the hospital."

"Is everybody ready?"

There was a pause. "Only two of the children had faces."

Li Yuen and I sat still and looked at each other. "It was a dream," we heard Grandma say. She added, in a businesslike voice, "Come, don't stand here like that, wasting time."

I caught a far-off look in Li Yuen's eyes that I had never seen before.

"Send one of the amahs to stay here and boil water," Grandma was saying as she stepped into the kitchen. "There is no need for all of them to be in Daisy's room— what are they doing there?" She looked at us while Auntie Lily hurried past the table and disappeared into the corridor. "Stay here," she said, looking at Li Yuen especially. "And stay together." Then she walked into the corridor and we got up from the table.

When we stepped onto the porch, Li Shin was standing near the steps with his hands on the rail, staring at the trees. He turned to us. "Are they gone?" he asked, and we nodded.

Then Li Yuen said to him, "What did Grandma want to talk to you about?" But Li Shin was staring off into the trees again, and he did not answer.

Li Yuen turned and walked off to a corner of the porch. I watched him climb onto the rail. He hugged his knees and leaned back on the wall and sat there facing us. After a while he said to me, "What are you staring at?" So I turned away and looked across the grass instead, and watched the grasscutter walk up and down out there, his singlet shifting pale white underneath the frangipanni tree.

"Is he waiting for the baby to come?" I asked, moving over to stand beside Li Shin.

He took my hand and said softly, "Yes, Chief." His fingers closed tightly over mine.

We stood there like that until we heard grown-ups running in the corridor, coming towards the kitchen. When I asked, "What's rape?" Li Shin did not answer. He was watching the back door. I moved closer to him, and he reached down and pulled me against him. He held me there with his hands over my chest and I watched the back door too. We could see through it into the soft kitchen light where our schoolbooks lay open on the round wooden table and two stools were pushed back the way Li Yuen and I had left them, forgetting to push them back in. I saw them and wondered if Grandma would notice that and if she would say anything about it, because Grandma always said you must put things back where you find them.

The grown-ups were coming closer and closer, and then we heard them in the kitchen. We watched Grandma come out the back door. Our uncles and aunties came out from behind both sides of her and then they were everywhere on the porch, standing and talking and picking up branches and putting them down and picking them up and putting them down. Then Auntie Lily noticed us standing near the rail and she pointed to us.

Li Shin kept his hands on my shoulders, pressing me to his body, and I knew that I was safe, even from Auntie Lily. I could see Li Yuen still sitting on the rail in the corner. He hugged his knees and kept quiet.

Grandma looked at us and was about to say something and then she changed her mind. She went into the kitchen, and when she came out she was carrying a kerosene lamp. "We must stop wasting time," she said. She went down the steps, holding the lamp carefully in front of her. The other grown-ups followed. They carried branches in their arms. They had stopped talking. We could hear them restless on the grass as they half walked, half ran across it, going to the grasscutter, who stood waiting at the frangipani tree.

"Something's gone wrong," Li Yuen whispered.

"Be quiet," Li Shin whispered back.

"Something's gone wrong."

"Be quiet, I tell you."

"What did Grandma want to talk to you about just now?"

"Nothing."

"I don't believe that. You think I'm a little kid like Chief?"

"I'm not a little kid."

"Shh."

Someone was coming back. When he came closer, we saw that it was Uncle Kuan. The other grown-ups stayed behind, under the frangipani tree. They gathered around the grasscutter and cut away the light from the kerosene lamp that sat burning on the grass. We could see the light now and then in between their legs. It burned a soft orange glow.

Uncle Kuan stopped at the bottom of the steps and looked at us and said softly, "Li Shin, your Grandma wants you to come with us."

Li Shin answered, "I don't have to do it."

"You have a duty to do it," said Uncle Kuan.

"I can choose."

"You cannot choose." Uncle Kuan's voice was quiet in the dark at the bottom of the steps. He stood there looking up at us, waiting. Then a soft shifting sound came from the corner of the porch and Uncle Kuan looked past us and now he was looking at Li Yuen. I turned to look too. Li Yuen swung his legs over the rail and slid down to the floor. He stood there looking at Li Shin.

"Only Li Shin can come with us," Uncle Kuan said to him.

"I know," Li Yuen said, coming over.

"You are not old enough."

"Yes, I am," Li Yuen said. "But no one knows it yet."

Uncle Kuan looked at Li Shin. "We have no more time to waste," he said. "Li Shin."

I could hear a wind building high in the treetops. Li Shin unfolded my arms from around his waist and pushed me away gently. Then he turned to Li Yuen and told him, "Stay with her." He brushed past me and ran lightly down the steps, and he and Uncle Kuan walked quickly out across the grass, where the other grown-ups had turned around by now and you could tell they were waiting.

I rubbed my toes on the sandy floorboards and then I ran down the steps and Li Yuen ran down after me and caught my hand from behind. "Chief," he said. "We can't go with them."

I turned to look at him. "I'm just going to stand here," I told him. "And I'm not a little kid."

"Come back up," he said, dragging me back to the porch. He was stronger than I. I climbed up the steps with him and then we stood at the rail, looking towards the frangipani tree, and he would not let go of my hand.

Out across the grass the kerosene lamp glowed orange, moving about the air. Someone had picked it up and was carrying it. We watched our aunties and uncles stooping to gather the sharpened branches into their arms, their

187

faces flickering like skin lanterns in the dancing light. Li Shin was carrying branches too. He was standing still in front of Grandma, so still you could tell that she was saying something to him and he was listening carefully.

Up on the porch we could hear only the wind and the leaves.

When Grandma finished talking to Li Shin, the other grown-ups started to walk into the cemetery. They pulled Li Shin in with them and then we could not see him anymore and we could see only the backs of the grown-ups and it was not that they were walking into the cemetery that made us scared. It was the way they did it, everybody not talking as if they knew they should not talk, as if that was a sacred thing that they were doing and a law. We could hear the twigs crack beneath them, and that told us they were not all walking on the path. We stayed on the porch and listened to the cracking come out from behind the unmoving trees and we could hear that the wind had left and the quiet that was rising. We stood in the quiet that rose like floodwater in darkness over the empty grass and it was like drowning and not hearing anything except a soft and distant thunder echoing like muddled water in your ears and wind when it blows while you are running.

"What are they doing?" I dared to say at last.

"I don't know, Chief."

"Yes, you do."

"No."

The cracking grew softer and softer and then it stopped. I tried to pull away, but Li Yuen held on firmly to my hand.

"Let go," I said.

"No," he said. "You'll make Grandma angry."

"She won't hear us," I said.

"Grandma hears everything."

"We can be quiet."

"Chief, Grandma hears everything."

I looked at him.

"Besides," he went on, "how are you going to be quiet in the cemetery? What are you going to do? Float?" He sat down on the steps and pulled me down beside him.

We sat there a long time and it was very quiet and then we heard the cracking again, and Li Yuen stood up and went down to the grass and I stood up too. We saw Grandma walking out of the cemetery. She was holding the kerosene lamp in front of her, and behind her came the grasscutter. Next to him we saw Li Shin, who was looking at the ground as he walked. Then we saw our aunties and uncles. Everyone was still carrying branches. As they came walking towards the porch, Li Yuen put his hands on my shoulders and dragged me off the path. We stood on the grass, waiting for them to pass.

Li Shin did not even look at us when he walked past. I watched him go up the steps. Except that he was looking at the ground, he walked the way he always walked, with his shoulders pushed back and his body moving straight, vertical, and if you asked him why he would tell you that that was the way a soldier walked.

They disappeared into the kitchen, and Li Yuen grabbed my hand and whispered, "Come on." We ran around the side of the house to the front, trying not to slip on the leaves that had fallen in thick damp layers underneath the treetops during the monsoon.

They came out the front door and went towards the

road. The grasscutter was carrying rope over his shoulder. I started to follow them but Li Yuen pulled me back.

"But they're going out," I said.

"No, they're not," he said.

So we stood by the side of the house, underneath the treetops, and watched from there.

He was right. They were not going out. They did not even step onto the road. Instead, they spread themselves along the fence and then they dropped their branches on the ground beside them, and the grasscutter took out his knife and sliced off bits of rope and dropped them near the branches. As he walked along the fence, each grown-up would bend to pick up a branch and start tying it to the top of the fence.

"What's that for?" I whispered.

"Quiet."

"What's it for?"

"Do you want them to hear us?"

"Tell me."

"Later."

"Promise?"

Li Yuen looked at me. "I promise, all right? Now shut up."

I turned back to watch them. They were tying the branches all along the fence, working at it silently and quickly, so familiar with the rope even in the dark, as if that was what they did, as if they did that every day, like going to work. The road sat black and empty on the other side of the fence, and we could hear it just as silent, and the rubber trees growing on the plantation were silent too. I turned to Li Yuen. He was leaning sideways on the wall, with his hands behind his back.

"What about the baby?" I said.

"Didn't I tell you to shut up?"

I turned back to the road.

When they had tied branches all along the fence, they walked over to the gate and stuck branches in the ground. Then they separated and moved towards the jungle trees on both sides of the house. They drilled branches into the earth all along the edges of the trees. Then they came back to the house, walking quickly now. Our aunties were clutching at their skirts, while our uncles had their hands in their pockets. We remained hidden at the corner of the veranda and listened as they went up the steps. They hurried into the house, and then it was quiet again. But when I looked around the corner, Li Shin was still outside. He stood on the veranda and stared towards the fence. We heard Grandma's voice at the door.

"Li Shin," she was calling to him gently. "Come inside now."

He glanced at the corner of the house where we were just before he walked inside. We could hear Grandma talking to him softly as she closed the door. It was hard to tell if he had seen us or not. He would have looked there all the same without knowing that we were there, just thinking that we might be. He would have guessed that we might be, because he was one of us. Or at least he used to be.

We stayed out there awhile, and then Li Yuen started to walk towards the fence.

Li Yuen had a way of walking, a slow and cautious way, but most times you could tell that it was not because there was anything to be slow and cautious about, it was just the way he walked, that was the way he was, he was a slow and cautious person. He moved as if always trying to cross mine fields that no one else could see. I watched him as he went towards the fence. I wanted to call him back, but I followed him instead, and the grass shifted beneath our bare feet, his bare feet walking ahead of mine. Out there all around us in the dark the branches stood tied with their sharpened ends pointing up. I could see them clearly as we moved closer and closer to the fence.

When we reached them, Li Yuen lifted his arm and pressed his palm on the tip of a branch. I was standing just behind him. "What are you doing?" I asked.

He did not answer.

"Li Yuen."

I saw him shiver, the way he would shiver in the morning when we had to wake him up. Then he turned to face me. I tried to ask him again, but I could not. So I just looked at him.

"We'd better go back," he said quietly.

I looked at the branches behind him.

"We'd better go back," he said again. "Come on."

I walked with him back to the house.

The front door was still closed, and Li Yuen ran up the steps and across the veranda and tried the knob. "Is it locked?" I asked, watching him from the grass. He came back down without answering.

We went around the side to the back, where we saw the grasscutter sitting on his box underneath the frangipani tree. Li Yuen pulled me up the wood steps to the porch. We walked across the porch and into the kitchen, our shadows falling across the floor as we entered. It was

very quiet everywhere inside the house. "Why is everyone being so quiet?" I whispered, because whispering
seemed to be the right thing to do.

Even Li Yuen whispered back, "I don't know. I suppose
they're all in Auntie Daisy's room."

"Let's go there," I suggested.

He said nothing. We stood for a while in the kitchen,
and I watched how still our shadows could be in the dim
altar light. Then Li Shin walked in and saw us, and he
stopped and said, "What are you doing?"

"Why is everybody so quiet?" I asked him.

He walked to the back door, opened it, and peered outside. Then he turned to me and said, "Want to go outside?" He came over and took my hand. "Come on, Chief.
It's cooler outside."

When we walked across the porch, he was so silent you
could not hear him and it was as if there were only one
person walking on the floorboards and that was me. We
went down the wood steps. Then we stepped onto the
grass and he stopped walking and we stood there awhile.
I could feel his hand holding my hand, holding it tight
but not so tight as to hurt.

When I looked up, he was staring towards the grasscutter and the cemetery trees. The night was very still.
We could not hear the leaves in the mango tree behind
us. In the quiet there was not even that far-off insisting
cry of crickets in the tall grass.

"Can you smell it, Chief?"

"Yes."

"It's the rain coming from the sea."

"When will it be here?"

"Oh, not yet."

"Will it come tonight?"

"Yes. Late tonight."

"Will it be like the monsoon?"

"Yes."

I heard him breathe beside me. He was still staring towards the grasscutter and the cemetery trees. He was very tall and very thin, and when he breathed in and out his tummy moved. He stood very straight, because that was the way soldiers stood.

"Let's go," he said.

We started to walk, and the grass shifted beneath us. I heard Li Yuen say in a quiet voice, "We're supposed to stay together." He had come out of the kitchen after us and was standing on the wood steps, watching. He spoke again, "Grandma said to stay together," into the still and silent night.

I could see the straw in the grasscutter's hat stick out all over, slanting on his head. I looked down to the grass where a red candle stood burning in a blue porcelain bowl. Around the candle the grass lit up green and soft. Then it melted away into the quiet and the dark.

"Are your legs tired, Chief? Do you want to sit down? Let's sit down, Chief."

We sat down. Now I could look into the grasscutter's face. In the candlelight the shadow of his hat fell across his eyes. He was looking at the ground, not doing anything else, as if he was waiting.

We were underneath the frangipani tree. Above the leaves there were no stars. I followed the sky back to the

roof of Great-Grandfather's house, where three windows
glowed bright into the dark. I knew Auntie Daisy's window, and Uncle Wilfred's window next door. The third
window was at the other corner of the wall, in the room
that Grandfather had slept in when he was sick. We had
never played there. We were not allowed. The room was
at the end of a short narrow corridor, and the door had
been locked for years. Three thin steps led up to it. We
were not allowed to play on them because the wood was
too old. The steps might break.

As I was looking at the window now, the light went
out.

"Our fathers worked for the government," Li Shin said.
"In Central Intelligence." He paused. "They were like
soldiers."

The grasscutter nodded underneath his hat. "You speak
Malay in school?" he asked.

"Yes."

I heard a sound come from inside the cemetery trees,
softly, and then it was gone.

"All your schoolfriends speak Malay?"

"No, only some of us."

When the sound came again it was on top of us and it
was a small breeze and the leaves were rubbing on one
another in it.

The grasscutter stood up. "You should speak Mandarin," he said. "Your second language should be Mandarin."

"Malay is our national language," Li Shin said, standing
up too, and pulling me up beside him.

"You are Chinese," said the grasscutter.

"I'm not from China."

I could hear the leaves. Then the sound was gone and the leaves became silent and I could not hear them.

"I was born on this island," Li Shin went on. "This is my home."

"It is the language of fishermen," the grasscutter said. "You speak it."

I could hear the silence and then another small breeze came. It came like a crack that broke into the silence, and then stopped, the silence receiving. Then the wind came. It came sudden in the treetops, blowing up dust from the ground into our hair and faces, and I could feel Li Shin pulling at me.

"Chief. What's the matter, you have something in your eye? Let me look."

I could hear the wind around us.

"Take away your hand, Chief, don't rub your eye like that."

He blew hard into my face, and after that I could see the grasscutter holding the red candle where there was no flame. The wind was all around us and I could hear it noisy in the dark beating the trees, and then Li Shin took my hand. We turned towards the house.

Grandma was standing on the porch, looking across the grass at us. She watched us as we walked towards her. We reached the wood steps, and she said quietly, "Li Shin." I turned to him as we went up the steps.

"Su Yen, go into the house."

Li Shin let go of my hand. The floorboards creaked as I walked across the porch. I stepped into the kitchen and stood just inside the doorway, and I heard Grandma say, "Your friends were looking for you again. Why did they come here tonight? They do not know you have important things to do?"

"I'm their captain."

"You did not tell them about your Auntie Daisy?"

"I have things to do with them, too, Grandma."

"They are more important than your family?"

"No."

"Li Shin, what am I to do with you?"

I tiptoed across the kitchen floor over to the corridor, and went to find Li Yuen.

He was in the red room, standing in front of the windows and watching the road. I looked around the room, at the wall of books sitting in dim light and colored shadows, and I tried to imagine a young pale-looking man, our great-grandfather Wei Hsu, sitting there with an open dictionary in his lap, writing long love letters to the Irish girl Ena, who had already vanished from his life but he did not know it yet.

Li Yuen turned around.

"Someone was in the room," I said, walking over to him. "You know, the one where Grandma says Grandfather slept?"

"It's locked," he said. "Why would anyone go there now?"

"Someone was there." I knew what I had seen. "I saw a light."

"It was probably someone else's room."

"No, it wasn't."

We stood looking out at the road. The air smelled warm and sweaty, and outside, that sudden wind was gone as if it had never come. "Can we go check?" I said after a while.

"Maybe later."

Since he did not think it so strange, I decided that maybe
it was not. Perhaps an amah had gone into the room to
dust it. Perhaps it was being prepared for the new baby.

"Li Shin's friends stopped by, on their way to a
meeting."

I nodded. "But so late at night?"

"That's what they said." Li Yuen threw up his hands
impatiently. "How do I know why there's a meeting this
late?"

I looked outside. It was dark out by the road, but you
could make out the fence if you knew it was there.

"You promised to tell me about the branches," I said.

Li Yuen slipped his hands into his pockets. "It's superstition," he said, looking at me sideways. "Not Chinese
superstition, Malay superstition."

"Grandma doesn't believe in Malay things," I said.

"Tonight's different," he said, turning back to the window. Something shook in the grass at the bottom of the
veranda steps, and he looked there for a moment. Then
he said, "Malay people say when a baby is born near
midnight, Pontianak will try to steal it."

"Why?"

"Don't interrupt." We could hear leaves scraping the
roof above us. Li Yuen went on, "If people want to protect
the baby, they must tie sharp sticks all around the front
of their house. When Pontianak comes, she will see the
sticks and she won't try to fly over."

"Why doesn't she fly higher?"

"She can't."

"Why not?"

"She can't, that's all."

Someone was walking in the corridor, and Li Yuen
turned around.

"What does she look like?" I asked.

"She has long hair," he said, sitting on the windowsill and watching the door.

"What does her dress look like?"

"She doesn't wear a dress."

"She wears trousers?"

He shook his head. "She doesn't wear anything."

"She's naked?"

He continued to watch the door. The footsteps in the corridor turned and started coming towards the red room.

"She's naked?" I said again.

"And she is very beautiful." He looked at me. "That's why men are afraid of her. She'll come to you and you'll think she is so beautiful, but if you follow her, you will die."

The footsteps in the corridor stopped. I turned and saw Auntie Lily standing in the doorway with her hands on her hips. She was looking at us as if she did not know what to do. "You two had better go to bed," she said finally. "Otherwise I'll tell Grandma. Hurry up."

The first time that I woke up, Li Yuen was still sleeping. But Li Shin's bed was empty, and I could hear him in the corridor with Grandma. Water was running somewhere behind the walls. Then Grandma stopped talking. I heard her walk away. I climbed out of bed and ran into the corridor.

Li Shin was leaning slightly on the wall, his hands in his pockets. He was staring at the floor. The light from the nearest candle flickered across his face. "You sound like a baby elephant," he said, without looking up.

I leaned on the wall, close to him.

"You must learn to walk like a girl," he said.

I could smell white Johnson's baby powder all over him.

"You listening to me, Chief?"

"Yes."

"You must learn to walk like a girl."

"I don't want to be a girl."

He ruffled my hair. "Why not?" he asked, kneeling down to face me.

"I want to be a boy," I said.

He laughed. "Why?"

I shrugged. "Because."

"Because what?"

I shrugged again. "Boys get to do more things."

"What kind of things do you want to do?"

I watched the candlelight dance on his face, making his eyes bright. Then voices came down the corridor, and he stood up. I looked around him and saw two amahs turning the corner. They saw us, too, and stopped talking.

"You can do things, Chief," Li Shin said. "You can do anything you want. I don't want you to be a boy."

We followed the amahs into the kitchen. They moved towards the sink, clanking empty kettles in their hands.

"Is Auntie Daisy all right?" Li Shin said to them.

They nodded and walked to the stove and lit fires with matches. I watched them set the kettles down. Then they turned and walked into the corridor again.

Li Shin looked at me. "I'd better take you back," he said, and he took my hand.

The second time I woke up, Li Yuen was standing at the window. I could make out his thin shape in the dark, his pajama shirt touching the back of his thighs. The shirt came down to just above his knees.

A breeze drifted in, and Li Yuen leaned against the window, pressing his palm on the sill. The curtains flicked into the dark. I got out of bed and tiptoed up behind him.

"Get back into bed," he said, glancing around. "You'll catch cold."

"What about you?" I said.

"I'm tough," he said.

The kitchen window was open, and we could see a block of light sloping across the porch floor outside, where there were crumbs of broken earth left by the grown-ups passing through when they came back from the cemetery.

Someone opened the back door. We heard grown-up voices talking and then the talking stopped and the grass-cutter stepped onto the porch. He hurried down the steps, cut across the grass to the frangipani tree, picked up his box, and carried it to the shed. We heard a breeze pass over the ground, stroking the fallen leaves. Then the grasscutter stepped back out of the shed. He closed the shed door and came towards where we were hiding behind our window.

The grasscutter moved softly on the grass. Dry dark leaves blew around his ankles. He passed us and went towards the side of the house and faded away around the corner.

An amah stepped out of the kitchen, holding a broom. She glanced at the trees and shivered and then she began to sweep, brushing the sand down the steps and off the edges of the porch. Then she hurried back into the kitchen and slammed the door shut.

A twig cracked in the trees. Then the night was quiet

again and I watched bits of cloud shred themselves thin in the sky. "The moon's almost full," I said, and pointed to the moon behind the trees.

Li Yuen said nothing.

"How come it's so dark when the moon's almost full?" I said.

He shrugged.

We could hear leaves and branches rustling to the side of the porch. I leaned out of the window to look at the rocking chair in the corner, and Li Yuen grabbed my shoulder and pulled me back in. "Stop that," he said. "You'll catch cold."

I stood beside him and tugged at the curtain hem. The air was getting cool. I could smell seaweed and salt water in it. "Where did Li Shin go?" I asked.

"I don't know," he said, walking back to his bed.

"Are you sure Pontianak is naked?" I left the window and followed him.

He got into bed and dragged the sheet over his legs, and I climbed onto Li Shin's bed and sat there, pulling my pajama shirt down over my knees.

"Li Shin says it's just superstition," he said quietly.

"How come she's naked?" I asked, listening to the alarm clock ticking on the dresser between us.

"I don't know." He kicked off the sheet and walked to the window again.

I watched the soft light glimmering underneath our door, coming from the candles in the blue glass bowls that our amahs had put down in the corridor outside, sacred bowls reserved for funerals and births.

"Chief."

"What?"

Li Yuen was standing with his back to me. "Auntie Daisy's baby died, you know," he said, looking out at the trees.

I watched a breeze lift his pajama shirt.

"Grandma came to tell us," he went on, "but you were sleeping, so she didn't wake you." Something rattled on the roof, and he looked up towards the sound. "Branches." He leaned on the windowsill, twirling the curtain hem around and around until it looked like a thick tail.

"Was the baby a boy or girl?" I asked at last.

"I don't know."

"Where is Li Shin?"

He let the curtain go and it started to unwind, spinning in the dark. He tiptoed back to his bed.

I watched him lie down. "Maybe Pontianak came tonight."

"Grandma says sometimes accidents happen," he said, staring straight up at the ceiling. Outside, the leaves shook softly in the trees. "I went to the kitchen with her." He turned on his side, facing away from me, and dragged the sheet over his head. "To pray," he said, through the sheet. "Maybe you can pray here."

I watched the window. Outside the rain was starting. I could hear it coming closer and closer from the sea.

❀

All that night the winds slashed rain from the sky and the rain fell threshing hard and fast, rocking the trees. When morning came and the rain stopped, we walked out to the porch, where the wood steps were damp. Li Shin held my hand and we stepped down to the grass. It was slippery walking on the grass. Around us, the trees stood still with their leaves torn out and we could smell them everywhere. The smell of them dripped into the sand, the ground becoming mud. It was so soft when we walked on it, we could hear leaves squash themselves into the dirt. The dirt made a sucking noise that could make you afraid, make you believe that if you stood still for one moment, that mud would lick you in and then you would be gone. I held on to Li Shin's hand and we did not stop walking until we were back on the porch, where Li Yuen was standing in the kitchen doorway watching.

Later that morning we could hear the grasscutter hammering down in the shed. Li Shin said that the grasscutter was making a coffin. He was using wood from the crates that the oranges came in.

When the coffin was ready, Grandma told me to go away from the kitchen. "Go to the red room, Su Yen," she said. "It will be bad luck if you look. You are not old enough yet."

I went to the red room and stayed there until an amah came to tell me I could come out of the room now because everybody was already in the cemetery. Then I went to the kitchen. It was just after two o'clock. I put ten cards, face down, on the table. When I looked up again, Auntie Daisy was in the corridor. She came tiptoeing to the table, where she stopped and grinned at me. "Esha," she said, "I've escaped."

I looked outside the window. A week ago someone at the office had given our twin aunties a set of wind chimes from Hong Kong, and our twin aunties had finally put them up. The chimes dangled from the porch roof like an aluminum pagoda, with the sunlight tinkling blue and green and red between the pagoda roofs. I turned back to Auntie Daisy, who was taking a card from the table.

She looked at it. "Queen of Hearts," she said. She put the card back on the table and pulled one from the deck. She looked at it. "Jack of Clubs." She slipped it into the bottom of the deck.

"You're playing backwards," I told her.

She laughed. "When I was eleven years old, I also played Fishing. Like you."

"I'm not like you."

She stopped laughing, and then she smiled.

I took a card from the top of the deck and looked at it. It was Seven of Diamonds. I picked a card from the table, but it was Seven of Clubs. I turned it back down and put the Seven of Diamonds into the bottom of the deck.

"Your Auntie Daisy was very smart, you know." She held up my chin to make me look at her. "People don't remember," she said. She dropped her hand and I looked down at the cards and then I looked up at her.

"You have to remember where things are," I said. "That's how to play Fishing."

"Who taught you?" she said.

"Li Shin."

"You know who taught him?"

I looked out the back door. There was a white dishtowel drying on the porch rail. A breeze moved over it and pulled up the soft edge. "Where is he today?" I heard her ask.

"Li Shin went to school," I said. "He couldn't go to the funeral. He has a meeting." I took a card from the deck and it was Queen of Diamonds, but when I turned over the card that was supposed to be Queen of Hearts, it was Four of Spades. I put my card back into the deck. Then I looked at Auntie Daisy. "You switched them."

The wind chimes jingled outside on the porch. "Maybe

you remember wrong," she said, gazing at the chimes, then past them, into the cemetery where her dead baby had been taken.

"It was here." I thumped the place on the table. "You switched them."

She got up and walked to the altar. When she came back, I saw an orange in her hand. She was stroking it like somebody's head. I shuffled the cards while she sat there peeling the orange. Then she bit into it and I watched the juice slide between her fingers. The orange peels rocked on the table between us, like small boats. "You're not supposed to take things from the altar," I said. But she went on biting into the orange. The juice dripped all over her wrists. When she had eaten the whole orange, she got up from the table and tiptoed back to the corridor. I watched her dress sway against her hips, yellow flowers loose on white cotton. I could tell that she was laughing quietly. She kept on laughing, holding her hand over her mouth.

When she was gone, I put my head down on the table. A breeze was blowing in the rocking chair outside, and I closed my eyes and listened.

When Grandma came back from the cemetery, she took out Li Shin's old school shirts and began to sew back missing buttons so that Li Yuen could wear the shirts. At five o'clock that afternoon I found her sitting by a window in the red room, with her face bent towards the needle. She stuck the needle between her lips and waved me towards her without looking up. I left the door and went to her, where I stood watching the needle fly in and out of the shirt as she continued to sew, tugging the white thread along. Finally she cut the thread, put down the scissors, and shook out the shirt. "Still too big," she said, looking at the shirt. "But what to do, his own shirts are already too small."

I watched her fold the shirt. Then Li Yuen's voice behind us said, "Grandma," and when I turned around, he was standing at the door. "Auntie Mei wants you to come quickly to Auntie Daisy's room," he said.

She took the shirt with her as she walked to the door. "Is Li Shin home yet?" she asked, and Li Yuen shook his head. He looked back at me as I followed Grandma into the corridor.

"You have homework to do, Su Yen?"

"I did it already." I turned to see if Li Yuen was coming with us, but he was still standing outside the red room.

"And your drawing," said Grandma. "Did you practice your drawing?"

"Last week I got B," I said.

"B is not A," she said.

We walked on, our shadows dancing on the walls opposite where the candles on the floor burned softly in their bowls. A pipe rattled as we passed the bathroom. Then we reached Auntie Daisy's room, where the door was closed. "Go and practice your drawing," Grandma said, turning to me.

"Is Auntie Daisy going to be well soon?" I asked.

"Perhaps soon," she said. "Your Auntie Daisy is very sick."

"Yesterday she screamed so loud."

Grandma touched my cheek. "Were you afraid?" she asked. I shook my head, even though I had followed Li

Yuen into the cemetery. Grandma stood there with her hand on the doorknob and looked at me. "Go and practice your drawing," she said.

Suddenly the door opened and Auntie Mei stood there, looking out at us. She wore a red apron, and a low yellow light soaked the room behind. "We'd better call the doctor," she said to Grandma.

I could hear sheets dragging inside the room. Then Auntie Lily came to the door. When she saw me, she said, "Your grandfather saw four children sitting by the roadside. The two in the middle had no faces."

Auntie Mei glanced at me. Then she pulled Auntie Lily into the room and closed the door.

"Su Yen."

I looked up from the floor, and Grandma pulled me to her. She straightened my collar and patted my arms. "Go and practice your drawing," she said.

"Yes, Grandma."

I started to walk, tracing my finger along one wall, watching the flames on the floor light up the bowls, the hollow blue glass. I heard the door behind me open and close.

I went to the red room to see if Li Yuen was still there, but he was not. Then I went to the kitchen. He was standing outside on the porch, and I could see him through the back door. Then he turned and came inside, and I said to him, "Want to play cards?" But he shook his head.

"Auntie Daisy has hair," he said.

I looked at him.

He went to the window and looked out. "At first Auntie Mei wasn't there," he said. "Auntie Daisy knew I was outside and she wanted me to go inside and visit her." He was still looking out the window. "She told me to look at her stomach. She told me, Li Yuen, come and look at my stomach, come and see where my baby used to sleep. That's what she said."

"So did you do it?" I asked.

"She pulled up her nightgown," he said, still facing the window. "She said, Li Yuen, come and look at my stomach."

"You looked?" I said. "You saw?"

"She has hair." He turned to me, looking shy. "I thought only boys grew hair down there."

I pretended not to know what he was talking about, and after a while he stopped looking at me, and we walked to the front of the house to wait for Li Shin. On our way past the dining room we saw our uncles gathered around the table, talking softly. The five-o'clock sun skated over their heads, and they looked almost like children.

I had never told anyone about that night I had caught Auntie Daisy out on the veranda. Daisy, let me touch your daisy. I had watched them from behind a curtain in the red room. I had watched Auntie Daisy spread herself to that voice. Breathless, willing, she had wanted his hand when it rushed between her thighs, where I could imagine his fingers rough in a shivery, longing way. I knew that whatever had happened the night she came back in the police car must have been different. But I also knew why our aunties and uncles needed to blame Auntie Daisy herself. A horror without a source could not be stopped. This was what they believed.

Eight

The night wind drifted into the trees, dragging seaweed through the dark. "Smell that, Chief?" Li Shin said, turning to me. "It's going to rain again. You can always smell rain before it comes." I nodded, and he squeezed my nose. "You'd better go inside now," he said. Then he walked to the door, stopped, and pulled it closed a little.

"Listen, Chief," he whispered, kneeling down so he could look into my face. "Can you keep a secret for me? Will you?"

"Yes."

"I'm going out for a while," he said. "But I don't want Grandma to know."

"Where are you going?" I asked. "Do you have a meeting?"

He hesitated. "Something like a meeting. It's called night patrol. I'm on duty tonight."

I rubbed my toes against the floor. "What are you all going to do? Patrol the beach?"

He stood up. "Just for an hour."

"Let me go with you," I said.

"No," he said. "You're not trained. But I'll be back soon." He turned and ran down the steps. The wood did not creak and I watched him walk over the grass in the blue-black light.

At the edge of the cemetery he looked back, and waved at me to go into the house.

When he walked out of Great-Grandfather's house that evening he was walking at a smooth and easy pace, not walking too fast or too slow, not hurrying the way a boy might hurry when he's afraid somebody will catch him and try to stop him. I watched him cross over the grass into the cemetery, and when he slipped behind the trees still he didn't hurry, walking at that smooth and easy pace all the time to let you know he was comfortable at it and know he was calm and not afraid and was a solitary kind of person used to it, the way you can tell when a boy walks too fast because you can hear the breath come out of him in short staccato sighs, and can tell when he walks too slow because then he looks as if he might be staring at too many things too long, and seeing each thing as if he might be seeing it for the first time, even when it is only a stop sign, that only says STOP. A boy might walk slow naturally and be comfortable doing it and that might just be his way, to come sauntering along the sidewalk whistling and gazing straight ahead, hands in his pockets. But you can tell when a boy is not comfortable walking slow, when he does it just to have something to do, just to have time to look at things, which he looks at over and over, to occupy that sudden time that falls upon people when they are going to a place they do not want to go to and they walk more slowly than they are used to and then there is so much time that there is nothing to do except look at things because if you do not look at things you have to think. And you must not think because you know the thoughts will come too fast, and then you will get confused. And yet the slower you walk the faster they come, rising out of that abyss you now discover lies within you, that nowhere out of which they just come and come. Coming so fast they escape your catch, so like dead leaves that rush in stray winds, featherweight, scattering far. You think of something and then you think of something else and then you realize that you are thinking a separate thought from what you were thinking just one minute ago. And then you cannot remember what you were thinking just one minute ago and sometimes you wonder about mad people and you wonder if this is what it is like to be a grandmother and watch the children that come out of the children that come out of you break away. How inevitable it is that they do, still, but you think they should be yours and they are not and you must watch them fall scattering and think of them as already dead because that is how they must seem to you because you watch them and are helpless to help them and cannot even catch them, to hold them long enough.

But he was not walking too fast or too slow that evening. He was walking at a smooth and easy pace, and when you see that your elder cousin walks so comfortably you tend to think of him as sure and not afraid, think that he knows what he is doing. You believe that. He never told me exactly where he was going. It did not occur to me to make him tell me. I was eleven and a half years old. He was seventeen, not very old for a boy, but on that night I still thought it was.

Li Yuen came into the dining room, shaking water off his hands, and sat down in his place next to me. Soon the grown-ups began to walk in. I looked straight out the window, hearing them pulling out chairs and sitting down.

It was dark outside and the tree leaves were still.

"Li Yuen?" I heard Grandma say. The room became quiet and I tried not to look at the empty chair on my other side.

"Where is Li Shin?" she asked.

Li Yuen answered, "I don't know, Grandma," and then he looked at me. I looked away and stared down at my plate.

"Su Yen?"

I picked up my spoon. "I don't know, Grandma," I said, running it through the puffy white rice.

"Look up when you speak to people."

I put down the spoon.

"Look at me," she said.

I could see the dark night air outside the window, and just faintly, the shapes of leaves.

"Su Yen."

I turned my head and looked up the table at her.

213

"Don't tell lies," she told me.

I could hear the electric fan spinning above our heads.

Outside the window there was the blackness that might have come from the forever where the trees emptied, that crept up to the walls of Great-Grandfather's house like a Japanese soldier. I poked at the cucumber slices in my rice. They were almost transparent because the amahs would throw them in when the rice was almost cooked.

"He went into the cemetery," I said, after a while, and Uncle Kuan pushed back his chair and stood up.

"When?" asked Grandma.

I kept on poking at the cucumber. "Just now."

She asked sharply, "Just now when?"

"After the grasscutter went home."

All the grown-ups were getting up now, kicking their chairs away and hurrying to the door without pushing their chairs back under the table. They ran into the corridor, and then we could hear them running towards the kitchen.

"That foolish boy," Grandma mumbled as she stepped into the corridor. "How did I raise a foolish boy like that? You say to him, The Prime Minister is not your father. He doesn't listen."

After she left, Li Yuen picked up his fork and spoon and started drumming on the table. "How come you're so stupid?" he said, without looking at me.

From the alcove in the living room the grandfather clock began to chime. I waited until all the rooms grew quiet, and when nobody was running in the corridor anymore I got up and went to the window.

"I'm not stupid," I said, putting my hand out of the window to touch the leaves.

"You're an idiot," he said, "that's what you are."

I stroked the leaves, feeling them warm and smooth in my right hand. I tried to imagine a Japanese soldier peering into the room. Then I turned back to Li Yuen. He was sitting quietly now and watching me. I stood there and looked at him and then he stood up. "Let's go," he said. He turned and walked out of the room, and I left the window and followed him.

It was dark that night like paint. Before the second rain the trees were quiet, and their stillness was of absolute waiting, of leaves frozen over the wet sand path. We walked through gatherings of their shapes laced about the air like hanging screens, and felt ourselves pass by like our own ghosts. Li Yuen walked ahead of me. He would disappear along the path, and reappear from shadows and tree trunks. I followed him, knowing the quiet like something certain, definite as a thing you could pick from the ground and hold in your hand and turn over to look at. It was that quiet that would come before the rain, and was there again after. Both Li Yuen and I knew that quiet. In it hushed winds were held, and raindrops dripped, measured slowly off the rough edges of leaves, and the rain kept on calm hot afternoons. The quiet was that, and was the leaving, too, was wet grass mixed with mud and sunlight trapped high in the trees. Once when Li Shin was nine years old, a long long time ago, he had taken both of us outside and held our hands as we were going down the steps, and we could hear his footsteps on the wood rise and hang like so meaningful sounds without which we knew we would vanish, turn transparent fast as fireflies into twilight, and then no one would remember the place where we had been or be able to find us.

But that night the quiet was water sliding underneath a tall closed door. We walked not understanding the movements behind the trees, and in the shuttered dark, we saw grown-ups bending, turning their heads, and we heard their voices. We heard younger voices, too, and recognized the boys, slowly, knew them from the way they stood together, all loyal to one another, all the same height. They stood watching over the boy on the ground, the one we did not recognize, the one we thought was cold because he was curled up on his side, wrapped in blanket, not moving.

Later, when we thought about it, we would know how it could happen, that whoever they had been, they never thought he could be seventeen years old and a schoolboy. He had grown tall, as tall as our uncles, and when he bent down to pick something up, he would glance around instinctively, just like a soldier. He could cross softly over wooden floors, and walk so straight. He was not wearing his cadet uniform that evening, but the nighttime came so fast it did not matter. In the cemetery they could not see anything except the way he walked. By the time he had walked past them, they were already behind, stealing through the trees so quietly he never heard them until the leaves moved behind his head, and he turned. If they had looked up, if they had looked for just one moment, they might have seen his face. They might have seen his eyes surprised. They might have seen his shoulders still too narrow for him to be a man. They might have seen his running shorts. They might have stopped when their fingers touched his skin.

But only he saw them. He saw their faces smeared with black shoe polish, saw their heads dimly in thin moonlight straying through the trees, saw their hair cut short like his. He must have remembered when he was younger, Grandma used to cut his hair for him. She would make him carry a chair from the kitchen out to the porch. Then she would make him sit in it, and he would be still while she cut his hair with her silver scissors. He must have heard her voice calling to him in Great-Grandfather's house that night. He must have called back. When they came for him, when he saw small rocks in their hands, he must have called to her. When they grabbed his waist, and they dragged him down—Grandma, he called—when soft grasses were shaking in a wind, and he could hear the grown-ups coming to him.

Outside Great-Grandfather's house the grown-ups hurried down the porch steps, making a loud noise, but there where the rain trees grew the grasses were shaking, shaking. And already it was too late.

❁

When we came back from the cemetery we went into the kitchen and sat down and waited until we could hear footsteps on the porch. Then we got up to go outside, but Grandma met us at the door. She pushed us back into the kitchen, saying, "Go and finish your dinner."

I heard Li Yuen ask her, "What about Li Shin?"

"Li Shin is sick," she said. "He has a fever. He cannot eat. Go and finish your dinner."

It was not the right time for us to disobey her, so we went back into the dining room. We ate quickly, standing at the table and holding up our plates. We saw our aunties and uncles walking close together as they passed by the room. When we carried our empty plates into the kitchen, Grandma was at the stove, boiling water. Li Yuen took my plate from me and walked over to the sink.

I watched Grandma as she arranged six frangipani flowers in a big white tin bowl on the counter beside the stove. I knew, from past times when my cousins and I would return from school with the flu, that she was going to pour the boiled water into the bowl, and that at first the flowers would be so light they would float. Then they would sink, and rest pinky-white at the bottom of the bowl. I knew that Grandma was going to stay up all night, washing Li Shin with the flower water so that she could make the fever go away.

Finished with arranging the flowers, she stood staring at the kettle. "Grandma, can I go to see him?" I asked. She shook her head, answering, "No, he's asleep."

"I won't disturb him."

"No, Su Yen, it is better if you let him sleep."

"Grandma?" came Li Yuen's voice from behind me, and she looked over my head at him.

"Was it Communists?" he asked.

"The Prime Minister," she said, suddenly angry. "This is all his doing." Then, quickly, she shook her head. "We must not question the gods. We must not show disrespect. Worse things can happen." She turned back to the stove, switched off the gas, and lifted the kettle.

"Go and brush your teeth," she told us, picking up the bowl of frangipani with her other hand. She moved slowly towards the corridor, her left shoulder drooping because the kettle was heavy.

Li Yuen picked up a spoon from the dish rack and started rattling the pots and pans hanging on the wall.

"Why didn't you carry the water for her?" I asked him.

"She'd say no," he answered, moving towards the refrigerator and banging on all the drawers on the way.

"Li Shin would have carried it."

"She would've said no."

"You could have asked."

"What for?"

He threw the spoon across the room and it fell clanging into the sink. Then he came and pulled me off the stool. "Grandma told us to brush our teeth," he said, dragging me into the corridor.

In the middle of the night the rain grew harder. We could hear the cemetery trees shaking, and water streaming off the edge of the roof. I pulled the sheet up to my chin, but I could not sleep, and after a while I threw off the sheet and got up.

Li Yuen sat up in his bed and watched me. I walked across the room and picked up Li Shin's gun, the one he used to carry when we were small. Then I walked to the door. In the corridor the candles were burning along the wall. I was careful. I did not knock them over with the gun.

I went to Grandma's room.

She was just coming out. She was carrying the white tin bowl. She looked up and saw me and she closed the door behind her. I followed her into the kitchen, not asking her any questions so that she would not shoo me away. In the kitchen I watched her pour the old water from the white tin bowl into the sink. She scooped up the wet flowers that flowed out with the water. She threw them in the trash can.

A kettle of water was boiling on the stove. I heard the back door open, and our amahs came in carrying baskets filled with fresh frangipani. Grandma looked at them, saying nothing.

I smelled their sweat when they passed me on their way into the corridor.

Grandma turned off the gas and took the kettle from the stove. I walked behind her, knowing to stay outside when she went into the room. After a while the amahs stepped out, closing the door behind them.

I sat down, keeping my fingers on the trigger of my gun. Li Shin had taught Li Yuen and me to do that so that we could be ready. I crossed my legs, and rested my gun across my thighs. I was ready.

In the morning I woke up in my own bed. I must have fallen asleep in the corridor, and someone had carried me back. From my bed, I could see that Li Yuen's bed was empty. The sun was just rising outside, and there was a silver light in the window. It was very quiet everywhere in the house, but I could tell that the grown-ups were already awake.

When I arrived at Grandma's room, the door was open. I walked in and saw Li Yuen sitting on the bed. Grandma was in the bathroom, I could hear. The bathroom door was open, so I walked over and looked in, where I saw

Grandma kneeling at the bathtub. Near the door, a basket of frangipani sat on the floor, and I could smell the flowers. Li Shin's body was lying in the tub, and Grandma was rubbing frangipani petals into his skin. I walked away.

Li Yuen was sitting on the bed, staring at his feet. He would not look up. I watched our amahs fold a faded blue blanket that I had never seen before. One of the amahs took the folded blanket to Grandma's cupboard and laid it on a shelf. As she closed the cupboard door, the other amah bent down to pick some towels off the floor. She picked up a pair of green underpants, too, rolling the underpants into the towels as she shuffled out of the room. The amah at the cupboard followed her.

I went to the window and looked out. An amah was standing on the grass, hanging up wet white sheets. When Li Yuen came to stand beside me, I asked him softly, "Did the amahs stay awake all night?" He looked out of the window, not answering. But I knew they must have stayed awake, the whole night, picking frangipani and washing sheets.

The grass outside shivered shiny in rainwater. There were bright thin cracks in the trees, the sun still rising. The amah threw a sheet over the bamboo pole and adjusted it so the edges did not touch the ground. She clipped the sides of the sheet together with plastic pegs, a blue one, a yellow one, and a pink one.

Li Yuen was dragging his fingertip along the windowsill. He lifted it up and stared at it. Then Grandma called to us.

I stopped just inside the bathroom door. Li Yuen walked in behind me, and I heard when he kicked the basket. We saw frangipani spilling all over the floor. They looked soft and crazy on the gray cement. "Never mind, there are enough," we heard Grandma say.

She was looking at me. "See if the water in the kettle is still hot, Su Yen." I stooped down and touched the kettle sitting beside the basket. It was warm, but not hot. I looked up and shook my head. She smiled. "Good," she said. "Bring it here."

I stood still a moment, then lifted the kettle and carried it to her.

"Pour it in."

I poured the water slowly into the tub, watching it run over his feet and between his toes. Grandma was peeling off more frangipani petals. She sprinkled them on his stomach, then lower down. I watched her tuck some of the white sweet-smelling petals safely around what my classmates at St. Catherine called "balls," down there cradling his pinky-brown birdie. By now I knew that his birdie had a grown-up name, a name that began with a P and that Sister Adeline had told us nice young ladies would not mention in public. I had never seen an almost-grown-up birdie before, so I looked, never imagining that it would appear so soft and helpless. Then I poured more water in. A puddle formed around his ankles, and the water ran along the tub and slid up his thighs, where the frangipani turned wet and dark.

Li Yuen stood near the door and watched us. He would not come closer.

When we were younger, we sailed small white paper boats in muddy floodwater swirling brown and deep. The boats tossed up and down, rising, sinking, rising, sinking, and we watched to see whose boat would be the first to disappear. Even though I was a girl, not allowed to play in the rain, on days when Grandma went to the temple to pray, Li Shin would let me run outside, and I would run along the monsoon drain with them, slipping in the puddles that filled the asphalt holes and splashed rainwater and sand on our feet. When the season wore on, and the rainwater turned sand to mud, the puddles left quick hard splattered crusts around our ankles, and we would have to wash them off before Grandma came home.

Nighttime in April, the rains would stop. Then we would lean out of windows, smelling grass, smelling frogs and crickets that kissed in leftover rain, what Li Shin used to say. He said, Chief, your mama and papa kissed. Like frogs and crickets, he said, kissing to make babies. That's how come you're here. And you too? I said. He said, Yes, me too, my mama and papa kissed, now I'm here. And Li Yuen too? I said. He said, Yes, my mama and papa kissed twice.

Nine

Grandma told us once that in China there used to grow a white country flower. This flower grew far off in the hills and bloomed only at night, because it had magic. When it bloomed, it gave off a powerful sweet scent, like the scent of the gods when they came to you, Grandma said. She also told us that in the village where she grew up, the villagers had a custom. When a family member fell sick, a grandfather would send his grandson into the hills, because in every family it was the grandson's duty to bring back the white flower. It was the grandfather's duty to teach the grandson how to recognize the flower in daylight, when the flower was not in bloom. Even so, she said, there would be grandsons who would bring back the wrong flower.

"What happened then?"

"Then the sick person would die."

"Did the family blame the grandson?"

"He should not have pretended to know what he did not know. The gods are not merciful towards vain, deceitful people."

"But that's not fair, Grandma."

"Why not fair, Li Shin?"

"Maybe the grandson was afraid, Grandma."

"He should not have lied."

I wondered, when he died, what exactly Grandma knew. She had fringed our lives with her stories of wars and ghosts, and when we were younger we would believe what she said, and do only what she said. But the older we had grown, the more Li Shin had said that we must not listen to Grandma, not listen to her too much. We must keep our ears wide open, he would say. That way we would hear what Prime Minister Lee was saying too. Prime Minister Lee would lead us into the future. Grandma only wanted us to remember China, a China that had once been a great empire, but then even in our great-grandfather's day it had already deteriorated into a dirty smelly country, filled with diseases and superstition. No modern Singaporean wanted to dwell on the China part of our past. And we had a right not to. As Singaporeans, our loyalty was to Singapore, a Singapore whose history was begun by Sir Stamford Raffles, the great explorer. With him, our immigrant ancestors, fleeing from feudalism and poverty, had found for themselves a fresh start. This, then, was our legacy—their fresh start, our new history.

I wondered if Li Shin's name would never again be spoken in Great-Grandfather's house, the way Uncle Tien's name was not spoken, and our parents' names were not spoken. I understood why the names had to disappear, put out like flames of unwatched candles that might burn down a house. It was not punishment for the dead. It was protection for the living.

But Li Shin I had loved.

I watched the cadets carrying his coffin into the cemetery, and by the time they came back out, it was almost evening. I was sitting on the porch steps, because Auntie Mei had told me to wait there. The stillness from the night before was still around, stretching stiff in the trees like glue. All afternoon I had felt it, sticky on my arms and legs. Now I could even feel it inside my panties, in the spot where I had found the blood.

The cadets were carrying their berets in their hands. They stepped single-file out of the trees. I could see Grandma walking behind them, with Li Yuen and Susan beside her. Li Yuen was dressed in long white trousers and a long-sleeved white shirt, and Susan wore a white dress with a lace collar. Her hair was tied back with a white ribbon. Our uncles stepped out after them, dressed in long white trousers and long-sleeved white shirts. They were followed by our aunties, who wore plain white dresses. Last of all came the grasscutter. He, too, was dressed in long white trousers and a long-sleeved white shirt. He was carrying a pile of shovels under his arm, and as he stepped out of the trees, he turned and moved towards the shed.

When Grandma came up the steps, I heard her say to an amah, "Pour orange juice for the children."

I left the steps and followed her into the kitchen.

"Grandma," I said. "Are you going to give Li Shin's
uniform to another cadet?"

She stopped at the entrance to the corridor and turned
around. "All his clothes will be given away," she said.
"Some nuns are coming tomorrow to pack them."

"I would like to keep his uniform, Grandma," I said.

"You," she said, not quite believing me. "Why, Su
Yen?"

The cadets were standing near the window, staring out
at the blue-green shadows sweeping over the grass while
they drank their orange juice. Susan and Li Yuen had
already left the kitchen. As soon as the amah had poured
out the orange juice, they had taken their glasses into the
corridor and now were somewhere else in the house. I
felt suddenly alone, distanced from everyone else by a
sadness I could not name.

"I think Li Shin would like that," I said.

"Your cousin has left us." She turned towards the corridor. "What we do no longer concerns him."

"I would like to keep the uniform, Grandma."

Our aunties and uncles, who had stayed outside to talk
softly among themselves, now left the porch and entered
the kitchen. They paused to look at Grandma and me, and
then all of them, except for Auntie Mei and Auntie Lily,
walked past us and disappeared into the corridor.

"Ma," said Auntie Mei. "You look tired. Why don't
you lie down for a bit? Come, I'll take you."

Auntie Lily was watching the cadets, who by now had
left the window. Over by the sink they were lining up
one behind the other. I saw the cadet at the front of the
line reach up to the shelf where our amahs kept piles of
clean white towels. He took a towel, unfolded it carefully,

and spread it over the countertop. The other cadets began to step up to the sink to wash their glasses. One by one, they handed their washed glasses to the first cadet, who arranged the glasses in neat rows, upside down, on the towel.

"Ma," said Auntie Mei. "Come, let's go to your room." She took Grandma by the elbow, and the two of them began to walk away.

"Don't forget to tell the nuns, Grandma," I called softly into the corridor after them. "Tell them don't pack Li Shin's uniform. All right, Grandma?"

Grandma did not turn around, but Auntie Mei did. She looked over her shoulder at Auntie Lily, who was still in the kitchen with me, and Auntie Lily asked me at once, "What are you talking about?"

"I want to keep it," I said.

Auntie Lily put her hands on her hips. "Don't talk rubbish," she said, and shook her head like a dog I had noticed one morning, flinging rainwater off its fur as it skulked around the school parlor after someone had forgotten to close the front gates.

The cadets left the sink and stood hovering around the back door. They put on their berets, then smoothed out their trousers with their hands as they prepared to step outside.

"It's unlucky to keep dead people's clothes," said Auntie Lily. "We must give them away, to people not related to us."

"Why?"

"You want to be followed around by a ghost for the rest of your life?"

"Li Shin's ghost?"

"Who knows? Could be anyone's ghost." Auntie Lily lowered her voice. "It has happened before. Someone else's ghost calling out your name in the dark, pretending to sound like your dead father or mother." She glanced past me into the corridor. "Remember," she murmured, "during the war, hundreds of Chinese were tortured to death. This island is haunted."

I could hear the cadets stepping out the back door, the sound of their boots rapping on the wood as they marched across the porch and went down the steps to the grass. A few seconds later they turned the corner, and I heard the ground leaves crackling where they walked.

"Think about what I've told you," said Auntie Lily, as she moved towards the corridor. "And don't bother your grandma with any more rubbish. Let her rest now."

I walked over to the back door and stood there awhile. I saw the grasscutter pacing around the frangipani tree, his shoulders hunched and troubled-looking in the waning light. With his hands stuck in his pockets, he seemed to be hunting the ground, searching for something he had lost.

I wondered if the grasscutter believed it was possible for a whole island, a whole country, to be haunted.

       I had heard how the nuns at St. Catherine woke themselves up at five o'clock in the morning to pray. They would wander down corridors to meet in the chapel, their sleepy fingers sifting rosary beads, their footsteps light as dust on walls. They traveled by the light of the moon, its Eucharist shape pulsing across the sky, a sign, a warning—I had heard that there were things only nuns could hear. They could hear grass stretching over water at midnight, and flowers, deep-planted by old women's hands, standing tender, naked to cool wind. They could hear the souls wailing and moaning in purgatory. This was why they woke up to pray, their pleas for mercy slipping off lips cold with sleep resounding, chanting, recanting.

Sister Adeline used to talk to us about an end to the world as we knew it. She called it Armageddon. Armageddon, she said, would come if there had been so much killing and torturing on this earth that the voices of the dead, crying out for justice, rattled open both the gates of heaven and the gates of hell. And if both gates came crashing down—could we imagine the chaos then? she said.

In all the rooms the air hung blue-green, hushed in the hollow dusk light. The grown-ups were gathered somewhere in the front of the house, and I could hear Susan and Li Yuen talking in the corridor outside our bedroom. I was inside the room, taking Li Shin's cadet uniform down from its hanger. I heard Susan ask, "What do you mean, password?" And Li Yuen replied, "Password." He was carrying his black toy gun. I saw him step into the doorway, blocking it with his body.

"I don't know any password," Susan said. She was taller than Li Yuen, so she could have pushed him aside easily, if she had wanted to. Or she could have snatched away his gun.

"No password, no entry," said Li Yuen. "That's the law."

"Whose law?"

"This country's law. Ask the police."

"All I want is to look for some books that I lent to him."

"You could be an enemy."

I heard Susan sigh. "You know I'm not your enemy," she said impatiently, walking away.

I started folding Li Shin's shirt, feeling it stiff and familiar in my hands. I laid the folded shirt on my bed and slid the trousers off their wooden hanger bar. I could hear Li Yuen walking in the corridor after Susan, calling out softly to her to wait.

I used to watch Li Shin wash his uniform himself, in the evening after he had returned home from a meeting. First he would soak both shirt and trousers for an hour, in cold water mixed with a spoonful of soap powder. Then he would rinse them, twice. The first time, he used plain cold water. The second time, he would stir a little starch into the water. After rinsing his shirt and trousers in the starchy water, he would drape them over separate hangers so that they would dry overnight and he could iron them in the morning. He always ironed his trousers first. And after ironing, he would hang both shirt and trousers on the same hanger.

I hid the folded uniform between my mattress and bedsprings. I had never tried to hide anything in Great-Grandfather's house before, so I did not think that anyone would know exactly where to look. I put the empty hanger back into the cupboard and left the room.

I went to the bathroom, where someone had left the louvered window above the toilet open, and outside tree leaves were pressing on the frosted-glass plates. When I was younger, Grandma used to bathe me, and the first thing that she would do would be to close that window. In the afternoon the leaves outside sometimes winked yellow and black, marking the passing of butterflies, but at night when Grandma called me there for my bath the leaves would be dark, and I would see nothing. I would stand by the door, while Grandma pulled back her sleeve and raised her arm, stretching. When she pushed upwards on the lever, I would listen for that sound of the plates snapping shut, flattening against each other, making me think of four thousand National Cadets clicking their heels when they came to attention. That was the sound that Grandma made when she closed the window so that I would not catch cold. Then she would say, Now you can take off your shorts and T-shirt, Su Yen.

I remembered how she would fill up the tub, testing the water's temperature with her fingers. Then she would pick up the yellow soap. I would climb into the tub and sit down. She would wet the soap, then slide it over my back and my shoulders, and after she had washed me all over, she would wash me between my legs, saying softly. Always remember to wash down here, Su Yen. Later, she would hold on to my arms while I was climbing out of the tub, so that I would not fall, and she would dry me with a big blue towel. She would rub white powder over my chest to make me smell nice. She would help me put on my pajamas. My pajamas were always good-luck red, with tiny white buttons. I would watch her fingers push each button into the buttonhole, and then I would feel clean, and satisfied, and safe.

I pulled off my panties. I had noticed the blood earlier that afternoon, and I had thought that it might stop. I had even thought that it might somehow disappear, that I had imagined it. But when I looked, the blood was still there, a pale transparent red. I put the round black plug in the sink. Then I turned on the water and picked up the soap. I stood in the bathroom a long time, scrubbing, until Li Yuen knocked on the door and said, "Chief, what are you doing?"

I pulled up my shorts and unplugged the sink. Then I picked up my panties and squeezed out the water. I threw my panties into the wastepaper basket near the toilet. I tore off long strips of toilet paper and crumpled them into small balls and dropped them in the basket as camouflage. Then I opened the door. Li Yuen was standing outside, still carrying his gun. He stepped past me into the bathroom, looked around, and said, "There's a funny smell in here."

"Where's Susan?" I asked.

"She went home." He was staring down at my legs, and when I looked, the blood was running in a thin line down my left thigh.

"Don't tell anyone," I said. "Please."

"You cut yourself?" he asked, his voice sounding scared.

"No," I said. "There's no pain."

He went on staring at the blood. "You sure?"

"No pain," I said, walking out into the corridor. I knew that he did not know what it meant that I was bleeding without pain, but I also knew that he would not tell. We were only two of us, now. Anyone else could be an enemy, and we did not know what the grown-ups might do.

I did not notice Auntie San and Auntie Lin walking in the corridor behind me, although Li Yuen said later that he had seen them pass by the bathroom, and that when he stepped out after them, he saw them following me.

I could not think why our twin aunties would be doing that, why they would want to follow me. They could not have heard Li Yuen and me talking about blood. After all, they were what the nuns at St. Catherine called "deaf-mutes." They had to watch your face to know what you were saying. They listened not to sounds but to lips, eye movements, hands that waved, and the shapes that people's bodies flowed into when the bodies sat down or stood up or walked about a room. It was true that they could hear vibrations in the floorboards, and that when the grown-ups gathered in the dining room to talk, our twin aunties could tell how fiercely the others were arguing just by placing their hands flat on the tabletop. But they could not possibly have heard Li Yuen's voice and mine in the bathroom.

Besides, I had walked from the bathroom straight to our bedroom, and when I had turned to close the door for privacy, I had seen no one in the corridor.

"Maybe they were hiding in one of the rooms," Li Yuen said, that night while we were talking.

"But why?" I said.

He shrugged his shoulders. "I don't know," he said. "But you'd better be careful. I'm telling you—they were following you."

Sometime during the night, as we were falling asleep, we heard the amahs carrying trays of tea-cups past our room. Once or twice, when a door opened, we could hear one of our aunties crying.

❀

Early the next morning we were woken by the sound of voices talking anxiously in the kitchen. Li Yuen slipped out of bed and tiptoed out into the corridor, with me following closely behind. We stopped just before we reached the kitchen. Then, standing with our backs against the wall, we listened while our aunties and uncles argued back and forth. Their voices flipped about like fish caught in a net, half hopeful, half hopeless. Perhaps Daisy had imagined the dream? Perhaps it was actually a story someone else had told her, one of those young men who used to park his car outside? Or could Daisy be lying, trying to arouse attention, to cause trouble? Perhaps she was bored, cooped up in the house like that. What if someone took her out shopping one of these days—it would be all right, probably, so long as Daisy was not left by herself.

Their voices wafted into the corridor, smelling of coffee and toasted bread. Li Yuen and I stood very still, straining our ears, almost holding our breaths. Auntie Daisy had had a dream. She had dreamt men climbing out of boats into seaweed, tangled seaweed strewn over seawater, lightless, a night without the moon. The men in the dream waded through the seaweed, then stepped out onto the sand. It was too dark, she could not see their faces. When Auntie Mei tried to wake her, Auntie Daisy opened her eyes and said, See them? Can't you see them? She told Auntie Mei that the men were starting to move into the trees. Smell them, she said. You can't see them anymore, but smell, there's salt water in their boots.

We heard Auntie Mei repeat what had happened. Last

night Auntie Daisy had jerked her head suddenly and, turning to the window, cried out, Li Shin. Look, listen. She had grabbed Auntie Mei's arm. Then again, Auntie Mei had heard her say, Li Shin.

Li Yuen looked at me in the corridor.

I, too, had dreamt of Li Shin during the night. He had come walking barefoot across the room, wearing pajama trousers. He had stopped beside my bed and said, Chief, don't be scared. Then he had taken my hand, pulled me out of bed and out into the corridor, and we had gone to the kitchen and out the back door, down the porch steps into cool damp air. We had stood out there, smelling grass and leftover rain. Then Grandma, looking out the back door and catching us, called out, Li Shin, What are you doing? In my dream I had heard her hurrying down the steps. She came and pulled at his arm. Have you no common sense? Look at Su Yen, wet all over. You want to catch cold, both of you? Grandma was rubbing my head, and pulling again at his arm. This time, Li Shin turned around. Sorry, Grandma, he said, and then he let her lead us back inside the house.

We knew not to tell the grown-ups about my dream. We knew to be careful.

At four o'clock, while the nuns were in our bedroom folding Li Shin's clothes into neat squares and stacking them like old newspapers to be tied up and taken away, Grandma was sitting in her room, staring out the window and rocking.

On the wall beside the window hung a painting. A boy, thirteen or fourteen years old, stood framed in the door-

way of a dark room. He was one of Grandma's old schoolmates. She had put up the painting a few years after
Grandfather's death. No one important, she had told us,
when Li Shin had asked her, Who was that boy? Just a
schoolmate. It was the painting itself that mattered. She
had brought it with her from China, the work of a local
artist from her village. She was putting it up simply because the time had arrived. What time, Grandma? Li Shin
had asked. Time to remember, she had replied, knowing
that we would not understand. Time to face up and see.

I stood now beside her at the window.

"Have the nuns left, Su Yen?" she asked quietly.

"No, Grandma, not yet."

She nodded and continued to rock. I watched dust float
above the windowsill, and listened to her rocking chair
wince softly on and off, on and off.

The boy in the painting had an ashy face. He wore a
gray shirt with a wrinkled collar, and dark blue trousers
rolled up around his ankles. He was barefoot. He stood
with his hands buried in his pockets, and I could see the
third button on his shirt dangling loosely on a thread.

"Grandma, can people change what they dream?"

"Depends on the dream."

Somewhere in the corridor an amah was walking, her
slippers sliding over the wooden boards. The sound came
closer and closer, and then moved into the room next door.
After a while I could hear the amah snapping open a clean
bedsheet.

I looked out the window. Li Yuen had come out onto
the porch and stepped down to the grass. Now he was
standing on the footpath looking towards the cemetery.
He was wearing only his running shorts, and I could see

how his back and shoulders glistened sunburnt brown, the skin of a boy who belonged on an official track team, who did not run just for fun anymore the way only very young children could.

"Grandma," I asked next, "can people change a warning given in a dream?"

"Depends on the warning." She stopped rocking and turned her head. "Why do you ask this, Su Yen?"

"I don't know," I said.

Her eyes were slightly curious. But already, whatever concern had entered her mind was leaving, and I could feel its weight, no heavier than a light-filled poof! I looked again at the boy in the painting. His eyes were ashy too, as if he had spent that whole day walking too close to something burning in the village. I was going to point this out to Grandma, but she had started rocking again. So I turned and tiptoed to the door, and let her have some peace.

Now she would stay there in her rocking chair all hours of the day. Staring out that window, she rocked and rocked, and waited for evening, believing that it must have been the time, believing that he must have started dying even as he crossed over the grass, that he had died already when he stepped into the trees. So she waited, staring out that window, her eyes running thick and black as the night. She watched twilight approach, darkness rising out of that earth where she knew soon thick wandering roots would claw the ground, burying the stone. Still she peered, fought her way from shadow to shadow. It was as if each evening he died again, and she would wait, hoping, as if the hope were still answerable, that the gods might change their minds and send him back, and then he would come home, walking in the last rays of the day.

At St. Catherine there was a priest, Father Damien, who came over daily from St. Peter's next door to say Holy Mass. In the dark noon chapel light, where nuns' fingers signed crosses in midair and the never-opened windows sharpened to the high trapped sound of the altar bell, my classmates and I had watched Father Damien hold the Host against Armageddon. Once we had heard feet running in the corridor downstairs, the kindergarten children playing hide-and-seek before a nun caught them and warned them it was the wrong hour. A five-year-old girl with her face on her hands, with her hands on the cold stone wall, had called out, Here I come. Here I come. We had heard her voice circling on itself, the voices of the other children gone now, softly into walls. And I had imagined I could see it, that girl's voice— a turning shape over the fields, whipping itself invisible, again and again. It echoed off the chapel windows, where we, inside, surrounded by green glass, soaked up the Ave Maria as the nuns began to sing. Nuns' hymns, we had heard, were born late at night and early morning, and hummed of oil, candles, souls peeled open.

The girl downstairs had laughed, finding a friend. Two were now racing for the wall, their rubber soles charging down the marble floor. Then a young reckless hand had slapped hard on the stone, and a voice had yelled, Home. I had noticed how the nuns turned their faces, and Father

Damien too, scattering Ave Maria to the gods like scraps of thin black paper. After Mass had ended and most of the candles were blown out, the wooden benches shifted and the older nuns got up. They stooped coming down the aisle, holding hands with one another, their skirts caressing. As they filtered through the chapel doors I saw—they had already left, gone somewhere else in their eyes.

In Great-Grandfather's house so did the grown-ups pray. But they prayed without daring to speak. Long ago, on the night that our parents were killed, the grown-ups had blamed Li Shin's father. But they had also blamed the gods. This was why they had shut up their voices, afraid that their anger might escape. It was too strong, too violent. It had to be pushed down, stifled out of memory. Otherwise, it threatened to lash out, shatter our family into a thousand screaming faces that would shout loud curses, not only at one another but also at the spirits of our dead relatives, the ancestral spirits that were supposed to protect us. And the faces would curse, too, at the gods, for having abandoned Li Shin's father. He had been Grandma's eldest son, the one who, most of all, should have been protected, who was supposed to have been born protected.

Now that I was old enough, I wondered if Li Shin's father had offered that exchange himself, when he chose freedom instead of duty. When he had decided not to enter the family business, but to work for the government instead, he had gone against Grandfather's wishes. He had pledged loyalty outside the family. I knew now that this was what Li Shin had done. But Li Shin's father had done something worse. He had influenced a younger brother, my father, into following in his footsteps. Perhaps this was how he had lost divine protection. Perhaps this was why all the ears listening from the heavens had turned away from him that night the speeding lorry came rambling down the Malayan highway.

I could almost hear it, the sound of that lorry smashing into the back of the car, a long sliding screech flung over the tops of the trees. I could almost see my mother, turning to look at my father, and my father, turning to look at his brother. I had never thought about my mother before, but she came to me now, a faceless shadow in the moving dark, surprised at how easily everything was coming to an end.

Li Yuen turned around as I crossed over the grass to him. He slipped his hands into his pockets and said, "I'm going into the cemetery. You want to come?"

"Yes," I said.

"We should bring a candle," he said. He walked over to the porch, went up the steps, and disappeared into the kitchen. Then he came out again. I could see his body in the doorway. I could see him looking down at the candle, his palm cupped around the flame, protecting it.

I walked over and stood at the bottom of the steps. As he came down, the flame shook and I watched his palm move closer. The skin of his palm was tight and I could see the lines in it.

We started to walk. I listened to his feet on the grass,

walking ahead of mine. Then we were in the cemetery, walking in that cool green light, on the path where if you stood still you could watch the big and the small leaves come floating down, and if you left to walk in the trees you must watch the ground. A breeze moved in the lalang. Li Yuen brushed away the rain tree vines. He kept walking. Then he moved off the path, and I followed. We crossed over the light gleaming through holes that baby butterflies ate into younger leaves. The dry twigs cracked again and again. Then he stopped. I looked around his shoulder, knowing before I saw it where that fresh white stone stood. Still too new for cracks or moss, there it was, silent among the broken twigs, silent in the gray-green shade.

Li Yuen made a clean place in the earth to put the candle. Then he sat down and crossed his legs. I found a tree not too far from him, where I could lie down. It was comforting to look up into the leaves, where the sky came through squinting like blue stars.

Once, Li Yuen looked over to me to ask, "Is there still blood?"

"A little bit," I told him. "There's still no pain."

We did not speak again after that. Then, as soon as the daylight was getting less, becoming more gray than green, becoming watery, we got up and made our way back to Great-Grandfather's house.

"They're Chinese," he said, as we were stepping out of the cemetery. "Not Japanese."

"Who?" I said.

"Communists," he said. "It's in the book I'm reading. Know what else is in this book? Chinese law of nationality. Grandma's right. We are citizens of China."

"What book are you talking about?"

"That book Susan lent him."

We sat down on the porch steps. "You don't like to read," I said. "You don't even have a library card."

Li Yuen sat there gazing at the trees. He shook his head and said, "Things are different now. And I do have a card."

I stared at his brown face and reminded myself that he was not going to be a soldier, that he was a runner, that when Grandfather was alive, he used to tap Li Yuen's legs, then say, Good, then push him back onto the road. Practice some more. Before Li Yuen had joined the school team he used to practice behind the house. He would run between the coconut trees that grew on either side of the path. I remembered one evening he had measured the distance between them. I remembered him crawling along the grass with his ruler, then grinning up at me and saying, It's almost one hundred meters, Chief. That was right for sprinting. He was kneeling on the grass then and smiling up at me because I was following him.

On those afternoons he used go to one of the trees and stand under it awhile. It did not matter which tree. Sometimes he would start with the one on the left, sometimes with the one on the right. The sun would fall between the leaves while he was under them, and the leaves would shake thin gray needles over his skin. Then he would look to me up on the porch, and I would call out the Ready Set Go. I would watch him run. I would watch him sprint over the grass, kicking up hot dust when he touched the path, and then he was back on the grass again. When he touched the second tree he would not stop, but swing around it and sprint back, then throw himself against the first tree back on the other side. There he would stay, leaning on that tree, taking in deep breaths, and when he threw his head back the thin gray needles would play on his face.

"They're not Malay?" I said. "The Communists?"

"All their leaders are Chinese," he said.

A breeze shifted the leaves. It was the moment that if we ran around the side of the house to the front, the sun would be winking in the trees across the road.

"How will you die?" I asked, after a while.

"Same as everybody else," he said.

"How?"

"I'll close my eyes."

"Is that all?"

"Sure."

"Will you lie down?"

"Yes. I'll lie down and then I'll close my eyes."

"When will you do it?"

"When I'm tired enough."

The sun was down and only that dark blue light still stayed, bathing the trees and the shed. A wind blew along the ground, and we could hear it in the grass. In the footpath, sand dust rose and fell and drifted.

We could hear Auntie Mei and Auntie Lily coming towards us across the kitchen floor. Then Auntie Mei was in the doorway, and I heard her voice behind us, asking, "Esha, did you take the uniform?"

I turned around, looked straight into her eyes, and said, "No."

She and Auntie Lily looked at each other, and then they walked away. I looked at Li Yuen, but he was watching the trees, knowing it would soon be dark.

❀

I was not surprised when at nine o'clock
that night, Auntie Mei came to our room. She did not
turn on the light, and as I sat up in my bed, I heard Li
Yuen sitting up, too. In the dark I saw him reach down
and pick up his gun, which now he always kept on the
floor beside his bed.

Outside the window, the tree leaves moved slightly in
a quiet wind. I watched Auntie Mei walking towards my
bed. She sat down, and asked me softly, "Is there something you want to tell me?" When I did not answer, she
went on, "Your Auntie Daisy also started menstruating
early."

I looked across the room at Li Yuen. His face was turned
towards the window, and he seemed to be listening to the
leaves. His gun lay across his thighs.

"Once a month, you bleed," said Auntie Mei. She spoke
slowly, and very gently. I knew that a lesson was waiting
to unfold, there in the dark space between us, and I could
not wish it away. I was not supposed to. "It happens to
all women. It usually begins when you are twelve or
thirteen years old."

"I'm almost twelve."

"I started when I was fourteen," she said. "So did your
other aunties. All of us except Daisy. She was eleven,
too."

I saw Li Yuen turn away from the window. He slipped
out of bed and, holding his gun by his side, walked over
to us. In the dark I noticed how he seemed taller, and
thinner. He was wearing only his pajama trousers, with
no shirt.

"Your Uncle Wilfred found the panties," said Auntie Mei. "Everyone knows now. We've talked about it, and everyone agrees that it will be the best thing."

"What will be the best thing?" Li Yuen asked.

Auntie Mei looked down and played with the pleats in her skirt. "Auntie Lily and I will pack your things for you," she went on. "Whatever toys or books you want to bring, put them on your bed in the morning. Tomorrow evening, when your uncles come home from the office, you must be ready. They will come home in a taxi. We will take that taxi to the convent."

"I'm going to tell Grandma," Li Yuen said.

Auntie Mei put a hand on his shoulder to stop him. "Your Grandma isn't feeling well these days," she said. "Don't disturb her."

"Why are you doing this?" Li Yuen began to poke at the mattress with his gun. "How long must Chief stay there?"

"Your Grandma made a mistake," said Auntie Mei, getting up from the bed. "We are trying to be more careful. Do you understand?" She walked slowly to the door and paused. "Esha, the nuns will take care of you." She left the room, closing the door behind her.

Still holding his gun, Li Yuen sat down on my bed. "Why didn't you tell her?" he said, now angry at me. "Why didn't you tell her you wouldn't go?"

I got out of bed and walked to the window, where I could look out to the leaves moving in that dark quiet wind. Grandfather had dreamt two children without faces. Blood on my panties so early after Li Shin's death could be another warning. Of what, our aunties and uncles did not know, but they had decided to take no more risks. In Great-Grandfather's house the family had to be protected.

That was the law. It had always been. It would always be.

From our window I could see the mango tree, now rattling in the rising wind. Long ago two boys had knelt, pushing the red-brown dirt into the hole, the older boy saying to the younger boy, Will you hold the tree still, you're moving it too much. Now I saw the red-brown dirt run soft and thick between the older boy's fingers, and then the younger boy slid his hands into the earth, too. The heat stuck damp to their skin, and that white light was in the sky, that same white light my cousins and I had played under, that if you tried to look up at it you had to shut your eyes.

After a while I heard Li Yuen breathe, soft, slowly, beside me. He smelled salty, like the night air, like seawater.

"Do you think he was tired?" I asked, only to ask.

He turned his head, looked at me, and answered softly, "I don't know."

We stood listening to the sound of our breathing in the dark. Then, for what would be the last time, I felt him take my hand. "You'll catch cold," I heard him say, and I wanted to tell him, No, I'm tough, too. But I had already begun to grow older that night. I knew a little of what Grandma must have felt, when she left China. I even knew why she had told us her stories, and why soon it would be time for me to begin. So I let Li Yuen pull me away.

The seawater smell flooded our room all night, rich and old with the years we remembered, lost sounds, voices, where once we had been three. Li Yuen and I stayed awake for as long as we could. We both knew the truth now. The gods did what they did. It was not our place to stop them. No one, not even grown-ups, could.